A SPY IN ALL BUT NAME

G. J. PARRY

D1176646

For my Wife and Children

Contents

MORE BY THIS AUTHOR

A SPY IN ALL BUT NAME

1
Covert Detail

High above the Russian shores of the Black Sea, on a tree-lined slope in the Caucasus Mountains, a man with a gun strode warily down a rocky escarpment. Where the trees merged to create dense woodland, he stopped and scanned the rising ground. The man carried himself with a natural ease, quietly confident, effortless. He had a dependable, lived-in sort of face, keen eyes wrinkled at the corners. On his feet he wore stout, high-laced climbing boots, his legs encased in a pair of black Levi jeans. His jacket of faded leather hung comfortably over a baggy, roll neck jumper. Powerful binoculars swung from a cord round his neck and the gun he held was a Swiss made Sig Sauer, a semi-automatic 9mm pistol. On his head he wore a fisherman's cap, Breton style, with a small peak.

The man answered to the name of Bowman, Michael Richard Bowman, and to those who gave the orders, Mike Bowman was 'deniable', an anonymous asset, attributable to no one.

He stopped to lean against a tree, listening to the forest. In the distance a woodpecker hammered, and a pigeon called, softly. It was hot and he used the moment to rest, to control his breathing. Close to his right eye a spider trembled on a gossamer thread. Fifteen paces to his left a woman lay prone, also a 'deniable', but young and inexperienced. She was dark haired, attractive, and head strong. Jessica Stewart watched the woodland on their left flank.

He called in a fierce whisper. 'Anything?'

There was a subtle movement of the ferns as she shook her head. 'Nothing.'

Bowman swivelled on one knee and brought the pistol chest high. He pushed through the low growing foliage and parted the leaves. A flicker of sunlight lanced into the forest glade, leafy shadows beyond. He concentrated on dark places, ground level, where a man might be hidden, searched for a full minute, probing the undergrowth. The target had certainly come this way and unless he and Jess made a wide detour, this was ambush territory. Easing back he twisted behind the gnarled trunk.

'We going round?' he whispered, trying to be inclusive, wanting her to know her opinion mattered.

Jessica Stewart turned her head slowly, eyes peering through the foliage. She turned her mouth down in a disapproving pout, a minimal shake of her hair.

Bowman narrowed his clear eyes; it was his choice, and if their quarry was still running, the longer he took to make a decision the further away he would be. Seconds passed as he fought to justify a move into the open. The 'Old Man' wouldn't take kindly to failure, too much time and money had already been expended. Frowning, he looked down at the 9mm Sig and slid the safety catch to off. It looked to be fifty or sixty paces to the clearing, another twenty to get across. Plenty of trees between him and the open ground. He glanced up and met her eyes, pointing towards eleven o'clock.

'Move up twenty and cover me.'

She gave a thumbs up, and crawled forward.

He tracked her by the moving ferns, but then lost her whereabouts. He waited, eyes up, watching. She rose ghostlike from the ground, shifted her head round a tree trunk and examined the way ahead. Holding up a hand for him to wait, she searched to her front. Finally, she half turned her head and nodded.

Bowman drew a deep breath and gathered himself for the lunge. He prayed there were no unseen holes to twist an ankle. Pistol ready, he came up at the run, sprinted across the fern covered ground and weaved, left and right, tree to tree. Bent at the waist he burst into the clearing, running hard. He swerved again, to the right, she needed a clear field of fire. Braced against the expected impact of a bullet he launched himself over the last of the open ground.

He landed hard and rolled away, lay still. Silence. He dragged in a lungful of air and cursed under his breath. Glancing back at the clearing he signalled she should wait, pulled himself to his feet and scouted forward, finger on the trigger, forcing himself on. In less than three minutes he'd covered a lot of ground. No sign of the quarry.

Doubling back to the clearing he slowly made himself visible. Wouldn't do to surprise her. He beckoned her across and turned to watch the forest, alert to the slightest movement. She joined and knelt alongside.

He felt her eyes on him, and waited for a question.

'Now what?' she asked.

'Couple of hours and we'll be out of daylight. If we push too hard he might hear us, could be difficult.'

Jessica smiled, pearl-white teeth sparkling in the late sunshine. 'No time like the present then?'

Bowman met her eyes, saw the raised brow and chuckled, a feeling of reckless determination coming to the fore. The laughter faded as he gave it some thought, keen eyes scanning the terrain. If he'd been alone there'd be no hesitation, but she was his responsibility. Make a rash decision and people died, something you learned over time, with experience. She was young, with a devil-may-care attitude, keen to be recognised in her own right, had volunteered for the mission. But Bowman was a senior officer in the National Directorate for Special Operations and the entire operation hung on his shoulders.

But he needed to get this done 'Alright, keep your distance and stay level.'

Jessica winked. 'You're the boss,' she said, and moved away to her left, opening the space between them.

Bowman extracted his fifteen round magazine, checked for movement against the spring, and clipped it back into place. Gun held loosely at his waist he began to move. For thirty minutes they pushed on, maintaining position, holding each other in sight, and all the while the forest grew darker. Above the dense canopy the sky shone blue, but the woodland hid the brightness and dusk fell quickly.

Bowman held up a hand and she froze. He opened his GPS tracker. The co-ordinates had them approaching the northern tree line, a mile distant.

A movement caught his eye; she'd dropped to one knee staring ahead. He crouched. The foliage had become silent, stilled of birdsong. Unblinking, he scoured ahead, willing the undergrowth to reveal something, anything. Peripheral vision went into overdrive, and still no sign.

A gun blasted, a single shot.

Jessica gasped at the bullet's impact, surprise on her face. Blood sprayed from the exit wound in her back. She fell sideways, eyes wide with shock, and collapsed with a muffled thump.

Bowman held stock still, only his eyes moving. He glimpsed a shadow that hadn't been there, almost black. He waited, patient now, forcing himself to ignore the girl. If she wasn't dead then she'd soon bleed out. Instinct tugged at him to help. But at this moment he was powerless, unable to offer assistance, if he made the slightest move . . . . A man's silhouette stepped forward from the shadow, walking steadily towards the girl, a long-barrelled pistol held forward. Bowman slowly raised the Sig, forefinger down the side of the barrel, and took careful aim. A moving target, slightly more than thirty paces.

He squeezed, and the pistol spat, jumped with recoil, and he fired again. Two rounds, a double-tap, and the target staggered backwards, struggling to stay upright. He crumpled and Bowman sprang to his feet, running gun outstretched, ready to shoot again. But on reaching the fallen man, death was self-evident; a bullet in the chest and one to the throat. Blood gathered at his neck, glistening red on the shirt.

Bowman left him and ran for the girl. She lay where she'd fallen; gore on the ground, eyes wide and vacant, sightless. He ripped open her top and felt for a pulse, an automatic reaction, knowing it was a futile gesture. The blood oozed from a neat puncture in her left breast close to the sternum. It was too late.

8

He sagged to both knees and cursed, and then mouthed a string of obscenities. God help him, but she was so very young. A speck of blood glistened on her cheek and he touched it, to wipe away the disfigurement. The sticky spot smeared, made worse by his clumsy attempt. He removed his finger, swallowed hard, and looked away. A sadness coursed through him. Where moments before the young woman had been full of life, a single gunshot had extinguished the spark, wiped away her future. He shook his head in bitter frustration. He cursed again and hoped the people upstairs appreciated the sacrifice. But even then he couldn't leave her in peace. Searching her pockets he recovered anything he thought might make for an identifiable trace. Not that there was anything significant, that had all been dealt with before the deployment. Rolling her to one side to get at the rear pockets of her jeans, he grimaced. Most of her back had been blasted away, a ragged mess. He forced himself to feel through the pockets and gently lowered her to the dirt. He found her gun, made certain the selector was on safe, and tucked it into his waistband.

Over to his left, a fallen tree made a natural shelter against the worst of the elements. It seemed proper to lift her up and gently place her body under the broken trunk. He thoughtfully arranged her hands on her chest and straightened her legs. In the end, kneeling at her side he reached out a hand to her lifeless eyes and gently brushed them closed.

Bowman came angrily to his feet, put the Sig away and walked back to the dead man. This is what Jessica Stewart had given her life for. Was the Russian worth it? That was a question for others. It wasn't within Bowman's remit to start wondering about the rights and wrongs. He'd only been given a name and an image of Mikhail Takonsky. Others had evaluated his potential as a worthwhile target, and Bowman had eventually been cleared for armed insertion. And now here he was on the forested slopes above Sochi, playground of Russia's elite, with two bodies. The one, a legitimate execution, (in the eyes of Bowman's masters) and the other, the brave daughter of soon to be grieving parents.

A thorough search of Takonsky's body revealed little, not that he expected much. In this game information was sacrosanct, professionals didn't carry documentation, of any sort. With night drawing in, he gave a final glance at the girl's body and turned away. The job was done, not the best outcome but at least he'd squared things up. The Russians would analyse her DNA for clues but the results would be inconclusive. Scottish mother, Canadian father, nothing firm to go on. A cynical grimace flickered across his strained features. For a war that didn't exist, this little skirmish had suddenly upped the ante.

Mike Bowman headed south for the Russian border with Georgia. It would be a long hike, a dangerous crossing, and more miles before he reached the safety of 'friendly' Georgia.

Night fell as he cleared the high peaks and pushed on down the ridges that ran parallel to the Black Sea.

It was late the following day before he made it to the British Consulate in Tbilisi, and there he took receipt of a passport and stamped visa. The officials issued him with an airline ticket for a Lufthansa flight departing Tbilisi International Airport, eight hours flying time to Munich in southern Germany. The flight turned out to be uneventful and in the seclusion of a first class seat, he eventually managed to grab some hard earned shut eye.

Altogether it was the thick end of seventy-two hours before he landed at Heathrow Airport. Border Force had been alerted to his coming and they whisked him through without interference. In the multi-storey carp park reserved for just these sort of circumstances, he climbed into his waiting Land Rover and called in notification. It was 10pm in West Drayton before he parked the Defender and managed to sink a whisky in the bar of a nondescript hotel. It became the first drink of many before the bar closed.

In a place called Jos Bay, on the south-east corner of Kent, chalk white cliffs overlook a gently sloping beach where the soft sand hisses at the water's edge. It is the waters of the English Channel that lap quietly on the shore.

At midnight, six miles out to sea, a Brazilian flagged 8,000 ton freighter radioed the Dover coastguard and reported a problem with her steering. The signal warned the coastguard of an unavoidable reduction in speed, down to five knots, in order to give the engineering department a chance to replace a faulty solenoid. They estimated thirty minutes to complete the repair.

Dover coastguard acknowledged, logged the bulk carrier's call, and warned all vessels in the immediate area. Surveillance of the busiest shipping lane in the world, watched over by a state-of-the-art radar installation, recorded what it expected to see. A bright blip on the screen slowed from fourteen knots to five and the operator turned his attention to a fresh target steaming in from Land's End.

Aboard the freighter, a rope ladder, quickly followed by a Jacob's ladder, were unfurled over the port waist and a three metre Gemini rubber dinghy lowered to the clinging crewmen. One of them grabbed the coiled painter, steadied himself, and trailed the dinghy to stream out below the aftermost ladder. A man in a wetsuit descended that second ladder, jumped aboard the swaying dinghy and fired up the Yamaha engine. Matching the freighter's speed through the waves he looked up, waiting. On the deck above, another wet-suited figure took his leave of the Captain and clambered down the wooden rungs. At the foot of the ladder he hesitated, waiting for the right moment, and jumped for the middle of the dinghy. A large waterproof haversack followed, hauled in by his outstretched hands, secured with a lashing.

On the forward ladder, the crewman tossed the line into the boat and waved them off. As the pitch of the outboard motor increased, the glistening back inflatable veered out from the ship's side and began her bouncing run for a small secluded cove.

The Captain of the bulk grain carrier returned to his hammer-head bridge and thanked Dover coastguard for their assistance, and then rang down for half ahead. A short while later, the 8,000 ton merchantman made a turn round the North Foreland and headed for the Thames estuary. The Customs officials at the Port of Tilbury would be none the wiser and the

Captain leaned back in his chair with a smile. His conscience was clear, and his crew all the richer for their silence.

Commander Robert Edward Fraser MBE, sharp eyed and craggy faced, frowned at the mug of black coffee and pursed his lips, deep in thought. Seated at his desk in the headquarters of the National Directorate for Special Operations, (NDSO), he glanced at the wall clock, took a tentative sip of the steaming liquid, and subconsciously listened to a murmur of subdued voices coming from the conference room next door. It was nigh on one in the morning and he was tired.

There was a knock on the door.

'Come,' he said.

His Personal Assistant, Carol Hearsden looked in. 'They're ready for you now, sir.'

'Right, I'll just be a moment.'

She withdrew and shut the door and Commander Robert Fraser, affectionately known as the 'Old Man', but never to his face, managed a rare smile of professional attachment. Carol came from Newcastle-upon-Tyne, a Geordie lass and proud of it. Having achieved a Doctorate in English Literature from Durham University, she'd joined the Civil Service and quickly achieved widespread recognition. An old colleague of Fraser's had recommended her as a highly adaptable, trustworthy PA. Now in her early forties, impeccably dressed in a white blouse, grey skirt and with a pair of elegant low heels, she exuded an air of unflappable reliability. What little makeup she wore was enhanced by her brilliant smile and carefully applied coral pink lipstick. Carol Hearsden had become indispensable to the Commander's peace of mind.

Robert Fraser ran his fingers through the iron-grey head of hair. He felt the long day's growth of stubble round his muscular jaw and sighed. The last few hours hadn't gone according to plan and he needed answers. He flicked an invisible speck of dust from the sleeve of his charcoal suit and straightened to his full height. At fifty-one years of age, broad shouldered and barrel-chested, he cut an imposing figure; time to put things in motion. He opened the door and made his appearance.

'Good morning, gentlemen. Somewhat earlier than we might have anticipated.'

The next three most senior men in NDSO sat round the conference table and muttered something unintelligible.

He grinned. 'Sorry, did I get you up?' He sat and produced a laptop and then placed a heavy palm on the lid.

'You're wondering why I called you in at such short notice' He looked at each of them in turn. 'Bowman's operation went tits up.' In an instant he had their full attention.

Ian Webster was the first to speak, a clipped, staccato bark, somehow at odds with his smooth, bald head. 'Meaning what, exactly?' he snapped.

A pair of heavy rimmed glasses framed piercing blue eyes and the permanent frown gave a hint to the man's exceptional powers of intelligence. A confirmed bachelor, he lived alone in a modest house in a nearby village. His only companion went by the name of 'Churchill', a black and white Cocker Spaniel. A decade earlier Fraser had head-hunted him from GCHQ. He'd been working on shared intelligence with the Americans and Israel's Mossad. At that time they were focussing all their efforts on Iran. Eventually he'd persuaded Webster to join the NDSO.

'Meaning,' Fraser elaborated, 'the target's been eliminated but unfortunately Jessica Stewart died during the mission.'

Webster rubbed his nose. 'Mmm . . . , awkward,' he said, and looked at the ceiling.

Jamaican born Winslow 'Tubby' Palmer, Head of Planning, turned his heavy black jowls towards Fraser and peered over a sheaf of papers.

'It's not just awkward, that might take a lot of explaining.' He drummed a podgy finger on the table to emphasize his point. 'Three months planning and the job is a bodge!' At fifty years of age he had the seniority and experience to be outspoken. His previous life had been spent as an army officer, a graduate of Sandhurst, rising through the ranks to become a Lieutenant-

General at NATO Headquarters managing Operational Command.

Fraser kept silent, letting the man's anger subside. Instead, he looked at the Assistant Director for Operational Deployment, Angus 'Jock' Monroe, and raised an eyebrow. 'What can you tell me, Jock?'

Monroe coughed and cleared his throat. Ex MI6, he'd seen service in Berlin as the 'wall' came down and the Cold War became a thing of the past. When the Russian Section had been decimated by cuts, NDSO managed to acquire his vast experience in the field of espionage. His pale-blue eyes landed on Fraser. 'Tubby's right. Something unexpected must have happened; it should have been relatively straightforward. We had no indications of anything untoward.'

'Well, *you* tell me what went wrong. Have you questioned him?'

'Not yet, seemed a bit insensitive, what with the girl dying. I thought he needed time, at least till the morning.'

Fraser shook his head in disbelief and scowled his displeasure. Bowman, he thought, held the rank of Field Officer, not some raw recruit in the Training School. 'I'm not having it. I want him brought here now.' He turned and barked. 'Carol!'

She slipped in from her office. 'Yes, sir?'

'I want Bowman brought in, immediately. No excuses, in person. We'll wait.'

Totally unflustered by Fraser's abruptness, she nodded. 'Yes, sir. I'll inform Despatch.'

Fraser softened. 'Thank you, and some coffee would be welcome.'

With a faint smile she was gone and he wondered how, after all these years, he'd managed to retain her services. And here she was, gone midnight, volunteering to stay on duty. He turned his attention back to the laptop and opened the file. Staring at the heading, 'Operation Ubique', he smiled at the appropriate choice of Latin for 'everywhere'. A very apt title in the context of this operation.

'Now, gentlemen. Assuming there's something to be salvaged from this mess, where do we go from here?'

Jock Monroe's angular, thin face looked up from his clasped hands. He reminded Fraser of a bird of prey, the gaunt profile and hooked nose; but behind the skeletal façade was one of the sharpest minds in the business.

'I think,' Monroe began, softly, 'that we shouldn't be too quick to condemn. The target has been eliminated, that's what we asked Bowman to do, and as usual he came up with the goods. Until we have his version of the operation. . , well, for example, the girl hadn't been on a mission before.' He spread his hands expressively. 'She obviously made a mistake, misjudged the situation, but at least she'd been with us long enough to become a 'deniable' asset.' He shook his head. 'We can't say it was Bowman's fault. If memory serves, he wasn't too keen on taking her along.'

Fraser winced and thought of the protracted argument that had taken place in this very room. Not too keen was an understatement, and it had taken all Fraser's powers of persuasion to get Bowman's acceptance. 'True,' he agreed at length. 'Do you think that Takonsky was warned? It wouldn't be the first time.'

Monroe gave him an old fashioned look. 'Not entirely, sir, I just worry that there might be too many Services involved with these operations. A leak is always possible. But excluding all that, until we hear from Bowman, all this is sheer conjecture.'

Commander Robert Fraser sat back, folded his arms and wished Carol would hurry with that coffee.

At 01.20 hours of that same morning, a shimmering black dinghy approached the crescent shaped shoreline of Joss Bay's secluded cove. The man in the bows prepared for the landing and unhitched the waterproof haversack. The man on the outboard motor throttled down, lifted the propeller clear of the water, and allowed the inflatable to ride the onshore tide. With a slithering crunch the Gemini met the sand and stopped.

Haversack slung over one shoulder the man in front stepped onto the beach, dropped the bag further up the sand, and bent to push the dinghy back into the waves. Without a word said, the inflatable swivelled out from the shore. The Yamaha was half submerged and burbled into life. A final hand raised in farewell, the rising note of the engine, and the black dinghy peeled out into the surrounding night.

On the beach the haversack was hoisted to a shoulder and the man walked up to the underside of the tall cliffs framing the cove. Unfastening the heavy duty zip he rummaged inside for the dry clothes and changed out of the wetsuit. In less than five minutes he stood dressed in a pair of black jeans, T shirt, a pair of Adidas black trainers, and a dark blue, hooded fleece. A baseball cap finished off the outfit. Before zipping up the bag he extracted a small 9mm pistol with a five round magazine and snugged it into the purpose made liner of the fleece.

He checked the contents of the wallet. Nat West debit card, American Express credit card, a hundred pounds in cash and a driving licence. The licence was in the name of David Hardcastle and the address was entered as Farm Cottage, Rose Lane, Ross-on-Wye, Gloucestershire. Date of birth coincided with an age of thirty-two (which was true).

And so the Russian SVK RF trained undercover agent, Anatoly Pushkin, alias David Hardcastle, penetrated British Sovereign territory.

2
Intrigue

Mike Bowman awoke to the sound of someone pounding on his hotel door. Painfully aware of how drunk he still remained at two in the morning, he instinctively felt for the gun and sat up. A nauseating throb drummed at his temple.

'Mike open the door! Mike!'

The shout was followed by more heavy knocking, but at least Bowman vaguely recognised the voice.

'All right for Christ's sake! Leave off with the bloody hammering.' He swung his feet to the floor and felt a rush of blood. How many whiskies had he knocked back? Too many by the feel of it. Unsure of his footing, he padded to the door and unlocked.

Geoff Allenby barged in and found the light switch.

Bowman squinted in the glare. He stood swaying, naked, gun hanging by his side. 'What?' he managed.

Allenby closed the door. 'It's the Old Man, he wants to see you. I've been sent to bring you in.' He walked past Bowman and peered round the room, found the shower cubicle and turned the handle. 'For Christ's sake get in,' he said. 'You'll need to be sober by the time you see Fraser.'

Bowman allowed himself to be manoeuvred into the stall and hunched his shoulders against the stinging needles. After a minute of agony he relaxed, letting the heat do its work, head bowed. He gave it a while longer, and when he began to feel half-human, killed the spray and wrapped a towel round his torso.

Allenby had made coffee. 'Here, drink,' he ordered, and sat in the only chair.

Bowman did as ordered. The scalding black liquid burnt its way down, but he persevered, and pulled a face at the bitter taste. He forced down a last mouthful and reached for his clothes. While he dressed he thought of the 'Old Man', guessing there would be unanswered questions, to which Bowman was the only witness.

Shrugging into a loose fitting rain jacket, he retrieved the gun from the bed, and then caught a glimpse of himself in the long mirror. On closer inspection a weary pair of bloodshot eyes stared back and he grinned crookedly at his reflection. Without a shave, a few days of beard had bushed round his chin. To hell with it, he thought, if Fraser wants me at this time of the morning, then he'll have to put up with it. About time the bloody 'desk jockeys' were reminded of life at the sharp end.

'Come on then,' he snapped, 'let's get on with it.'

In the downstairs foyer they settled the bill with the night manager and Allenby led them out to a BMW. 'Get in.'

'Whoa,' Bowman said, 'what about my Rover?'

Allenby nodded to a man climbing out of the passenger door. 'Give him the keys. You'll find it in Motor Transport.'

Reluctantly, Bowman handed them over. He found a cigarette and flicked his lighter, watching while the man climbed in the Defender and drove away.

'Wait,' he insisted to Allenby, and strolled off across the car park. The cool of the night air engulfed him and he mixed it with nicotine. He squinted up at a quarter moon hanging low on the horizon, a few stars glinting through the intermittent cloud. It would be the predawn grey of another morning soon, he thought, and turned back for the car. Allenby was drumming impatiently on the roof and Bowman grinned. Do him good to wait, and he slowed, enjoying the man's dilemma. Fraser on the one hand, a drunken sot of a senior officer on the other.

He dropped the butt and squashed it on the tarmac. 'Okay, let's go play games.'

Allenby snatched open the back door, ushered Bowman inside, and slammed it, hard. With exaggerated calm he moved to the driver's door, eased in behind the wheel and hit the starter. The BMW purred into life.

Bowman watched all this with amusement, felt Allenby stamp the accelerator, and as the car powered out onto the main road, he settled into the comfort of the back seat. Let the man get it out of his system. If that's all he had to worry about then he was lucky. Seemed a bit uptight, wouldn't do to have him as a 'number two'. Probably only ever used weapons on a firing range anyway. Not that Bowman relished the thought of killing, but that's what he was trained to do and it was no good being squeamish. He stretched and sighed, a man always has a choice, and he'd made his bed a long time ago.

Of course, there was always the whisky, that beautiful amber nectar that helped a man to forget, when needed. And the death of the girl had warranted a bit of over indulgence. Collateral damage they called it, a crying bloody shame in his eyes. Partly his fault too; he could have called it off, not pushed. Mistakes got people killed.

The BMW hit a bend at speed, too fast for comfort, and Bowman felt Allenby ease off the accelerator. The powerful beam of the headlights flashed over a white sign. They'd just picked up the westbound M4 and Allenby hit the blue light. Bowman stopped watching the speedometer after it went through 120 miles per hour. They made it to Bird Lip Hill in record time, dropped into the valley and hit the A40. Bowman grimaced. Not long now.

In Her Majesty's Coastguard Station overlooking the Channel from high on the cliffs at Dover, the radar operator took note of a fleeting echo moving north by east off Margate's headland. He watched the echo for a short time before it faded. He logged the sighting. Fast moving, estimated at twenty-five knots, and when he entered the possible heading from projected bearing, noted the contact was on a course that intersected with the bulk carrier.

He frowned. Erroneous sightings did happen, any number of factors might come into play, but in this case the radar signature was strong enough to make the entry official and he forwarded it marked 'unidentified observation'. He said as much to the Shift Commander and went back to his watch keeping. Currently the radar had seventeen solid, identifiable blips on the trace, more than enough to keep him occupied.

The Shift Commander wasn't unduly concerned, but with the steady increase in people trafficking he thought it prudent to inform Border Force. Illegal immigration had become a high profile issue since Brexit. A quick phone call to the South-East Sector's duty officer absolved him of all further responsibility; if they thought the sighting important they could send a cutter to investigate. He looked at the time and yawned; a few more hours to change of shift, and more importantly, only another forty-two days until he retired. The radar observation post went back to the 24/7, year round routine of coastal watch.

Bowman looked up through the windshield. An enormous set of wrought iron gates brought the BMW to a halt outside the grounds of Salerton Hall. This was the well guarded, isolated headquarters of NDSO. A man in a peaked cap leant through the gatehouse window and peered at Allenby, who held up his ID card.

'Very nice, Mr Allenby, sir,' he said sarcastically, 'and who's that in the back?'

Bowman shuffled across and pressed his face to the glass, grinning.

'Oh it's you Mr Bowman,' he said, his face lighting up. 'Lovely to see you again, sir. Been a while.'

Bowman pressed a switch in the armrest and the window slid down. 'Hello, Jim. How's the missus?'

'More trouble than she's worth, don't know why I keeps her on.' He reached across to a button and the big gates swung silently to the sides. 'Mind how you go, sir,' he called, and touched the peak of his cap.

Bowman nodded in return, reminding himself that Jim had spent nine years with the SAS; he was a lot sharper than the image he liked to portray. The car rolled forward onto the gravel driveway and pushed out into the darkness. Twelve hundred yards further on across the open meadow the BMW eased left around a circular bed of roses and pulled to a stop at the front entrance. He climbed out next to a colonnaded porch, the red brick walls shrouded in Boston Ivy. The lights were on, glowing from every window. It could have been any one of the countless stately homes that dotted the English countryside, but it wasn't. This was the heart of the National Directorate for

Special Operations, 'UK eyes up' only, and very few people knew the location, or that it even existed. GCHQ had the well documented 'doughnut', along with the National Cyber Security Centre (NCSC), their civilian counterpart in London; MI6 was located in 'legoland', and MI5 at Millbank on the River Thames. Bowman pursed his lips. Of all the so called 'Secret' Services only NDSO had never made it onto a journalist's radar, only this one had been kept under wraps; and therefore this house, set in almost six-hundred acres of prime real estate had kept its anonymity.

Allenby walked towards the entrance. 'They're waiting.'

Bowman nodded and crunched across the gravel.

In the PA's office, Carol looked up with a warm smile.

'What's all the excitement,' he queried.

'The Commander wants a debrief, Mike.' She studied him for a moment. 'Are you okay?' She seemed genuinely concerned.

He grinned. 'I've been better. Had a few too many whiskies, triple distilled.'

The shake of her head spoke volumes. She stood and moved to a side door. 'Wait.'

His presence was announced and he heard Fraser's gruff, 'Send him in.'

Carol stood to one side and inclined her head. As he walked by she whispered, 'Good luck, Pet.'

Bowman entered, wondering why he felt like a schoolboy called to the headmaster's study. The room reinforced his sense of foreboding, hung with a vast array of book shelves; the Grand Library as was, with a highly polished conference table filling most of the remaining space.

Commander Fraser indicated a chair. 'Take a seat.'

He did as asked, better on his backside than standing. Four pairs of eyes scrutinised his every movement.

Fraser gave him time to settle. 'Okay, Mike, tell us exactly what happened.'

Bowman took a deep breath, looking at each of them in turn. 'Well . . . , we moved to our position before dawn, on the

21

wooded hillside above the chalet. Our first sight of Takonsky was mid-afternoon.' He paused and directed his explanation to Fraser. 'He came out the back, through the kitchen door, walked up the lane towards the forest and stopped at the footbridge. He took time to look around, checked behind him, and then suddenly cut up into the woods. By this time he was three-hundred metres away.' Again he paused, hesitant. 'It was a case of move quickly or lose him. I made the decision. We separated, trying to stay quiet but pushing on. It was twenty minutes before we made contact. We found him walking along a track of sorts. I took another step forward and trod on a dead branch. He heard the noise, took one look over his shoulder and ran.' Bowman sat back, gathering his thoughts. The hangover didn't help. 'We were compromised, he definitely clocked me. So what do I do, leave him? I went for it. Tracked him down a rocky escarpment. In retrospect, I guess it was a bad call. He shot the girl and I took him out. One less Russian assassin.' He stared at their faces, belligerent. Damned if he would apologise for doing his job.

Monroe leaned forward. 'Pity you gave the game away.'

Bowman bristled but held his tongue.

Fraser intervened. 'These things happen. Question is, what next?'

Silence followed his query and Bowman let them stew. His head throbbed and his mouth had turned to sandpaper.

Ian Webster scraped his chair back from the table and came to his feet. He walked very deliberately down the length of the room, stopped and turned to face them. 'I wonder if Jock's right and he *was* warned?'

Fraser snorted his doubt. 'No chance, why would he run. He could have called in half the local GRU.'

Webster shook his head. 'I doubt that. He spotted at least one person apparently following him. We know he had a weapon, he chose to take the gamble, and it nearly came off.'

Bowman thought about the argument and chipped in. 'With all due respect, sir,' he said to Fraser, 'there's no reason to think he was trying to avoid us, not until he saw me, that's when he took off.'

22

The Old Man stared at him, reflecting, and slowly nodded. 'Point taken, why hang around to be shot.'

Webster came back to his chair and sat. 'I think we need to reassess the phraseology of our report to Whitehall.'

Fraser nodded gravely. 'I agree,' he said, and then paused to stare at Bowman, 'Go home, Mike. Get some rest. We need to put a few things in order.'

Fraser stood and leaned on the conference table, staring at the far end of the library. When he spoke, it was so quietly Bowman had trouble hearing. 'What I don't like is how close we came to failing. There are always those who want to make cuts in the budget. They don't need much of an excuse to close us down.' He looked up from under his eyebrows.

Bowman came to his feet; they'd be tossing this about for hours.

Fraser noticed the move and nodded. 'You might not hear for a while, but stay sharp.'

He half-heard, turning for the door.

'And a little less of the whisky wouldn't harm. You stink.'

Bowman paused in mid-stride, acknowledging the rebuke, and then walked into Carol's office.

'Can you really smell it that much?' he asked.

She pinched her nose and waved him away.

Head bowed in mock shame he walked out and found the exit. The light from a window cast a long beam over the driveway and a man stepped into the glow. He held a set of keys. 'Allenby said you'd want these.'

Bowman caught them and followed the outstretched finger. The Land Rover was parked in semi-darkness on the far side of the drive, and he ambled over and hauled himself wearily into the cab. He sat and lit a cigarette, thinking.

What the hell did it matter that the girl had died. For the mandarins in Whitehall NDSO's report would highlight the facts; Mikhail Takonsky eliminated, therefore a successful mission. Perhaps their attention would be drawn to Jessica Stewart's unfortunate demise, and glossed over with a knowing look, an acceptable casualty in pursuit of a permanent solution. Bowman rubbed his forehead. To her parents, when the police

23

arrived on their doorstep, it would matter a great deal. And of course there would be a few artefacts, the small consolation of personal possessions to help alleviate the pain. In all likelihood they would be presented by a woman trained in the heartbreak of bereavement. But no corpse for a funereal, just the grateful thanks of Downing Street and how she'd given her life for her country.

But to Mike Bowman it also mattered. Should the same set of circumstances crop up again, he'd do whatever it took to ensure there was no repeat. Not on his watch.

He yawned and flipped the cigarette outside. Time to head home.

At 06.30 hours in the Harwich International Port, the overnight Stenna Line ferry from the Hook of Holland docked at the Parkeston Quay. As the vehicles and foot passengers began to disembark, Her Majesty's Border Force swung into action. But since the economic downturn of 2008, cutbacks had reduced the number of officers to less than the bare minimum required for efficient handling.

Barry Taylor, having avoided mandatory redundancy, should have turned up for his shift at six o'clock, but instead hurried into the office at five past the hour. It was the third time he'd been late this month and he'd been warned about time keeping. Apologising for his lateness, he squeezed to the back of the briefing room and listened while the shift commander ran through the latest list of 'illegals' to keep watch for. Dismissed at last, he grabbed a coffee from the machine and made his way into UK Immigration Passport Control.

Settling himself behind the desk he turned on the computer, checked the camera worked, and managed to finish the last of his coffee just before the new arrivals began to filter in. For a moment he thought about his young wife, heavily pregnant and due to give birth any time soon. Luckily, her mother lived a few streets away and was due to make her daily mid-morning visit. But the pregnancy had not been without its problems and Barry Taylor couldn't help but worry. It was a distraction he could have done without.

A family of four waited and he beckoned them forward. The Dutch parents were relatives of people living in Norwich, the two kids were tired and irritable, and he wasted no time in clearing them through. Next up were a man and his wife from Luxembourg, pensioners on a weeks holiday touring the Fens.

Then a red haired woman stepped forward and presented her Swedish passport. He checked the date of birth and examined the photo. Glancing up to verify the similarity he was immediately taken by how beautiful she was in the flesh.

'Miss Andreasson?'

She nodded.

He flicked through to the stamped visa. 'Where will you be staying?'

'I have a two week reservation at the Hilton in London.'

He inserted the passport under the electronic scanner. The computer verified the visa, acknowledged the genuine issue. 'And the reason for your visit?' Her eyes were gorgeous.

'To visit the Tate Gallery and go shopping.' She gave a shy smile and patted her red hair and he noticed a broad black bracelet on her wrist, a delicate silver chain hanging in a loop. 'I love to shop, especially in England. You have such pretty things.' The full red lips parted in a gentle smile and Taylor was momentarily transfixed by her mouth. Forcing himself to concentrate, he took a lingering glance at her passport and handed it back.

'Enjoy your stay,' he said automatically.

'Thank you so much,' she said softly, and tucked the passport inside a Prada handbag.

He watched her walk off, admiring the elegant poise, the shapely calves above her glossy, black high heels. Reluctantly he returned to the queue and waved for the next person to approach. A middle aged man with a fat beer gut strode forward and brandished his passport.

Taylor sighed and opened it up.

If he'd been a little more focussed, a little less distracted, he might have noticed that the young Swedish woman's passport was not all that it seemed. But she wasn't on the list of 'illegals' and Barry Taylor had other things on his mind.

He checked the man against his photo, a German from Hamburg, on a business trip to London.

'How long will you be in the country?'

'I think . . . , for three days only,' he managed, and Taylor handed it back. 'Enjoy your stay.' He looked round to see a party of school kids, their teachers looking harassed. 'Next!' he demanded brusquely, and steeled himself for the encounter.

The woman in high heels walked out onto the quayside and headed for the railway station. At 06.45 she bought a one way ticket to London's Liverpool Street Station, due to depart at 07.21 hours and making a direct journey.

Helena Goreya found the train waiting at the platform and picked a carriage. She was due at the Russian Embassy by twelve noon.

3
Checkpoint

More than a thousand miles east of London, the NATO aligned country of Latvia guards her borders against the dangers of the all encompassing power of the Russian Federation. At an insignificant checkpoint between the two countries, as the sun lifted clear of the horizon, the Latvian military prepared to begin the process of opening the barriers to the flow of traffic.

Racing south towards the safety of Latvia, a young woman by the name of Anna Kuznetsova grimaced as her old saloon skittered over the badly maintained road. Out here in the wastes of the Russian borderland it was deemed unnecessary to spend scarce resources on the upkeep of little used highways. Amongst the scattered pockets of forested hills, the terrain broadened out into vast swathes of rolling lowlands, ideally suited to the deployment of tanks. And the young woman knew enough about the military to appreciate roads were not needed for rapid movement through this country. At the same time, she wondered whether to keep pushing so hard over such a ruinous surface. A broken spring wouldn't help.

Her rear-view mirror showed a drift of dust from the Lada's wheels, no sign of anyone following. But her skin crawled with the fear of being caught. With every passing kilometre she expected to be overhauled by the GRU. The speed of their Mercedes Sports cars would easily outstrip the ancient Lada. Again she wondered if those at last night's drunken party remembered talking to an attentive young waitress. And if they did, would they also remember what had been said, the information they had inadvertently let slip. Her foot stayed pressed to the floor.

Twelve kilometres north of the crossing the road curved to the right, skirting the edge of a sprawling forest. Up ahead, where a logging trail exited the woods, a dark car had parked at the roadside and Anna tensed. Had they got ahead of her? She eased off the accelerator, not wanting to appear too hurried, and the Lada drifted down to eighty kilometres an hour. Her hands felt weak on the steering, a wave of apprehension encompassing her body. Driving past she dared to glance over and breathed a sigh of relief. An old man was walking back to the car, fiddling with his trouser buttons. He must have answered a call of nature. A grey haired woman sat in the passenger seat, waiting.

Anna smiled grimly and picked up speed. If the car held together, a few more minutes would see her at the checkpoint.

She drove on, thinking of her Uncle. Forty-eight year old Gvido Medris held the post of Forest Ranger. He was a carpenter by trade and when the work came his way travelled far and wide making furniture. And she was very fond of Uncle Gvido. A kindly, bearded father figure; she visited at least three times a year, more if she could. He would be surprised to see Anna on the doorstep, but his laughter would echo loudly as he enveloped her in an enormous, welcoming bear hug.

The checkpoint came into view and she slowed. As far as she could tell, today appeared much the same as normal. People queued in their cars waiting for the big sliding steel barriers to be opened. Only official vehicles crossed at night, it was 07.00am for the public.

And so she joined the line of cars. She pulled to a halt behind an old VW Polo, switched off and stepped out to count the cars ahead. There were fourteen. With luck she might be across in twenty minutes. Back inside the car she tried to relax. In normal times Anna visited Uncle Medris three times a year, coinciding with the main holidays. This was an unscheduled vacation and she hoped the Russians on the barrier wouldn't be suspicious. She felt hot, even though the morning air was cool, knew she was suffering from nerves.

The clock on her dashboard ticked over to 07.00 and up ahead the steel barriers slid back and the cars shuffled forward.

Nervously she turned and checked the road behind. Still no sign of the dreaded GRU. She switched on the engine, moved up two cars length, and switched off. Closer now, so near. She could see the Russian officials checking documents; travel papers, passports for those who needed them, engaging the drivers in quick but thorough questioning.

Then came the sound of a fast moving car snarling up the road from behind and Anna trembled, felt sick. Her rear-view mirror showed a black Mercedes, and as it flashed past she caught sight of three men inside. The driver hit the brakes, hard. It slewed to a halt in a cloud of dust and two men jumped out, armed with submachine-guns.

Anna froze, alarmed by what was happening. Harsh voices issued orders and a young man and woman were manhandled back into their Fiat. The Mercedes growled, edging forward, moving menacingly toward the front of the queue. Striding along the line of cars the men of the GRU hesitated by each vehicle, checking the occupants.

When the black Mercedes drew level with a battered Audi, the driver seemed to panic and the door flew open. She saw that the driver was pleading with the armed men, hands spread wide, but couldn't distinguish the words. Shouts were exchanged and the man took a step backwards. The Mercedes stopped moving and the soldiers up at the checkpoint turned to watch. One of the machine-gunners cocked his weapon and the man threw his arms in the air, vigorously shaking his head.

Anna heard the shout of 'traitor!' and the man screamed a denial. 'Nyet! Nyet!' He broke and ran, and the machine gun stuttered, a staccato blast of shots. The man made it as far as the front of his Audi and staggered. He reached for the radiator grill, desperate to keep from falling, clawing at the metalwork. He fell, head bouncing on the road. Crimson blood ran over the dusty surface, spreading in a glistening pool.

Shocked by the brutal execution, Anna felt tears stinging her eyes. A haze of gun smoke lifted from the barrel and an oppressive silence settled over the scene.

The machine-gunner broke the stillness, walked across to the body and pushed with the toe of his boot. The lifeless figure lifted and then flopped face down

Anna shrank in her seat, struggling to comprehend. The Mercedes made a tight turn and drove towards her, coming back at a snail's pace. From the checkpoint's compound a number of soldiers marched out to the body, began to lift it away. The two machine-gunners walked very deliberately to each waiting vehicle, pausing to look inside before moving on. Nearing Anna's Lada, the leading man stopped, dark eyes flitting over the car's interior. She cringed, he seemed to be taking longer with his inspection. Reluctantly she glanced up. He stood there grinning suggestively and opened the door.

'All alone?' he asked, leering at her low neckline.

She managed to nod, mouth dry.

He bent forward and she smelt bad breath, heavy with onion.

'I could escort you to the checkpoint,' he suggested. 'A man like me, I could help you jump the queue.'

Anna summoned up her courage. These men didn't seem to be aware of her status, not yet anyway. She looked him in the eye. 'I *am* in a hurry. My Uncle is unwell, he needs me.'

The GRU man giggled, a strange high pitched cackle. 'I'll bet he does,' he said, peering down at the swell of her breasts.

Anna swallowed, shook her head slightly. 'You don't understand. He is old and frail, not like you fit and healthy.' Flattery might work.

He grinned and straightened from the door. 'Vasili, see to the others,' he ordered, and walked round the front of the car to the passenger side. He squeezed his bulk into the front seat, submachine-gun between his legs and leaned close to her ear. 'A pretty girl like you should not be alone. How are you called?'

'Anna,' she whispered. 'Can I start the car?'

'If I let you, do I get a kiss?'

Inside, she shivered at the thought, but gave way. After the shooting no-one would care. 'If you must,' she said, and turned the key. The engine coughed and caught, and she blipped the throttle.

Strong fingers gripped her jaw forcing her face towards him. His lips crushed down on hers, painful against her teeth, wet and onion sour, and she struggled free. He laughed and slapped a knee. 'Ha!. ., a real woman, a real man's woman.'

Anna found first gear and pulled left out of the queue. The driver of the Polo averted his eyes. She waited for her passenger to try something else, a hand on her thigh, or worse. But he sat relaxed and let her drive, up to the barrier at the head of the line.

The soldiers from the compound carried the body to a truck, trailing drops of blood on the ground. Afraid of what might happen next, she pulled on the handbrake.

'You have papers?' he demanded.

'Yes,' she said, and pointed. 'In the glove box.'

He looked down in front of him and slowly smiled. 'Then give them to me.'

Anna frowned. She would have to lean across him and didn't like the idea. But along the road, four-hundred metres away, the Latvian flag hung limply on the pole. She mustn't waver now. Heart in her mouth, she leaned over the gear lever, across his legs and pressed the release catch. Her fingers found the envelope and she quickly leant back, holding them out for inspection.

Reading through, a thin smile played across the cruel mouth. 'So, Anna Kuznetsova, you work in Pskov, at the Kayanashki Hotel. I have been to this hotel. Maybe we can meet there when you come back? I could take you to the theatre.'

It was the last thing she would have thought of, but she managed a small smile. 'I would like that,' she simpered, knowing she would never return.

'Good, . . . , good. These all seem in order. I will clear it with the border guards.' He handed them over and began to climb out, stopped and leaned close.

'Anna . . . , one more thing. You will kiss me, here on the cheek. And you press very hard.' Another grin, and that stupid giggle. 'Your lipstick will be for all to see.'

She sighed. If that's what it took to be free, then why not? She planted her lips on his face, slightly apart and pressed. Pulling away she looked and nodded. 'There can be no doubt a woman has kissed you.'

He slapped her thigh and squeezed, let go and climbed out. Slamming the door, he called for her to wait and beckoned to a guard. She saw the guard nod, and her gruesome man from the GRU gestured to the exit.

'Take care, Anna,' he called after her.

31

The Lada trundled forward, out of the Russian zone and into the no-man's land between east and west. There was a sign, speed limit, 5kph. There were tears now, tears of exquisite relief, she could hardly see for the moisture rolling down her cheeks. Her body trembled, shocked by the ordeal.

And then there was a friendly voice in her own language, asking if she was all right, and could he see her papers. Now it was tears of joy holding out the envelope, sobbing with laughter.

The man shook his head, perplexed, obviously thinking she was crazy. She managed to sober up and made her apology. He smiled gently and handed her the envelope. 'If you're sure you're alright?' he tried to clarify.

'Oh, yes,' Anna laughed, wiping away the last of the tears. 'More than alright, I'm free!'

'Off you go then. Drive carefully.'

Still shaking with laughter, Anna Kuznetsova released the hand brake and left the border crossing behind her. It would be another thirty kilometres before she arrived at her Uncle's home.

To the east of Canterbury at a lay-by on the A28 the proprietor of 'Tom's Café' had opened for business. The first of the day's lorry drivers were tucking into breakfast, the warm aroma of fried bacon drifting on the still air.

Anatoly Pushkin walked the last few yards and dropped the haversack onto a white plastic chair. He ordered coffee and a large bacon roll. With his back to the morning sun he nursed the polystyrene cup and watched the cook flip sizzling rashers. And he smiled. There were many things the English did well; a fried bacon roll was one of them.

His watch showed 06.58. Another hour should see him at Canterbury West Station and he was scheduled to catch the 08.25 high speed for St Pancras.

'Bacon roll!' Tom called, and Pushkin took it from the hot plate to the table.

Ten minutes later, meal devoured and coffee emptied, the Russian set off at a brisk walk along the grass verge of the main carriageway. A police siren approached from behind, wailing closer. He put his head down and hunched into the dark blue fleece, and the car flashed by in answer to some emergency; the occupants were far too immersed in their current crisis to worry about an isolated figure wandering along the grass verge.

Pushkin smiled thinly. If they had the slightest inkling as to who or what he was, an armed response unit would be on its way. He pushed on, lengthening his stride. Time was of the essence.

4
Shadows

Hugh Atkinson reached a hand over to the bedside cabinet and killed the alarm. He lay in the half light of drawn curtains and listened to his wife's soft breathing. The hushed electronic beep of the digital clock hardly ever disturbed her sleep, at worst she might turn over. He slipped out of bed, tiptoed across the thick carpet and grabbed his robe. Not wanting to wake the kids, he crept downstairs. Toast and chilled butter with a cafetiere of strong Brazilian coffee was the daily routine. While he waited for the toast Atkinson opened the back door and stepped onto the raised patio. A tree-lined garden met his gaze, and Miranda's choice of flowers took the first of the sun's rays, gently warming the neatly mowed lawn. Beyond the end of the garden, fenced off acres of rolling grassland surrounded a distant mansion, a grand building which he knew very well. It was his place of work.

Nigh on five years back, his Section leader in GCHQ had interrupted his work and ordered him to report to 'B' Section's main office. The man who interviewed him was Commander Robert Fraser. At the end of the grilling he asked Atkinson if he'd like to go and work for another unit, very hush-hush. He explained it would be a lot more rewarding than his present job, both with the variety of assignments involved, and in his annual remuneration. The 'Old Man' as he came to know him, indicated his bank manager might even call him 'sir' when he visited the local branch.

The toaster jumped and he ambled inside and spread butter. Coffee brewed, he pressed the plunger and poured.

Hugh Atkinson took his breakfast outside, sat at the small scrollwork table, and relaxed with a mouthful of crisp toast, remembering an intensive few weeks of interrogation. Over the course of the next month he'd been questioned and tested by a number of computer whiz kids, all of whom had failed to ruffle his feathers. The main sticking point had been the intervention of his then boss, Peter Drysdale who had no intention of letting one of his star men get whisked away by this fledgling operation.

In the end, a direct order from Whitehall secured his release and the following week he took on the responsibilities of Senior Cryptanalysis for NDSO.

He surveyed the rose bordered grass with a good deal of pride. Miranda made for such a good wife. She looked after the kids, saw to their schooling and ran the luxurious four bed roomed house without a murmur. And she also managed to work flexi-time hours as an accountant for Harrington-Stafford Solicitors in Cheltenham's up-market financial street; a welcome addition to the family finances. They'd stretched themselves to purchase the property and the mortgage took a large chunk of money. Above all that, she didn't ask questions. As far as she was concerned, he was a civil servant working for the MOD in a 'sensitive' position. That was enough for her.

He checked his watch, time for a wash and shave. It was a ten minute drive to the mansion's only entranceway on the south side of the estate, and on top of that, he needed petrol. The Audi drank fuel as if there was no tomorrow. After using the bathroom, he crept back into the bedroom and dressed in an open neck shirt and sports jacket, smart-casual. Miranda turned over, one slim leg appearing outside the duvet. It would be so easy to slide in beside her, warm and soft. But the office awaited. The latest batch of Signals-Intel would be waiting for his mathematical analysis. Commander Fraser required his skills.

At the boy's bedroom door, Hugh leant to listen. Christopher's seventh birthday party was coming up; Hugh must remember to order that bicycle from Halfords. He left him sleeping peacefully. Tina's door stood slightly ajar and he peeked in. She lay with the covers over her shoulders, her blonde hair straying across the pillow. A precocious five year old bundle of energy. The smile lingered as he went downstairs.

His Audi sat next to Miranda's Ford Focus and he squeezed between the two and clambered aboard. Leaving the front gate he turned left, then indicated to pull round a parked Toyota pick-up. At the crossroads he made another left onto the A40 and joined the eastbound traffic. There was a BP station up the road and he turned on the radio for traffic and travel. The short morning commute had begun.

A few hundred yards from Hugh Atkinson's house, the occupant of the Toyota pick-up jotted down the time of the Audi's departure and reached for his flask of coffee. It would be the wife and kids next, on their way to school. Time enough to stretch his legs before returning to conceal himself inside the cab.

North-west of Moscow, the once grand Principality of Pskov basks in the glory of her ancient past. Stately buildings of the Russian Orthodox Church litter the countryside, and broad swathes of tall pine trees dominate the skyline. Forty kilometres due east of the Latvian border and hidden in the densely forested landscape, a well guarded military establishment acts as a base camp for Russia's Special Forces, specifically, the elite formation known as the Spetsnaz.

Under the watchful eye of an army Lieutenant, a double barrier to the north of the compound guards the main entrance. Razor wire, tank traps and dogs reinforce the perimeter fence. It was during the morning roll-call that a GRU licensed Mercedes drove up to the outer barrier and stopped. The soldier on guard duty checked the driver's documents and studied them carefully before handing them back. He then wandered slowly round the car and peered in through the windows. Having seen the driver's identification, and verified the car belonged to Major Shinsky, a liaison officer for Military Intelligence, the guard fully understood the seniority of the man behind the wheel. But the guard hid a smile and continued to meander round the vehicle. Members of Military Intelligence and the elite forces of Spetsnaz rarely saw eye to eye. Eventually the guard felt he'd delayed enough.

36

In the guardroom, standing well back from the windows, a full Colonel smiled thinly as the guard ambled towards the barrier and looked over for permission to allow the car through. The duty Lieutenant gave an exaggerated nod and the pole swung up to the vertical.

The Mercedes rolled forward and drove to the second barrier where the next guard saluted and waved him over to the holding compound.

Inside the guardroom the Colonel stubbed out his cigarette and nodded to the Lieutenant in command.

'Arrest him,' he ordered.

A signal went out to the waiting soldiers and the driver found himself abruptly dragged from his seat and frog marched into the guardroom. Vehemently shouting his protestations the man from the GRU struggled to a halt in front of the Colonel.

'What is wrong here?' he demanded. 'Do you know who I am?'

The Colonel took a threatening pace forward and studied him closely.

'Yes, I know who you are. If my information is correct you are Major Shinsky and I understand that you cannot control a very loose tongue. I have therefore been authorised to detain you for questioning.'

Shinsky blustered. 'And who gave you that authority?'

'Your Commanding Officer, Major. Your own Commanding Officer.'

Shinsky hesitated, some of the defiance subsiding. 'On what grounds?'

'Passing on state secrets while under the influence of drink for a start.'

'Who says so?'

The Colonel's hard eyes narrowed. 'Right now,' he said menacingly, 'I do, and for the moment that is more than enough.'

The Major blinked, paling under the Colonel's grim countenance. 'Where is your evidence?' he tried meekly.

'Silence!' shouted the Colonel, the first time he had raised his voice. 'You are a traitor to the Motherland and I act on behalf of the Presidium.' He turned to the Lieutenant. 'Take him to the interrogation block. I will attend to him shortly.'

Shinsky wilted, physically drained. What little time he had left would now be in the hands of the Spetsnaz. Their methods of inquisition were talked of in hushed whispers. His future looked very uncertain.

Miranda Atkinson came awake to the sound of her radio alarm pumping out Chris Rhea's Road to Hell and she stretched languidly. The sun lanced in through a gap in the curtains and she threw back the duvet to feel the warm on her naked body. She lay there until the news came on, slid out of bed and drew back the curtains. She stood in the sunshine watching the sparrows flit amongst the trees and then slipped into her wrap-around kimono.

She showered and dressed before calling the children. In the kitchen she prepared Weetabix and a boiled egg for herself. The kids came downstairs wide awake and giggling, full of life.

'Up the table you two,' she insisted, and when they'd wriggled onto their seats, she dished up their bowls of cereal.

As she cracked her boiled egg, Miranda looked at the kids and thought how wonderful it was to have such a contented pair; happy to go to a well regarded school that excelled in the local performance tables. They finished their breakfast, drank the freshly squeezed juice, and waited for permission to leave the table.

'All done?' she teased, and their heads bobbed in unison. 'Alright,' she nodded, 'and don't forget to clean your teeth.'

Thirty minutes later they were standing inside the front door, school bags packed and ready to go.

Miranda checked them over, ran a comb through Tina's hair, and straightened Christopher's tie.

'Are we ready then?' she smiled.

'Yes, Mummy,' Tina said, 'time to go, time to go, time to . . .'

'Enough!' Miranda warned, frowning.

Tina stopped chanting, eyes downcast, a petulant bottom lip.

A kiss on the cheek brought the smile back and Miranda opened the door. They ran to the car and she opened the doors. Only when she was sure they were securely strapped into the child seats did she start the car and reverse. Out in the narrow road she swerved past a parked pick-up and turned right for Cheltenham. Five minutes down the A40 she peeled off into a quiet suburb and pulled up fifty feet from the school gate. Christopher and Tina slid out onto the pavement and she kissed them goodbye. They ran to join their friends and waved as they walked in.

'Hi, Miranda.'

She turned in surprise. 'Hello, Cynthia, off to the gym?'

The tall blonde laughed. 'Only forty minutes, then coffee at Starbucks. You?'

'Work today. Big client coming in. I might make it tomorrow.'

Cynthia beamed. 'That would be good, I'll look forward to it.'

'Okay, sorry, have to fly. Bye,' she smiled, and bent into the driver's seat. Cynthia was so nice, she thought, one of the mums she could rely on to baby sit or offer a helping hand. It was good to have lots of friends. She pulled out from the kerb, turned back to the main road, and headed for the office. Life was sweet.

A hundred yards away on the far side of the road, a man in a red Post Office van lowered his camera and started the engine. He pulled out into the traffic and set off in pursuit of the woman's Ford Focus. Tailing a normal member of the public required no special skills, the innocents caught up in the world of international espionage were an easy target.

Outside the Atkinson's home, the man in the Toyota pick-up climbed out and shrugged into a high-vis, fluorescent yellow jacket. He reached across behind the passenger seat and grabbed a red metal tool box.

Having locked the vehicle he walked the short distance to the driveway, just one more tradesman about to start work; a common sight amongst the affluent dwellings of a middle class hamlet. At the front door, hidden from the road by a line of trees, he produced a set of locksmiths picks and let himself in. His visit took him to the master bedroom, then the open plan kitchen-diner, and finally the spacious living room. It took eleven minutes to install the five 'implants'. Before leaving he returned to each room and quietly voiced the same numerical sequence.

'One-two-thee-four.'

An acknowledgement in his earpiece confirmed the miniature microphones detected his transmission. In less than fifteen minutes, the man closed the door and walked back to the Toyota. He checked his watch; surveillance of the Atkinson property was 'live'.

5
White Noise

In Moscow, Colonel-General Viktor Leonid Zherlenko, Deputy Chief of the Russian Military Intelligence Directorate (GRU), strode purposefully into the office building on the south-west corner of Khodynka Aerodrome. With a disdainful grunt he dodged the many muttered greetings from passing members of the Headquarters staff and took the lift to the top floor of the eastern wing. When the lift whispered to a halt he stepped out into an empty corridor and crossed to his office overlooking the inner quadrangle.

'Good morning, General.' The greeting came from Major Oleg Stapanovich of the in house secretariat.

Viktor Zherlenko moved his heavy bulk across to the long window adjacent to his desk. Sunlight bathed the manicured lawn below where flowering bushes of scarlet and purple nestled in the precision edged borders.

'It is a *very* good morning, Major. Today we strike fear into the people of Britannia, is that not so?'

Stapanovich, an intellectual scholar of military history, looked up from arranging the paperwork. 'Yes, General. Not since the beginning of the new Russian Federation have we launched such a mission.'

Zherlenko turned from the window, his thick eyebrows briefly knitted in a frown. He gestured at the desk. 'Not too much of that paperwork is there?'

The Major swallowed, winced. 'None that need your urgent attention. If you wish it, then I could manage them on your behalf.'

Zherlenko's mood of optimism for the day took a turn for the better. Stapanovich could indeed take over the inconsequential signing of mundane reports. It would leave him free to enjoy the forthcoming encounter.

41

'Good,' he said, and squeezed his large frame into the chair.

The Major whipped away the stack of papers and walked them over to his own small desk in a corner behind the door. By the time he found space at the side of the computer screen there was little room for anything else.

In comparison, the General's spacious oak desk lay empty. Computers and their associated paraphernalia were not for him; his underlings might wish to play with the latest gadgets but Zherlenko preferred to not have his desk cluttered with electronics. An old fashioned flip calendar, a leather topped writing pad and pen holder, and the indispensable telephones were the tools of his profession. His final addition to the needs of a senior planner, two large wall maps indicating Russia's current military dispositions across the world.

He selected a Cuban cigar from the silver case, snipped the end and struck a match. Blue smoke snaked lazily above his thick white hair. He leaned back in the chair and watched the smoke rise to the ceiling, reflecting on the orders that had brought this mission to fruition. Following a routine monthly meeting in the Kremlin, a Senior Senator of the Upper House had approached him with an important proposition. The Senator informed Zherlenko that the Russian President, infuriated by the West's continued accusations of so called 'hacking', and political subterfuge, required an immediate plan on retaliatory action against the British Secret Service.

Zherlenko had consulted widely, and with information acquired from his Special Forces, settled on a plan to go after the most secret British unit. And the President, whose many close friends continued to suffer because of financial sanctions imposed on Russia's banking sector, took one look at the proposal and agreed without reservation.

The strident ring of the black telephone cut short his enjoyment and he lifted the receiver. 'Zherlenko,' he grunted.

A metallic voice echoed as if from far away. 'General, this is Colonel Ilya Bayalin of the 12th Directorate in Pskov.'

Zherlenko narrowed his dark eyes. The region of Pskov housed the training facilities of 'Niagara', an elite unit of Special Forces responsible for covert military operations.

'Go on,' he ordered.

'Bad news, General. I have arrested an officer, a Major Shinsky of the GRU. There was a party at the Kayanashki Hotel in Pskov, and too much vodka. He boasted of the operation and now a Latvian waitress has fled over the border. She said her uncle was ill.'

Zherlenko swore into the phone, putting two and two together. It didn't take a genius to work out this woman had overheard more than was good for her. This could unhinge the entire operation.

'When did you know of this?'

'Not until 08.30 hours. A member of the GRU later remembered her at the southern checkpoint. That was at 07.00, two hours before we began to search.'

'Do we have anybody in Latvia looking?'

'Yes, General. They located the Uncle's dwelling, but no sign of the girl or him. I called them off for now. Our contacts in Riga have heard nothing.'

Zherlenko thought hard. If the girl had run, it could only mean she wanted to talk to the British or Americans. She wouldn't dare talk to the Latvian authorities, too many ethnic Russians involved. So . . . , he mused, she might well be hiding in the forest. And the forests of the borderland crossed boundaries, ideal for the men of 'Niagara'.

'Now listen to me, Colonel Bayalin, this is important. You will locate for me a Lieutenant Boris Tsegler. You will use my name and tell him I want a small unit to infiltrate border territory and find the girl. If he can bring her out unharmed, so be it. If not, kill her.'

The silence lasted too long.

'Do you hear me, Bayalin?' he demanded.

'What if they should come across NATO forces, General?'

'Believe me Colonel, Lieutenant Tsegler is too experienced to make such an error.'

'And if he does get her out?'

'I will send someone to question her. Now I suggest you get on with it!'

Colonel Ilya Bayalin got the message. 'Of course, General. I will see to it now.'

Zherlenko heard the phone go down and slowly replaced the handset. Boris Tsegler had served the Motherland well. A veteran of covert assassination the man could be relied upon to get the job done. Twice promoted on the field and well versed in handling unexpected situations, he'd risen quickly through the ranks. And General Zherlenko had come to rely on the Lieutenant's expertise. And even if the worst should happen and they ran into NATO forces, little would come of it. Of recent years the Western Alliance had grown timid, risk averse.

But some of the gloss had been rubbed off the General's day. Operation Lightning was the culmination of much detailed planning, and now some snip of a girl might ruin everything. As for Major Shinsky, death would be too kind for him.

Hugh Atkinson sat in his office on the third floor of NDSO's headquarters and studied the latest batch of intercepts. Three screens filtered the data streaming in from the outside sources; one for MI6, another for MI5, and the last, more importantly, from GCHQ. Beneath the dormer window overlooking the gravel driveway, a second workstation housed four individual computers running complex cryptanalysis software, delving into the latest COMINT. A large black IBM mainframe took up most of the far wall, a multi-coloured array of LEDs flickering as it worked with its underlying machine code.

Atkinson's sharp brain analysed the information presented with robotic precision, retrieving and discarding countless transmissions, highlighting, logging and filing. His fingers were a constant blur on the keyboard, sifting through the myriad gigabytes of data.

But without the complex processing power of these hybrid systems, he well knew his limited human expertise would be floundering in the dark. He gave the computers direction, told the programmes how to concentrate their terabytes of search capabilities. And every now and then, through a combination of human and electronic brainpower, a screen would blink, flag up a warning. In that moment, Hugh Atkinson's unparalleled instinct for hunting down a new Electronic Signal Emitter, came into their own. Today was no different to many other days, the listening stations dotted about the globe retrieved their many and varied signals. Radio waves and cable transmissions: surface to air relays, fighter aircraft, ship to shore, and battlefield comms. Police, ambulance, fire and rescue, satellites, and even Russia's feed to the International Space Station, all had to be looked at to ascertain their normal patterns of predictability. If their usage fell within the normal parameters of application they could be eliminated from the search. It was the unexpected new frequency, an unrelated pulse that had to be investigated.

And then a screen on the remote workstation stopped scrolling. A line of digital data lit up, flashing bright green. Seconds later the far screen also stopped, blinking in unison.

Atkinson bounded across the room and threw himself into the swivel seat. He grabbed the mouse, highlighted the flashing data and isolated its properties. The transmission time recorded at two seconds. That ruled out a digital burst which would have been milliseconds. Initial evaluation ascribed the signal as a short-wave radio frequency falling into a possible 'instruction' capacity.

He switched computers, to the far screen. Again he extracted the data. The results presented him with the modern equivalent of 'triangulation', pinpointing the target by geo-mapping the predicted location.

Atkinson moved to his main desk and downloaded the Intel into a fresh document. He named it: Signal-Trace 4270043/12, and stored it via an encrypted USB. Adjusting his glasses, he moved back to the remote station. At the left hand terminal he called up the internal programming software and began to write a new set of instructions. When he'd finished inputting and passing the data through a test cycle, he uploaded to the mainframe and requested verification. The IBM hummed, a sequence of LEDs flashed, and the onboard monitor flickered once; "accepted . . finished".

Hugh Atkinson smiled and smoothed his hair. If that Signal Emitter repeated with the same digital signature, then the IBM, utilising the newly installed algorithm, would instigate an official response. Until then he was prepared to wait. Miranda wouldn't be too happy but it was time for an office sleepover, this was too important to ignore.

In London, a meeting of the Joint Intelligence Committee had been convened in MI5's Millbank offices overlooking the Thames. Representatives of GCHQ, MI6, the Metropolitan Anti-terrorist Police Division, and the Military attended, and MI5's Director General chaired the meeting. In total, seventeen officials presented themselves to the conference, and they included a significant proportion of Britain's most senior personnel of the Secret Service.

Finally, seated anonymously in the far corner of the room, a man by the name of Sir Hillary Montague had also answered the summons and now waited patiently should he be called upon, to answer the case on behalf of the National Directorate for Special Operations.

When called to order, the meeting opened with an address by Rear-Admiral Francis Barrington, Assistant Deputy Commander at the Ministry of Defence. He gave a brief overview of the MOD's current dispositions and emphasised the twin threats of Russian intervention in both their Middle East, Mediterranean operations, and that of their subversion of the Baltic states. He emphasised the recent threat to European cities by the Russian deployment of Nuclear-capable Iskander missiles on the Polish border.

GCHQ in turn, confirmed an upsurge in both Signals Intelligence (SigIntel) and Human Intelligence (HumIntel), and that the CIA and FBI were providing round the clock satellite imagery as and when required, particularly in conjunction with NATO's build up of forces in the east.

MI6 reported on recent covert operations in Europe, extensive co-operation with Belgium, France and Italy, and the ongoing threat from the far east, namely North Korea. The British Embassy in the Malaysian capital of Kuala Lumpur still required a substantial reassignment of resources.

In conclusion, the Director General declared, MI5 was itself inundated with a multitude of investigations, struggling to meet requirements, and was involved in heated discussions with the Home Office in an attempt to reverse the recent cuts in the budget.

Fifty minutes after the briefing had begun the DG then rose from his seat to congratulate his colleagues on a splendid effort in the face of unprecedented levels of foreign espionage, and the meeting officially closed. Unofficially, as the support staff began to disperse, five of the most senior officers withdrew to a corner of the conference room and continued to discuss current issues, not least, the urgent need to resolve a 'situation' that had arisen in the Baltic state of Latvia. It was agreed, off the record, that as the main agencies had their hands full it would be an opportune moment for Montague's NDSO to take the reins.

Sir Hillary accepted the undertaking and added the proviso that NDSO would confine disclosure of the operation to only those with 'a need-to-know', thereby limiting any interference.

Agreement reached, he made his excuses and left. Arriving at his office on the Chelsea Embankment his first call went to Commander Robert Fraser. An unscheduled meeting was set for the following morning.

It was late morning when Mike Bowman meandered out into the back garden of his Herefordshire cottage and stood watching a distant line of sheep wander down a slope. At the base of the hill the flock dispersed to graze, browsing the fresh found grass. Just below their new pasture, the River Wye wound serenely along the valley, and three brightly coloured kayaks drifted lazily down stream. Bowman breathed out, luxuriating in some well earned down-time.

Here at the cottage, alone in the rolling hills and valleys, any thoughts of the 'service' melted into the background. This was a place to relax and forget about the bad stuff. There was always peace and tranquillity, a place to get his head straight. The old house looked a bit ramshackle but he'd bought it cheap and loved its quirkiness. Access was by a narrow lane leading to the front gate and terminating at the entrance to an old outhouse that served as his garage. Four and a half acres of gently sloping pasture allowed for an uninterrupted field of vision. In his line of work it paid to be cautious. His nearest neighbour lived half a mile up river, the nearest road, a quarter mile down the other end of the lane.

He lifted his head to the sky and felt the hot sun on his face. Next month he would turn twenty-seven. Born in a British Military Hospital in Germany, his mother Mary, and his father, Brigadier Anthony Bowman, had seen to his early upbringing and schooled him in the way of the world. For the best part of the last nine years there'd been some kind of a gun in his hand. Way back in basic training the instructors had singled him out as a natural, and later, whether it was against terrorist or insurgents, he'd proved them right. Now he used those skills on behalf of the Government, a legitimate weapon in the defence of the realm.

Bowman's only contact with the outside world would come via a Personal Radio Transceiver operating on a modified Tetra network. No phone line, no computer, no mobile; other then the secure radio, his isolation was complete.

So the unexpected noise of a nearby car engine brought him to back to the present. It was a muted growl, in low gear approaching along the lane. He dived through to the kitchen, scooped up the pistol and moved cautiously to the side of the sitting room window. Two hundred yards down the rutted track a short wheel-base Land Rover swayed awkwardly over the pot holes. The dull green paint job bore a striking similarity to his Defender. Then he shook his head in disbelief.

Sarah Campbell sat behind the wheel wrestling the Rover over the worst of the undulating surface. Three years she'd been with the team, recruited from an armed response unit at the Metropolitan Police, and Bowman had worked with her two summers back. It had been Kent, and six weeks of hunting down a gun smuggling syndicate operating out of Faversham's muddy creeks. There was a violent ending. Sarah Campbell knew how to handle herself. Two dead gun-runners and three wounded. But a stray bullet found its mark and after a short stay in hospital, he'd brought here to recuperate from the flesh wound to her thigh. And for a while, as the long summer days had drifted towards the Autumn, they'd found an easy compatibility that went far beyond professional relationship. When the wound healed and fitness returned she'd reported back for duty, out of his life.

But why the hell had she turned up now? Walking round to the front door he gave the handle a sharp tug to force it free of the jamb. He stepped onto the crazy paving, folded his arms and waited.

The Land Rover bounced over an extra large hump and rumbled to a halt.

Sarah stepped down on the far side of the cab, lounged over the bonnet and smiled.

Bowman found himself torn between the pleasure of seeing her again and the unwelcome intrusion into his peaceful sanctuary. She'd invaded his personal space and yet he couldn't find reason enough to be angry.

He smiled gently. 'Hello, Angel, sight for sore eyes.' She had a lovely face. Her dark hair, cut into a short bob, framed her softly rounded cheekbones, and tiny dimples only served to accentuate her generous mouth. Her eyes drew him in, liquid dark, welcoming.

She moved out from behind the vehicle, walking elegantly towards him. Beneath the loose fitting jacket her body swayed in unison, her long legs emphasised by the tightness of a pair of jeggings. She closed the gap until he felt her breath on his face.

'Hello, Mike Bowman. Remember me?' Her eyes twinkled as she reached up and pecked his cheek. Her fragrance filled the air, delicate, intoxicating.

'There are certain things a man never forgets.'

She met his eyes, held them, and then looked away. Her jawbone clenched. 'This is business.'

Bowman grinned wickedly. 'Alright, it's business. Come inside and tell me all about it.' He turned and led her to the kitchen 'Grab a chair. Can I get you anything?'

'Tea would be nice.'

'Then tea you shall have.' He filled the kettle, rummaged for a clean mug and popped in a tea bag.

Raising her voice above the hiss of the kettle she said, 'Fraser sent me; might be a new job for us.'

Bowman leant back, palms supporting him on the edge of the worktop. 'Go on.'

'Long story or short?'

He grinned. 'Short will do.'

She brushed a stray hair from the corner of her mouth. 'Last night, Border Force received a call from Dover Coastguard. An unidentified sighting off the North Foreland. Then early this morning a dog walker found footsteps leading up the beach from the high water mark at Jos Bay. All the residents had been asked to report anything unusual. Kent police later spotted a hiker on the A28 heading towards Canterbury. He attracted their attention because he was on the grass verge banking. But they were on a blue light and couldn't stop.'

The kettle boiled, clicked off. He turned to make the tea. 'And?' he prompted over his shoulder.

'Nothing really. Fraser called me in, said you were resting, and would I mind waiting here. He'd be in touch. Short enough?'

He placed the mug on the table and sat opposite. 'Sounds more like a job for MI5. Nothing more?'

She sipped at her hot tea. 'Not at the moment.'

Bowman fumbled for a cigarette. 'Do you mind?'

'Your house.'

He flicked the lighter, drew smoke and let it rise to the ceiling. 'He tell you what happened with me?'

She shook her dark hair.

Bowman recounted the events leading up to his coming home and finished by stating the obvious. 'I couldn't save her. He used semi-armour piercing. Nothing I could do.' He wasn't making excuses, it was just a statement of fact.

She nodded in sympathy, not immune to the sadness in his voice, a professional understanding of the situation. They sat in companionable silence; she drinking the mug of tea and Bowman smoking. They were very experienced at waiting.

At the Russian Embassy in London's Kensington Palace Gardens, a smartly dressed woman stepped out of a cab, paid the driver and walked up to the entrance. She spoke quietly to the man on the door who then beckoned to an aide. He formally escorted her through to the richly decorated main reception.

The Ambassador greeted Helena Goreya from behind an intricately carved desk. He was fat, bald and short. His chin bore signs of grey stubble and she guessed he was well in his fifties. Thankfully the meeting lasted only long enough for formal introductions. A female attendant whisked her away to a lift and showed her a room on the upper floor. In the bathroom she stripped, removed the wig and heavy make up and dressed. She chose faded denim jeans, a grey singlet and a black imitation bomber jacket. Nike trainers finished the look.

In the attic, in the so called 'penthouse', the Senior Signals Specialist took over from the duty watch keeper and coded up a short message. He transferred the encrypted signal to the transmitting station. The software took receipt of three, five-letter blocks of coding and stored them for sending. The transmission would be sent as a 'one-time-pad', virtually unbreakable, in a single electronic burst. When all was ready, the Specialist checked the time, and pressed the send key. Before he removed his finger, a signal lasting less than a 100th of a second in duration hit the air waves.

At Moscow's Signals Intelligence Command, the operator tasked specifically with UK surveillance, took the incoming message, decrypted the three blocks of letters, and flashed the result to the monitor. Final translation read, "mission under way". Moscow's duty Telegraphist acknowledged.

Down one flight of stairs, Helena Goreya answered the knock on her door. 'Come.'

The Deputy Assistant Attaché breezed in. 'Helena! How long has it been?'

She smiled, but not with her eyes. This man made her skin crawl and she avoided the small talk.

'Do you have news for me?' she asked instead.

He dropped the charm offensive. 'Moscow has sent confirmation of the signal. Your mission can begin.'

51

'Good, is everything in place?'

He hesitated, and Helena caught the brief pause. 'Tell me what's wrong.'

'Maybe nothing. Markoff's last contact failed. We don't know why yet; he's investigating.'

She thought it over. That contact was important, a high priority. 'Has it been long?

'No, not even twenty-four hours.'

She relaxed a little. Delays in passing information happened, the reasons were many and varied. 'And is Markoff still staying in the 'main' house?'

'Yes.'

'In that case leave it with me. Make sure a diplomatic car is available for my use. I will call when I'm ready.'

The Attaché nodded, all pretence of geniality gone, deflated. 'As you say, Helena. I will see to it.'

She looked away. He was dismissed, and when the door closed behind him, she allowed herself a grim smile. There was much to do and time was short.

In the village of Longhope, near Gloucestershire's ancient Forest of Dean, a man by the name of Alexander Nokolai Markoff sat in the semi-darkness of the damp cellar and chose a bullet. He placed it carefully into the magazine and pressed down against the spring's resistance. There came a click as the bullet nestled under the top flange, and he let go. He reached for the next round and repeated the process.

Continuing to feed the magazine, Markoff's mind worked feverishly. He wondered if his agent had been caught. There'd been no sign of the expected signal to indicate a 'letter' would be waiting. And it was long overdue. There might well be a rational explanation; an illness or some emergency out of the man's control. But Markoff had been too long in the game not to heed his instincts. He'd been highly trained in the subtleties of espionage. SVF training not only taught a man the accumulated wisdom of under-cover warfare, but also the psychological evaluations necessary to overcome the mental puzzles that invariably surfaced.

He clipped the twenty-sixth bullet into the magazine. It was designed to take twenty-eight but it was best not to overload he spring. The open box contained another fifty rounds of 7.62 mm NATO ammunition, more than enough to spare. He closed the lid, picked up the rifle and began to strip it down, his thoughts lingering on the man's absence. There was no real justification for his conclusion, just a cautionary hunch. A tight smile played across the cruel mouth. He was alive today because he relied on that inexplicable sixth sense, and once again that feeling had come to the fore.

Alexander Markoff bent to the task of cleaning the gun. In the meantime he had an important mission to fulfil.

6
Deployment

The following day, Commander Robert Fraser, in answer to Sir Montague's summons, arrived at an inconspicuous London apartment on the Chelsea Embankment. The six storey red brick building overlooked the north bank of the Thames, sandwiched between the Albert Bridge upstream to the right and Chelsea Bridge left.

He entered by swiping his card down the exterior reader before walking inside the ground floor's plain, totally unadorned foyer. A stainless steel door faced him across the room, a second layer of security, and again the swipe of his card in conjunction with a four digit pin number produced a muted hiss and he entered the inner sanctum of the United Kingdom's hidden intelligence community. A uniformed receptionist looked up and nodded, and Fraser moved to a pair of lift doors. He rode it to the sixth floor and stepped out to the hum of an open plan office space, a dozen or so operatives beavering away at their consoles.

Walking along the narrow partitioned corridor to the far end, a single silver door awaited. He pressed the green glow of a panel button and stared at the CCTV lens. Biometrics satisfied, and entry granted, the door buzzed. He pushed and stepped inside.

As he walked towards two men standing by the heavy glass picture window, the bland, spacious room echoed to his footsteps. He was conscious of an ill concealed tension. He stopped beside two grey leather sofas that ran parallel to a long oak coffee table

'Morning, Robert.'

Fraser nodded. 'Morning, sir,' he said respectfully, deferring to Sir Hillary Montague's seniority.

'And this is Brian Gilmore.' Sir Montague gestured towards his colleague.

Fraser shook the extended hand and guessed the man to be in his early fifties. Black hair running to grey at the temples, brown eyes set wide in a well tanned face, and a trim figure inside a dark city suit.

'Good morning,' Gilmore said. 'We've met before, long time ago.'

Fraser studied him, reserving judgement, he didn't usually forget a face. Gave up. 'Mind my asking where?'

Gilmore grinned. 'On a firing range in the Brecon Beacons. Snow coming down so hard they ordered us to take shelter. Later on you were in the butt party and the instructor ordered you to stand up next to a target. I heard you answer down the field telephone, thought the handset was going to melt. When he eventually managed to get a word in edgeways you came out and stood there on the snow covered sandbank. That was the first time we knew what a man actually looked like at a 1000yards in comparison to one of those NATO man targets. They had a name for you after that, what did they call you, dead centre? . . . , no, it was Bullseye.' He laughed.

Fraser gave him a slow smile as the memories flooded back. 'That was a long time ago. I'm surprised you remember.'

The laughter faded to a chuckle. 'Not likely to forget that sort of thing, a man standing up on a live fire exercise.'

Sir Montague coughed. 'Sorry to break up this fond reminiscence but I do want to get on.'

Almost imperceptibly, Brian Gilmore winked at Fraser. 'Of course, Sir Hillary, we're all ears.'

'Take a seat,' Sir Montague said, and lowered his chunky frame onto the opposite sofa. The sharp eyes fixed on Fraser and he rubbed his chin.

'We have ourselves a problem, Robert. Not entirely unwelcome, but nonetheless a problem. How well do you know Latvia?'

Fraser, momentarily caught off guard, wracked his memory for recent information. 'Baltic state, ex USSR, now a NATO member. Small contingent of British troops out there near the Russian border.'

Sir Montague cleared his throat. 'Quite so, very concise.' He turned to Gilmore. 'Perhaps you should explain.'

The brown eyes flickered. 'The army uses Riga International Airport, gives us easy access, two and a half hours flying time. At the British Embassy our Assistant Military Attaché has reported a contact that's been made by a Latvian citizen, a certain Gvido Medris. Legitimate, a Forest Ranger, in his late forties.' Gilmore broke off, staring down at the oak coffee table, lost in thought.

'Anyway, this man is the Uncle of a young woman called Anna, and he's her only surviving relative. The parents died three years ago, a boating accident in the Baltic Sea. And this woman has some information she wants to give us, or more precisely, our Secret Service. She's absolutely adamant, it has to be the British, no one else. She won't trust anyone in the Latvian government. We've done some very basic background stuff and it all checks out. She works in a Russian hotel in Pskov, or did.' He stopped and looked inquiringly at Sir Montague who nodded and heaved himself up off the sofa.

He moved over to a solitary workstation and turned a large monitor to face the room. A tap on the keyboard and the screen came to life.

'This is a satellite image of Latvia, taken yesterday at 11.32hrs local time; an American GEO VII on an orbital flyby. As you can see, we have Riga to the west, and over here to the east, the border with Russia.'

Montague held 'Shift-F8' on the keyboard and the image zoomed in, expanding.

'From what we know,' and he pointed to a brighter spot on the image, 'this is the Uncle's house. Unfortunately, he's hidden the girl in the forest. It seems that he spotted a car full of what he thought were men of the GRU looking for her. He wasn't about to take any chances and moved location. The Uncle's not made any further contact. Before he left, he said his niece had found very important information and the British should come quickly.'

Montague swivelled the monitor to where it was and perched on the corner of the desk, fixing Fraser with a hard stare.

'Your analysis of the current situation is correct. We do have a contingent of troops deployed near the Russian border; about forty miles due south of the Uncle's house.' He lapsed into silence, then glanced up. 'In addition, US Special Forces are scattered down the length and breadth of Lithuania, Latvia and Estonia. The US Army's 3rd Armoured Brigade Combat Team, part of the 4th Infantry Division, has stationed itself on the Polish-Russia border, a spearhead of up to 25,000 troops.

Fraser watched his face, saw him battling to clarify his next statement.

Sir Montague stood up and thrust his hands deep into the pockets of his jacket. He ambled off round the room, head down in thought, coming to a halt in front of the big window and gazing out over the Thames.

'The thing is, Robert, we can't have the army boys thrashing about trying to find this girl. If the Latvian authorities found out about it, if they got to hear she didn't want to talk to them, well we don't want any misunderstandings.'

He turned with his back to the window. 'We . . . , that is the Joint Intelligence Committee, feel it would be prudent to have this matter handled with a touch more delicacy, off the record you might say. What do you think, Robert, could you resolve our little problem?'

It was Fraser's turn to pace the room. He wasn't so naïve as to imagine anything other than this entire meeting was 'off the record'. The NDSO were only called upon when all other avenues had been exhausted. The whys and wherefores didn't matter. Sir Hillary Montague would not pose the question unless ordered to do so.

Fraser stopped wandering round the room and turned to face the two men.

'Given everything you've told me, my initial instinct is to say yes. But it would involve my people passing themselves off as army personnel.'

Gilmore interrupted. 'Won't that mean the British army becoming a potential embarrassment if things go wrong?'

'Of course,' Fraser said smoothly, 'but it shouldn't be a major problem. It could be excused as a mistake followed by a Court Martial. Diplomacy restored, and a lot better than the truth. My people are Special Operatives, totally 'deniable', no way would the Service be dragged into it.'

Sir Montague rubbed his chin, frowning, tight lipped. 'Anyone in particular in mind?'

'Yes, sir. Experienced in covert operations, chap by the name of Mike Bowman.'

Hillary Montague exploded. 'What, surely not? The man's a bloody maverick.'

Fraser hit back, stung by the criticism. 'A maverick he may well be, but he's *my* bloody maverick and there's no one better.'

Clearly irritated, Montague turned away.

'You said people, who else?'

Fraser tugged an earlobe, thinking aloud. 'Just the one, a woman operative, Sarah Campbell. It strikes me that this 'Anna' might be more amenable towards the presence of another female.'

Sir Montague looked at Gilmore, obviously disgruntled 'What do you think, Brian? A bloody rogue upstart, and a damned woman.' He was plainly disgusted at the proposal.

Brian Gilmore glanced from one to the other but slowly nodded. 'No argument from me. I'm aware of this Bowman, his record speaks for itself. He certainly doesn't conform, but he's good at what he does. As for the woman . . . if Robert thinks they can handle things, let's go with it.'

Montague snorted his astonishment at Gilmore's deductions and strode off to circle the room, head down in thought, struggling to come to terms with deploying a man and a woman in whom he had no faith. Eventually he stopped his pacing and Fraser detected the hint of a smile playing round the man's mouth. For the first time since he'd entered the room, he sensed a change of mood.

Sir Hillary stared at him, unblinking, as though seeing Fraser for the first time. He came across and placed a hand on Fraser's shoulder.

'I might argue against the one, but I'll not disagree with both of you. If you're convinced that you have the right people, so be it, Commander. I'll leave it in your capable hands.' He abruptly turned away and Fraser recognised he was dismissed.

With the briefest of farewells he took his leave and descended to the ground floor. He ignored his waiting car and crossed the road to the Embankment, resting his elbows on the wall. A freshening breeze rippled the grey-blue water and from downstream a tug hooted loudly. A bright yellow pleasure cruiser full of excited tourists drifted past, angling for the far bank. Away to his left, down by Chelsea Bridge, a Union flag fluttered in the soft wind, a familiar red white and blue in stark contrast to the pale sky.

Fraser straightened. He was not one to show emotion, generally keeping it hidden, steeped in the old tradition, stiff upper lip. Many thought him cynical, a hard taskmaster, didn't suffer fools gladly. And that was essentially true, but above all else, Commander Robert Fraser was a patriot. He believed in Great Britain, in her democratic rights, and the rights of citizens to choose how they were governed by Parliament. He gazed at the flag and subconsciously straightened his shoulders. Yes, he thought, a small island nation we may be, but the underlying ideology of the British way of life extended half way round the globe.

He wasn't about to let Russia prevent a young woman from reaching out to the Western world.

He turned and beckoned his driver, almost embarrassed by his sudden bout of fervour. But then of course there was another man, a man who felt the same as he did, for whom Fraser had the greatest respect. Michael Richard Bowman also believed in that overriding sense of justice, was imbued with that same understanding of right and wrong. Not that he was overtly jingoistic, it was more to do with an understated call of duty, a deep seated conviction that the world needed looking after. And Mike Bowman could be relied upon to shoulder a great deal of that responsibility.

The car pulled into the kerb and Fraser ducked into the back seat.

At Bowman's run down cottage, Sarah Campbell ran a bath, dropped the towel from her waist and sank up to her neck in the perfumed bubbles. The old house didn't run to a shower and the only toilet sat outside behind a wooden door with a heart shaped cut-out. Primitive, she thought, but at least there was running water and it flushed.

Splashing bubbles on her face, she sighed quietly. She liked being around Bowman. He didn't go in for all that macho stuff, none of that pumping iron down the gym. But he certainly was fit; well proportioned and smoothly muscled. He had a few wrinkles round those keen eyes; a weathered frown on the intelligent forehead. Of all the men she'd come across, she thought Bowman was the most reliable and trustworthy of his breed. And when it came down to professional capability, you'd be glad of him at your back. She sank a little lower in the water, up to her bottom lip. Yes, Mike Bowman was good people.

The bathwater began to cool. She washed her body and then shampooed her hair, rinsing it under a flexible shower hose from the taps. Stepping out onto the exposed floorboards, she towelled vigorously until she felt her skin glow. A partially misted full length mirror revealed her naked self and she cast a critical gaze over the reflection. Tousled dark hair framing an elfin face, pert breasts and a flat stomach. Apart from the bullet scar on her thigh she looked good. Her only criticism; she thought her thighs were too well muscled. The downside of all that running.

She dressed slowly, applied a minimal amount of eyeliner and lipstick, and was done. Sarah smiled at her appearance. The salmon-pink lippy set off her even white teeth perfectly. She was ready for the day.

Sarah found Bowman in the back garden, blowing smoke as he wandered along the crazy paving.

'Penny for your thoughts,' she said.

Bowman's eyes found her face, and he smiled thinly. 'Can't help thinking about Jessica, sorry.' He stared down at the broken paving, obviously still coming to terms with her death. Then he gave her a lopsided grin and chuckled. 'It's okay, I'm a big boy now. Have to move on. Not the only time I've lost a colleague in action.'

Sarah felt guilty, intruding on his private grief. It might be better if she hadn't come. 'Mike, I don't have to wait here, not if you'd rather be . . .'

'Hey,' he interrupted, 'I'm fine, and having you here is probably just what I need.'

'If you're sure?'

'Course I'm sure, and anyway, it was the Old Man's suggestion. God forbid we don't do as we're told.'

A half-formed smile lit his face and he looked at her with such warmth she knew instantly that she wasn't going anywhere. She moved closer and tucked a hand under his good arm. 'Then that's settled, 'cause I can only be a good nurse if I'm here to tend your every need.' She smiled suggestively up at his sombre features and squeezed his arm.

He arched a lazy eyebrow, closing one eye. 'Is that so, an Angel and nurse all rolled into one. Lucky me.'

They continued his walk up the garden and she felt that long forgotten pull of emotional need.

On the top of the hill on the far side of the River Wye, a man with a powerful pair of binoculars let them drop to his chest and strolled out from a small stand of trees. There would be little else for him today. He put away the glasses in his backpack and retraced his steps to a bicycle leaning against a fence post halfway down the far side of the hill. He peddled away with a taut grin. At long last he'd established the whereabouts of the man's home.

Anatoly Pushkin parked the car in the narrow drive and killed the engine. He climbed stiffly from behind the wheel and stamped his feet to restore circulation. It had been a long drive. There'd been a crash between a truck and the central barrier. By the time the air ambulance departed he'd sat in traffic for three hours.

The detached house was hidden well back from the road, central to a quarter acre plot. As he walked up the winding path

61

the front door opened to reveal a well built man in his late twenties. He spoke perfect English.

'Hello, David. Long time no see.'

Pushkin grunted, not in the mood for banalities. And now he would have to answer to 'David Hardcastle', and everything would be in English. He pushed past and closed the door to the outside world. They could relax, a little. One false step and their mission would be over.

Late that afternoon, at the Russian Embassy in Kensington Palace Gardens, a black limousine swept out of the gates and headed south for Kensington High Street. An Intelligence Officer of MI5 immediately activated the well rehearsed procedure for surveillance of the car's movements and four separate observers commenced operations.

From Bayswater Road, a London taxi peeled into Palace Avenue and took up pursuit. The surveillance officer at the wheel held back behind three other cars, a talk-through at his throat passing a live feed to the central monitoring station. Ahead of him the limousine steadily negotiated the traffic and eventually pulled up at the junction with Kensington High Street. As the lights changed to green the target turned left. The London taxi discontinued tracking and turned in the opposite direction.

A blue Suzuki motorbike took up the chase along Kensington High Street followed past the Royal Albert Hall and took a right down Exhibition Road. At the next junction the limousine made a left into Brompton Road and the Suzuki drove straight on for Kensington Station.

A Renault Scenic crossed the junction from Cromwell Road and took up the tail. When the black car arrived opposite Harrods it stopped before a lights controlled pedestrian crossing and the chauffeur hopped out to open the back door. The yellow lines made little difference; the car sported diplomatic plates. An elegantly dressed, red-haired woman stepped out, checked the flow of traffic and crossed to the central reservation.

In the Renault Scenic the driver pulled to the kerb at a discreet distance and watched the woman cross the oncoming vehicles and called it in.

'Red-haired woman entering Harrods. Stay with the limo or wait for the woman?'

A brief pause and a firm instruction. 'Wait for the woman,' said the voice in his ear.

'Wilco,' he confirmed and settled down to wait.

The limousine pulled out from the kerb and the taxi-cab reappeared, trailing along behind at a discreet distance.

Halfway down the road the traffic lights turned to red. The embassy car stopped just as a double-decker steered out from the bus lane and partially obscured the taxi driver's view.

The trained officer wasn't worried, he could still see the offside rear of the limousine. But blinded by the bulk of the bus, he failed to spot the car's kerb-side rear door open. A boyish looking woman in jeans and bomber jacket slipped out from the back seat and walked off down the road. When the lights changed to green and traffic began to move the taxi held station behind the bus, every now and then swerving gently to the outside to verify the limousine cruised on regardless.

On the pavement Helena Goreya slowed to a casual stroll, just one more pedestrian in England's crowded city. Russian infiltration continued as planned.

At five o'clock that same afternoon, Bowman walked into Salerton Hall's library and with Sarah at his side took a seat at the conference table. The usual suspects were in attendance. Ian Webster, 'Tubby' Palmer, Head of Planning, Angus 'Jock' Monroe, and the Old Man seated at the head of the table.

'How's your knowledge of the Baltic states, Mike?' Fraser began, thoughtfully rubbing his jaw.

Bowman looked up at the ceiling, recalling the map of the Baltic Sea and neighbouring countries. 'North to south, Estonia, Latvia and Lithuania. Capital cities . . . , Tallinn, Riga and Vilnius.' He looked down.

'Not bad,' Fraser said with a hint of approval. 'In this case, Latvia's the one that concerns us.'

Bowman raised an eyebrow and Sarah shifted in her seat.

Fraser's bushy eyebrows came together with a frown. 'I was called to a briefing yesterday, to see Sir Hillary Montague. It appears there's a problem, and we've been volunteered.' He looked round the table to accompanying nods. 'I decided the two of you would be best suited to handle it and you'll fly out to Riga this evening from Brize Norton.'

Bowman glanced at Sarah, caught a gleam in her eye. 'Yes, sir,' was all he said.

The Old Man cleared his throat. 'There's a young Latvian woman by the name of Anna Kuznetsova, she's on the run from the Russians. Apparently she has important information and wants to speak to the British. Won't talk to anybody but us, and that means here in the UK, specifically the Secret Service, so I'm told.'

'Might I ask why NDSO, sir?' Bowman queried.

Fraser allowed a faint smile to lighten the muscular face. 'Everyone else seems rather busy, sort of came down to availability, and we were available.' He grinned at Jock Monroe. 'Nice to be needed.'

He fixed Bowman with a stern appraisal. 'You'll be going as Royal Engineer officers, you as Captain, and Sarah as Lieutenant, in your own names. ID and uniforms will be waiting with the RAF. Theoretically the job is simple. You join an Engineer Squadron near the Russian border. Under the guise of Mine Warfare reconnaissance you will be free to roam the area while you locate this girl. We're not expecting any trouble, should be a straight forward in and out. From a diplomatic point of view, anything happens to upset the Latvian government and you're to make your excuses on behalf of the British Army. 'Deniable' is still the watchword and you'll probably be facing a Courts Martial.'

Bowman gave him a lopsided smile. 'Thanks for that.'

The Old Man grinned in return, eyes twinkling with amusement. 'There's a chap called Baxter who'll meet you at the airport, Assistant Military Attaché. A Brigadier Spalding will be waiting at the Embassy. He'll bring you up to date and answer any questions.'

Sarah raised a finger. 'Will we have access to weapons?'

Fraser beamed at her. 'More than you could ever wish for. The Engineers are there on a NATO war footing, so called 'training exercise', but they're primed for action with all the guns and live ammunition that warrants.' He looked at Bowman. 'Anything else?'

Bowman considered whether it was worth asking, then asked anyway. 'If these Russians that she's running from, if they come visiting I assume lethal force is still an option?'

The Old Man stood up and leaned his fists on the table, eyes blazing. 'Let us be very clear. That is exactly what you may assume.'

Bowman stared right back, a mutual understanding of the task ahead, knowing that the Old Man backed him to the hilt. 'Thank you,' he said simply.

Fraser came round the side of the conference table and stuck out a big paw. 'Good luck, Mike. And you, young lady,' he said, shaking her hand as well. 'I'll leave you in the expert care of these three gentlemen. They'll run you through it all in more detail.' He looked at his watch. 'Must dash,' and he was gone.

Bowman looked at Monroe and sighed. He was a necessary evil, long winded but informative, and he was only the first in line.

The RAF's Airbus A330 landed at 21.32 hours local, and taxied down Riga's International Airport, coming to a standstill on a reserved section of the apron specifically designated for NATO inbound cargos. The flight from Brize Norton had taken just over two and a half hours and Bowman was quick to get to his feet and stretch his legs. Sarah joined him at the cabin door and together they ducked out into the darkness, descended the ramp and made their way over to the arrivals hall. A tall, suited civilian stepped forward from a roped off gangway and offered his hand.

'I'm Baxter, Military Attaché. Bowman isn't it?'

Bowman accepted the handshake and subconsciously checked the identification pass on Baxter's breast pocket.

Theoretically, it showed him to be a member of the British Consulate.

'And this must be the lovely Sarah Campbell.' Again he extended his hand. 'I have a car waiting. Shall we?'

Under the bright lights of the concourse, Bowman took a moment to scrutinise the man from the Secret Service. He judged him to be in his mid-thirties, dark haired and on closer observation, gaunt with high cheekbones. The eyes were sunken above a large bony nose and the overall impression reminded Bowman of an anorexic scarecrow. His dark grey suit had room to spare.

'This way,' Baxter said and led them outside to the wide pavement. From behind a line of waiting taxis, a pair of blinding headlights swept in towards the kerb and a chauffeur driven Mercedes sighed to a stop.

Baxter opened the nearside rear door and ushered Sarah inside, leaving Bowman to walk round the offside and drop in behind the driver. He relaxed into leather luxury. The MI6 man folded his lanky frame into the passenger seat and turned to Bowman.

'First stop is the Embassy. Brigadier Spalding will bring you up to speed, and then you'll stay the night with us.' He smiled. 'Early start tomorrow I'm afraid.'

Bowman thought the smile came naturally enough but wondered if he wasn't a bit on edge. 'Thank you,' he said. 'Is it far?'

'No, not far,' Baxter said brusquely, and lapsed into silence. The Mercedes eased out from the kerb, weaved through a few cars dropping passengers, and found a main road.

Bowman glanced at Sarah. Street lights flickered across her face and he caught a faint smile in return. The smile got bigger and she frowned and looked away. She had something to say, but not right now. Eight minutes later, in a quietly lit main avenue in the heart of the city, the Mercedes turned left through a pair of remotely controlled iron gates and drew up inside the hidden courtyard. At the top of a flight of steps a man in combat uniform stood waiting. Baxter paused, led them across the yard and stepped to one side.

'Brigadier Spalding,' he said. 'May I introduce Mike Bowman and Sarah Campbell.'

Bowman accepted the firm handshake with a quick appraisal of the man. He appeared to be in his late thirties or early forties, a weathered complexion and penetrating pale eyes.

'Glad to have you aboard,' he beamed, and waved them through into a bright reception hall. Baxter had a quiet word in the Brigadier's ear and walked back to the car.

'Right,' Spalding gestured towards a door, 'we're in here.'

Bowman strode in. The office was small but comfortably furnished, with a coffee table and deeply upholstered, dark leather chairs, and he guessed that dignitaries waited here for an audience. He and Sarah sat, and Spalding perched on the arm of a chair opposite.

'I'll not beat about the bush, the situation is this. The young lady in question is in a spot of bother. Her Uncle managed to contact us via a trusted family member, a brother-in-law so I'm told.' His pale eyes flitted from one to the other. 'She's still in hiding, holed up in the woods. Apparently the Uncle spotted a car on the main road with strangers inside. They were moving slowly, obviously looking for something or someone. He thought it was suspicious and as they hadn't seen him, got the girl into a hideaway.' He stood up, hands on his hips.

'Trouble is we've heard nothing since and as you wanted to keep a lid on things, I didn't want to go blundering around looking for God knows what.'

Bowman caught Sarah's eye and addressed Spalding. 'That's why we're here. I take it you know where the house is?'

'We do, it's up on the north-east border area. Baxter has it pinpointed. I'll sort that for you shortly.'

'And where are your troops?'

The Brigadier grimaced. 'In about the worst place you could think of. About thirty miles south next to a bloody gnat infested lake.'

Bowman grinned at the exasperated reply. 'Better than mosquitoes though?'

'Marginally,' Spalding muttered, and paced round the chair.

'And what form of transport do we use?'

'I have a squadron of Royal Engineers, which I gather you'll be using as cover. They'll supply you with a Panther. All terrain light armoured vehicle, carries four; versatile, everything you need really.'

Bowman pursed his lips. 'Sorry to bother you with this, but what about weapons?'

The Brigadier looked at him, stony faced. Reluctantly, he gave his answer, voice hushed. 'I was warned you'd need side arms, but I hope to God you don't start a war. The Sappers have everything you might need. Sharpshooter rifles, night sights, Glock pistols . . . ,' he smiled. 'booby traps if you want them. It's a NATO deployment so there's live ammo.'

Bowman stuck out his bottom lip, thinking it over, and nodded slowly. He looked at Sarah. 'Anything I've missed?'

'Uniforms?'

Spalding pointed to the ceiling. 'Upstairs in your rooms. "Black Bags" we call them.' He looked at Sarah. 'We were given your measurements and it's a woman's uniform. Should be okay. Any more questions?'

'No, I don't think so,' Bowman said, 'but as a matter of interest . . . , why won't she talk to anyone here?'

Spalding sighed. 'Simple really, she doesn't trust the Latvian authorities.

Bowman framed his question as a frown.

'Too many people on this side of the border are polluted with Russian ideology. Don't forget this was Soviet territory until the Berlin wall came down.'

Bowman accepted the logic. 'In that case we'll get our heads down. I gather it'll be an early start.'

'Indeed,' the Brigadier said. 'I'm returning to the troops tonight. The Mercedes will take you two in the morning. The local population, what there is of it, are used to seeing staff visits. When you get there ask for Major Vince Holliman. He's aware of your arrival, a mine warfare recce for strategic analysis.' With that, Spalding moved to the door. 'Goodnight, young lady. I do hope things work out.'

Sarah smiled graciously. 'Thank you, sir. I'm sure they will.'

He nodded curtly at Bowman and the two of them followed him out. In reception a woman on the desk gave them each a key and led them to a flight of stairs.

'Third floor, room three for the lady, and number seven for you, sir.'

Alexander Markoff hid the motorbike in the hollow of an old sheep dip and looped the helmet round the handlebars. He checked the time; 10.30pm and darkness had fallen to leave a moonless night, the Welsh landscape lit only by the faint light of countless stars.

His destination lay six kilometres due north of his present position and he struck out at a fast walk. Following a month's worth of prior reconnaissance he'd discovered the ideal route to take him unseen to within yards of the target. For Alexander Markoff, well versed in covert operations, this short forced march came as a welcome distraction from the mundane routine of surveillance. Tough and wiry, hardened by the extremes of mountain and jungle manoeuvres, he relished this opportunity to stretch his muscles in compliance with the Kremlin's orders. He carried only the bare minimum required to complete the task ahead. The most essential piece of equipment, a Kevlar helmet with a set of Night Vision goggles, and he'd stored those in the side compartment of his backpack. In addition he'd selected a handgun and silencer, a fighting knife tucked in his boot, and a folding pair of bolt croppers.

Markoff's objective was an open-cast slate quarry operating under the name of Advanced Mining Solutions Inc., more specifically, the compound designated High Security. His initial concern would be the disablement of all telecommunications that linked to outside forces. Police interference could then be discounted, leaving him with a clear hand.

On site personnel consisted of two shifts of four men, relieving each other every two hours. On each shift, one man patrolled the inner compound, one monitored the outer, and a third man, a dog handler, roamed freely with his Alsatian off the lead. The fourth man, the shift commander, remained in charge of the office and manned the phone lines.

Markoff pushed on through the undulating landscape, over barren hills and down shallow ditches. A dry stone wall took him east to a broken fence. He ducked under a wooden slat and came to the base of a steep incline. Scrambling up the loose shale, he finally emerged onto a wide, high plateau. By the faint light of the stars, Markoff could see the cavernous quarry spread out below. From the main compound to his left a dirt roadway descended in a long winding curve round the walls of blasted rock. Far below, giant trucks and diggers waited for a new day to commence.

Having confirmed the layout, he backed off from the high ground and made a wide detour to the west.

When he next crawled up to the outer fencing, Markoff wore his helmet and night vision goggles. Lying prone on the ridge he gazed at the compound just below. Six power saving orange lamps covered the entire area, a relatively feeble pattern of lighting. There were three buildings in total. To the right, nearest the quarry walls, a semi-permanent stack of Portakabins served as canteen, changing room and sleeping quarters for the drivers, quarrymen and off duty nightshift. To the left and closer to Markoff, a long wooden hut housed the main office with the communications hub. Beyond that, half hidden inside a protective deep-dug sandpit, sat a brick and concrete storehouse containing the high explosive for blasting out seams of slate bearing rock. Some of that explosive, PE-4, is what Markoff had come for. It was the British equivalent of Semtex, a plasticized mouldable form of military RDX, commonly used by the mining industry. And it tended to be a lot easier to steal it from mining companies than well guarded military installations.

Markoff looked at the rudimentary defences. The first obstacle barring his way was a three metre high, chain-link outer fence topped with coils of razor wire. He edged to his left, aiming for a concrete post and bellied forward. Bolt croppers to hand, Markoff sheared through a number of intersecting strands and then bent the area of tangled wires away from him, lessening the chance of getting caught up on sharp ends. Squeezing his body through the opening, he paused to take stock.

The dog caught his attention, loping along and fully alert, head up, tail swaying. His handler walked out from behind the wooden hut, gave a low whistle, and the dog trotted obediently to his side.

With his enhanced night vision, Markoff then spotted a patrolling guard strolling round the far boundary, two-hundred metres across the compound. They were far enough away for Markoff to take a chance on a run to his left. That would position him on the west end of the hut and allow access to the rear door. At the moment he lay down breeze of the Alsatian. He swapped bolt croppers for the silenced pistol and made his move.

Running hard along the fence he then tracked right and merged into the shadow of the building. He listened intently, waiting for any sound of alarm. When none came he crept down the side of the hut until he came to the end. A quick glance showed him all was clear and he turned the corner. At the rear door, he took a last look behind, gently grasped the handle and cracked it open. A room full of tools and clothing met his gaze and he slipped inside. Careful to avoid knocking any of the equipment he stepped across to an internal door and stood listening. The faint sound of music reached his ears, a radio or TV in the background. He folded the night goggles up onto his helmet and tested the handle. Without a sound Markoff pushed the door quietly on its hinges and crouched.

A middle aged man sat side-on reading a magazine. Whether it was a draught or sixth sense, he realised Markoff had entered. All in one movement he looked round, dropped the magazine and lunged for an alarm.

Markoff fired from the waist and the pistol spat three rounds. The bullets caught the side of his chest, three blotches of blood as they thumped into flesh. Hand flailing at the table the man crashed to the floor and lay groaning. Markoff took two paces and put a bullet in his temple. This was no time for niceties.

He sank to one knee below the windows and glanced round the room. Two landline phones and a wireless transceiver. Tracing the landline wires he disconnected them from a socket and pulled his fighting knife, slicing off the end terminals and discarding them. The wireless transceiver he destroyed with a bullet and then changed to a fresh magazine. The music from the radio played on, and staying low, Markoff backed out of the office and into the storeroom. At the outer door, he flipped down the night goggles and emerged cautiously into the relative darkness of the compound. It was now a simple process of elimination. He strode boldly out under the cone of light from a lamp, watched the Alsatian sniffing the air, and waited for the handler. The dog sensed Markoff, turned his head and growled, a deep penetrating warning.

His handler appeared and froze. Before the man could react Markoff raised his pistol and put a pair of bullets in his chest. The dog snarled, and charged, ears back. A frenzied mouthful of canine teeth came barrelling across the compound. Markoff swung the pistol, steadied on the dog's breast bone and squeezed, twice. The Alsatian yelped, lost it's footing and somersaulted into the dirt. It lay panting, tongue lolling sideways, eyes wide in pain.

Markoff ignored the animal, checking the buildings for signs of movement. He'd lost the patrolman's whereabouts, so moved clear of the dog and over to the solid protection of the wooden hut. He bent to one knee, knowing his man would appear, if only to raise the alarm.

The guard came from behind, around the rear of the hut. Hearing his footsteps, Markoff twisted and fired. The man grunted and staggered forward. Two aimed shots put him down.

Markoff walked over and stared down at his victim. Shallow breathing, frothing blood, a face contorted in agony. The man would be dead in minutes, no need to waste a bullet. Three down, one to go, not including the off duty shift of four. He glanced over at the Portakabins, no sign of movement, no light. Time was critical, but he deliberately waited and checked his watch. He had forty minutes to grab the explosives and make good his escape. If not, he'd have to deal with the other shift coming on at midnight.

He looked over to where the demolitions were stored and began to walk. The inner fence had been made from a double layer of square galvanised mesh, capped with spikes and razor wire. Inside that, the high walls of sand obscured any chance of a visual, unless the guard approached to inspect his perimeter.

Again the bolt croppers proved their worth, chewing through the layers of steel. It took five minutes of determined effort to wrestle a hole big enough to crawl through, but finally Markoff wriggled into the inner compound. Now for the entrance and the guard. He moved to his right, between the fence and the high wall of sand. Two overhead lights lit the compound, one either end of the building. The sand banked up at a 45° angle. Tufts of grass and sparse patches of moss covered the slope and he probed with his foot to test for stability. It took his weight, holding firm, and he climbed up traversing the slope. Nearing the top he crouched, minimising his profile, and peered over.

The roof extended left and right with no windows in the brick and concrete walls. A well trodden path led round the building. To his right, a low retaining wall allowed for a paved driveway which ran out of sight to the front entrance. He slithered along the crest of the sand bank until he had eyes on a sliding steel door, big enough for a truck to easily pass inside. A small personnel door had been let into the main panel, shoot bolts and padlocks firmly in place. Whoever patrolled this inner sanctum had still not made an appearance.

Markoff readied himself and then slid over the top, feet first down the other side. He landed in an uncontrolled rush of arms and legs but managed to keep from falling. Poised on the balls of his feet he stalked towards the front, tucked in tight to the concrete wall. At the end he stopped with his back to the wall and prepared to take a look round the corner.

'Stand still and drop the gun.'

The man's voice came as a shock, and he didn't sound like an amateur. From close behind, but not so near as to fall victim to a sudden move.

'Do it!'

Markoff eased out from the wall, pistol outstretched to his right, and let it fall.

'Hands above your head.'

He complied.

'Turn round . . . , slowly.'

Again he followed orders and found himself looking at the muzzle of a pistol. Another surprise; from what he knew these men were not armed. Big mistake, obviously the rules for the inner compound were different.

'Back up,' the man demanded.

He took a pace to his rear, and another, and stopped under the orange glow of a lamp.

'Far enough, take off the helmet.'

Markoff slowly lowered his both hands, flipped the night goggles up and thought about hurling the helmet at his adversary.

'Easy,' the man warned, as if reading his mind.

The helmet came off and he stood holding it in front of his waist.

'Who are you?'

Markoff thought fast. 'SAS, here to test your security. Seems like you're on the ball. Made me jump anyway.' He gave him a friendly grin.

The man maintained his stance but the gun wavered fractionally, uncertainty undermining his confidence.

'Why didn't we hear about it? They warn us about inspections.'

'Not this time, sunshine. No warnings they said, keep it realistic. You know how they think.' He took a hand off the helmet and spread it wide in a sympathetic gesture, relaxed.

The man almost swallowed the story . . . , but not quite. 'Show us your ID card.'

Markoff managed an easy laugh and raised the helmet. 'Inside pocket, let me put this down.' Before the man could argue he bent from the waist and lowered the helmet with his left hand. His right hand went for his boot and tugged out the fighting knife.

In one seamless movement he threw the blade through the air. The point sliced deep into the man's stomach and tore through his internal organs. He gasped with pain, dropped the gun and clasped his hands to his midriff.

Markoff lunged forward, grabbed the hilt and twisted upwards. The tip of the knife ruptured a lung. With a savage tug he pulled on the serrated blade. As it wrenched free the man cried out in agony and Markoff pushed his face. He toppled to the sand, choking for breath.

Kneeling at his side, Markoff whipped the knife across his windpipe and wiped the bloodied blade on the dying man's jacket.

A perfunctory search revealed empty pockets, no keys. He listened for a moment and then turned for the sliding door. Collecting his gun and helmet he walked to the personnel door and inspected the hinges. As he suspected, a standard hinge pin secured the halves together and unlike the hardened steel of the Yale padlock, the pins were manufactured from standard engineering steel. Shrugging off his backpack he extracted a battery operated Dremel multi-tool and selected a cutting disc. There were three hinges, each with a domed pin, and working from the bottom hinge upwards he sliced off the tops leaving the pins to drop out when he rocked the door. With his fighting knife inserted into the narrow crevice he prised the door from its recess and left it hanging from the padlock.

A glance at his watch showed twenty-five minutes before the second shift came on duty, more than enough time. Night goggles in place he entered the magazine, found a shelf crammed with PE-4 and removed three rectangular blocks. Measuring just thirty centimetres in length they were an easy fit inside his backpack and he fed his arms through the straps and prepared to leave.

Alexander Nickolai Markoff took a final look round the compound. With a twisted smile of satisfaction, he made his way back to the hole in the wire. In the outer compound, the bodies of his victims lay where they'd fallen, congealed blood dark in the night vision goggles. He strode past and wriggled out through the final barrier. A light came on in the Portakabins; the next shift preparing for duty.

He broke into a long striding run, a pace that swallowed distance, and a pace he well knew how to endure. Another piece of a the jigsaw had came together and a short while later, a man on a motorbike headed south.

7
Skirmish

Bowman woke to a tap on the door. '05.00, sir.'

'I'm awake.'

'There'll be a light breakfast in thirty minutes,' said the voice in the corridor.

'Be right down,' Bowman said, thinking how quickly things had changed. This time yesterday he'd been at home in bed, now the Russian border loomed large on the horizon. He wondered if Sarah had any second thoughts. This was her first foreign operation.

He swung his feet to the floor and stretched. The 'Black Bag' lay open in the corner, combat jacket hanging on the back of a chair; it was a while since he'd been in uniform. Ten minutes later, washed, shaved, and dressed in the latest camouflage pattern, he closed the 'bag' and moved out into the corridor.

Sarah appeared from room three looking every inch the warrior princess.

'Morning, Mike.'

'Morning, Angel. Bright eyed and bushy tailed?'

She grinned happily. 'Aren't I always?'

He chose not to answer, just smiled and followed her down the stairs to reception. The soft glow of subdued lighting revealed the first hint of pre-dawn grey outside and the man on the desk indicated a door to the rear. 'Dining room in the back, breakfast is ready.'

'Thanks,' Bowman said. 'Is the car ready?'

'As soon as you are, sir.'

He nodded and headed for the dining room. There were four small tables with chairs, obviously for the staff. A hotplate took up the length of the far wall and a chef waited to take their order.

Sarah dropped her black bag, ambled over to the chef and made a tentative inquiry. 'Do you have muesli?'

'Of course,' the chef said, sounding thoroughly offended.

'Then yes please, and a black coffee.'

Bowman walked to the hotplate. 'A sausage sandwich and make that two black coffees.'

'I'll bring it over.'

'Cheers,' Bowman said and wandered back to the table.

Sarah leaned forward, elbows on the table, chin cupped in her hands, an inquisitive look on her face. 'What do you make of Baxter?' she asked quietly.

'Meaning?'

'Can't imagine him being in uniform.'

Bowman chuckled then lowered his voice. 'That's probably because he's never worn one. He's MI6.'

'Ah . . . ,' she murmured. 'I did wonder.'

Five hundred metres outside Latvia's eastern border, a Russian Armoured Personnel Carrier arrived at the end of a narrow forest track, turned in a tight circle and pulled up facing the way it had come. Four men dressed in the combat uniform of Spetsnaz dismounted from the drop ramp and gathered around their Officer Commanding.

Lieutenant Boris Tsegler ordered a weapons check and consulted his map. He delved into a side pocket and produced a Russian military version of Glonass-K, the Federal Space Agency's Global tracking system. The full array of twenty-four satellites guaranteed a positioning accuracy of two metres and the co-ordinates verified his exact location. Hidden by the trees ahead, the border ran north to south across their path. Satisfied, Tsegler turned to his elite, highly trained section of volunteers.

'I remind you we are about to enter foreign territory.' He flung out an arm pointing behind at the invisible border. 'The NATO allies play war games beyond that border and the British have secured this sector, do not underestimate them. They are on high alert. If we are discovered you will be in a major fire fight. They are all volunteers, such is the nature of their army. They want to be soldiers, much as we do, not like the conscripts.' He paused, meeting the eyes of each man. Grigori, Stepan, Yuri and Alik. He took a pace closer.

'But I do not anticipate discovery. We will be as the Mongolian wind, soft in the morning, a whisper in the long grass. And when we leave, the grasses will straighten, there will be no sign of our presence.'

A muffled grunt greeted his words, camouflaged faces wreathed in smiles.

Tsegler clenched his jaw in approval. These men were highly motivated and he knew each of them better than their own mothers. Three of the four had been with him in Syria; the other man had killed two Israeli Secret Servicemen in Jerusalem. His reward for exceptional bravery in the face of the enemy was the granting of a medal, the Order of Military Merit. A rare honour. Tsegler had no doubts as to the capabilities of the men under his command.

'We go,' he said simply, and turned away to the trees and the hidden border. A few hundred metres and they would violate Latvian sovereign territory. The hunt was on.

Bowman drank the last of his coffee and leant back in the seat. 'All done?'

Sarah dabbed her lips with a paper napkin and nodded. 'Ready when you are,' she answered, businesslike.

He stood and grabbed his black bag, and with a cursory nod to the chef moved out into reception.

Baxter sat cross legged waiting on a bench seat.

'Morning,' he said. 'Fat and full?'

Bowman humoured him. 'We've eaten.'

'Good,' said Baxter, lifting his lanky frame from the seat. 'Driver's waiting.'

Outside, in the cool of the morning air, Sarah dropped her bag in the open boot and Bowman followed suit, closing the lid firmly shut. Again, he sat behind the driver who half turned in his seat. 'All set?'

Sarah nodded. 'We are.'

Baxter closed the passenger door and belted up. 'Right then, we'll be off.'

The iron-railing gates swung inward and the Mercedes nosed out of the Embassy compound onto the broad avenue, and Bowman leaned sideways to look over the driver's shoulder. At this time of day the road was empty allowing the car to quickly gain speed.

Within ten minutes they cleared Riga's sprawling suburbs and hit a main road east, driving directly into the sun's blinding ball of fire. Undaunted the driver lowered his visor, slipped on a pair of reflective sunglasses, and powered on up the road. The speedometer showed the equivalent of eighty miles an hour, ninety when the road straightened.

Bowman settled back and closed his eyes. Might as well snatch some shut eye, it would be a while yet.

In fact it was just over two hours later when Bowman opened his eyes to a jolt as the Mercedes braked and turned off the main road. The relatively smooth ride changed to a choppy bounce as the suspension met the wheel tracks recently created by a convoy of military vehicles. Ahead of them, what appeared to be an impenetrable wall of pine trees barred their way. The driver braked again, engaged second gear and turned off the trail bumping over dust strewn waste ground towards a previously unnoticed gap in the trees.

Bowman pushed himself up against the seatbelt and peered through the windscreen. Row after row of tall tree trunks darkened their passage, the driver working the wheel, picking his way with care. A few minutes of tortuous manoeuvring and the trees began to thin. A large expanse of water came into view from the right and they emerged from the line of trees to follow the banks of the lake.

Sarah tapped his arm. 'Over there.' She gestured with her chin.

Where the shoreline curved to the right he spotted a camouflaged vehicle hidden under the Scots pines. Beyond the netting he found tell tale signs of tented bivouacs and soldiers moving around tracked Armoured Personnel Carriers.

The Mercedes climbed a low rise into the trees and lurched to a halt by a marquee sized Command Post. Three heavily armed squaddies stepped forward and Baxter climbed out to speak to them. A moment later he put his head inside the door. 'Everybody out,' he said cheerfully. 'End of the road.'

Sarah alighted first and the three soldiers sprang to attention; the Corporal saluted. Bowman saw her hesitate and then return the salute with a wry smile. This had just become part of a fast learning curve. He climbed out to another salute, returned it casually and followed Baxter inside the flap of the tent. At the rear of the marquee the back door of an APC protruded inside the canvas wall, and a Signals NCO sat listening through a pair of headphones.

A bare headed Major Vince Holliman rose from a folding seat with a warm smile. 'Welcome to Camp Wilderness. How was the trip? Do have a seat, or perhaps you'd prefer to stretch you legs. Whatever . . . , some tea maybe.' He glanced beyond them. 'Orderly! Tea for our guests.'

'Yes, sir,' a voice answered, and the Major offered Sarah his hand. 'Lieutenant Campbell if my information is right? Very nice to meet you.' He turned away. 'And Captain Bowman.' There was a twinkle in his eye, a secretive smile, a hint of understanding. He shook hands vigorously before returning to his camp chair. 'Sorry about the accommodation.' He waved a hand airily about the inside of the tent and then reached for a pack of cigarettes. 'Smoke if you want to, we don't stand on ceremony out here.'

Bowman breathed a sigh of relief. It would be his first chance of nicotine today.

Major Holliman puffed a neat ring of blue smoke and brushed it aside. 'I have an order to the effect that you will be undertaking a detailed reconnaissance of the border with a view to laying a minefield. I should warn you that there's been a marked increase in Russian troop movements over the other side, and any transgression into their territory could be taken as a hostile move.' He gave a solemn wink.

Bowman glanced round the tent. Other than Baxter, there were two young officers standing by a large map board. He assumed some of the Major's oratory was for their benefit rather than Sarah and himself. He suppressed a smile. 'We do understand, sir. I promise we won't step over the border.'

80

'Glad to hear it. Where's that tea?' he barked. Then calmly, weighing his words, 'you know we have a Lynx helicopter, might be useful.'

'I'd prefer to stay on the ground, sir. Get to know the lay of the land better.'

'By all means,' Holliman agreed, 'and the trees don't offer too many landing spots; just thought I'd ask.'

The orderly hurried in with two mugs and handed one each to Sarah and Bowman. Holliman coughed impatiently.

'Just coming, sir,' the orderly responded, and disappeared.

The Major grinned. 'We'll have a walk round the perimeter when you're done. I could do with the exercise.'

His tea arrived.

North of the British encampment, two thousand metres inside the Latvian border, Lieutenant Boris Tsegler glanced over his shoulder. Weapons poised, his men advanced in single file, alert to the slightest sound. They were well armed. Two carried AN94 assault rifles, silencers fitted, and the other pair nursed Marksman's rifles, specially adapted suppressors screwed on tight. His own weapon of choice, a Dragunov SVD, a laser equipped, high velocity semi-automatic, capable of piercing lightly armoured vehicles at fifteen-hundred metres.

He spoke softly using his throat transmitter. 'Line abreast twenty metres apart.'

A sniper and an assault rifle peeled off left, the other two went right, a mirror image.

'Audio check,' he ordered. One after the other voices came into his left ear, clearly discernible over the background hiss. 'All good,' he acknowledged. 'Move out.'

Silently, rubber soled combat boots trod warily through the cushion of fallen pine needles. Perfectly camouflaged in the grey-brown of their environment, the five men of Special Forces melted into the shadows.

Tsegler smiled grimly. The wind blew softly.

Anna Kuznetsova lay on a rough hewn cot in an old abandoned hut. What remained of the shingle roof, supported by rotting timbers, offered scant cover from the elements, but she was grateful for Uncle Gvido's quick reaction in secreting her away. This long abandoned ruin of a home had become a temporary life-line. If her Uncle had not seen the car . . . ? There was no knowing where she might be now. And yet fear tugged at her soul, her very isolation made her vulnerable. Once during the night she'd woken with a start, lying there holding her breath, petrified of the unknown. Eventually she drifted into a fitful sleep.

The rough cot dug into her shoulder blades and she sat up.

Swinging her feet to the floor, her mind raced; the brutal killing of the man at the border flooding back. Even with all those witnesses the machine-gunner had shown no compunction, not a moment's hesitation. She shuddered, partly the cool air, more significantly, the memory of the blood dripping as he was carried away.

Anna came to her feet and crossed to the haphazardly skewed door. Outside, the dappled woodland helped banish her mood of despair, and she walked a little, round the hut, kicking her way through twigs and pine needles. For the third time in an hour she checked her watch and frowned. Uncle Gvido should have been here before this; he'd promised, and her imagination took over, presenting a never ending list as to why he was late, all of them bad. Wandering back inside, Anna sat on the cot, head in her hands, wishing it would all go away. If only the British would come.

A breeze whispered through the high pine branches, stirring the needles, hissing together as they shimmered.

She stared disconsolately at the floor. In the full light of day the hut stood out like a sore thumb, the man-made clearing highlighted its isolation. She hugged herself, rocking forward in thought. If the GRU stumbled across this place she would inevitably be found. It might be better to hide amongst the trees, away from the obvious.

'Hello Two-Niner, this is Zero, send . . . , over.'

Bowman glanced up to see the Signalman in the back of the APC scribbling on a message pad. He finished jotting notes and reached for the handset. 'Ah . . . . Two-Niner this is Zero. Roger, out.' He looked round, tore off the top page and brought it to the back door.

'Message, sir.'

'I'll have it,' Holliman said, reaching out.

Bowman watched as he peered down and studied the handwritten scrawl, saw the cigarette burning down to the filter, the tea forgotten.

'I'll be damned,' the Major eventually said. 'I think we'll have that walk now.'

Sarah raised an eyebrow and Bowman understood Holliman's suggestion was more of an order. He rolled his eyes at the tent flap. Baxter took the hint and led the way out.

Holliman joined them and strode off towards the lake and once away from any chance of being overheard, he paused at the water's edge. Staring at the rippling surface he shook his head.

'The bastards have probably crossed the border!'

Baxter looked nonplussed, spoke for all of them. 'Sir?'

Major Holliman turned to face them. 'A small squad of Russian infantry, to the north. An APC dropped them off and they marched into the forest, straight for the border.'

Bowman wondered how the information had been found. 'Who reported it?'

Holliman sighed, rubbed his hands together. 'Modern technology. A geostationary satellite that we're using to monitor their troop movements.'

Sarah spoke up. 'When did they cross, sir?'

The Major looked at his watch. 'Two hours ago.' He took a step closer to Bowman, looked him in the eyes. 'This changes everything. We can guess why they're here, but the Brigadier's worried about how long we can afford not to intervene. In other words, how long before he's forced to include NATO command?' He rubbed his chin. 'This is the first incursion we're aware of, could be bloody dangerous. So the Brigadier wants you back by sunset. After that, either way, he'll deploy the infantry. Can't afford to have the Russians roaming about willy-nilly.' He broke off to walk back to the marquee.

Sarah caught up with him. 'Have we heard anything more from the Uncle?'

He shook his head. 'Since yesterday, nothing.'

They filed through into the tent and Holliman moved to the back of the APC.

'The map, please,' and the Corporal handed him an Ordnance Survey sheet.

Bowman stepped in closer.

The Major smoothed out the folds and spread it on the end of the side seat. He traced a finger along a line marked in bold red marker pen.

'That's the border. For God's sake don't get it wrong. The situation's bad enough without us making it worse.' He paused and put a hand on Bowman's shoulder. 'The Panther's radio is set to our squadron frequency, the secondary waveband. Stay in touch. However long you're out there we won't change frequency.' He dropped his hand away and glanced at the Sigs NCO. 'Anything else?'

The Corporal grinned and Bowman felt his eyes on him. 'I'm Zero, sir, you will be Alpha-Foxtrot. If the signal's poor, try moving location.' He looked at Sarah. 'Don't touch the aerial when transmitting, it gets hot.' He hesitated and turned back to Bowman. 'One last thing, sir, security. No grid references. Use the twelve hour clock and distance from here.'

Bowman remembered the training; twelve o'clock was north, three o'clock east, etc, etc. Map co-ordinates were universal, better to fix location from a relatively unknown location. He met the signalman's eyes and smiled. 'Wilco, out.'

The Corporal seemed satisfied and addressed Holliman. 'That's it, sir.'

The Major rubbed his chin. 'Need a driver?'

'No,' Bowman said. 'We'll manage.'

'Right, let's get you some transport.'

Five hundred yards across the encampment, Major Holliman handed them over to Sergeant-Major Stannard, a lean and wiry veteran. He immediately took charge and led them to a

84

previously isolated Panther. Its primary purpose, forward reconnaissance and rapid assault fire support.

Bowman knew of the vehicle's reputation; a fast, all terrain, lightly armoured fighting vehicle with a Browning heavy machine gun up top and a 7.62mm GPMG. He was fully conversant with those weapons, understood their stopping power.

'Familiar with this, sir?' Stannard came across as respectfully cynical.

Bowman chuckled and leaned towards him, lowering his voice. 'I could do with a quick rundown.'

Stannard laughed in turn. 'Then I'm your man, sir. Jump in.'

In the space of five minutes, sat behind the GPMG, the Sergeant-Major swiftly but thoroughly instructed Bowman on all the relevant controls and a few idiosyncrasies peculiar to the type. Finally he reached across Bowman's legs and switched on the dash mounted radio. Headset and remote microphone ready, he nodded. 'Better make sure, sir.'

Bowman spoke. 'Hello Zero, this is Alpha-Foxtrot. Radio check, over.'

An almost instant reply echoed in his ear. 'Hello Alpha-Foxtrot, this is Zero. Strength ten. Out.'

Stannard grinned. 'Looks like you're all set, Major.'

'Not quite,' Bowman said. 'Personal weapons?'

Stannard pointed at the securely clipped guns. 'Two 7.62mm Sharpshooter rifles, two M4 assault rifles and in here,' he hinged down a storage lid, 'two Glock 9mm pistols. Expecting trouble?'

Sarah leaned in. 'Hopefully not,' she said evenly, 'but better safe than sorry.'

'Yes, Ma'am,' Stannard agreed, and swung himself to the ground.

Sarah hoisted herself in, swivelled the butt of the GPMG out to the side, and spread the map on her knees. Mounted low-centre of the driver's position was a GPS under its waterproof cover and she turned it on. Tapping the map, she said; 'That's her Uncle's house.'

Bowman glanced over to get the general picture.

Sarah pointed ahead, slightly left. 'There's a logging trail over there, runs north-north-east. Should get us to within a couple of miles.'

He pursed his lips, started the engine and the Panther rumbled into life. He gave it a touch of throttle, miscued the clutch, and graunched it into first gear. The four wheel drive scrabbled in the loose needles, bit through and lurched forward.

He grinned wryly. 'Sorry, Angel, out of practice.'

She smirked. 'Did you actually pass a test?'

Ignoring the sarcasm he aimed for a gap between two trees. He held his breath as they squeezed through. A grinding scrape rang from the offside rear and Bowman nodded his approval. Not bad for an initial judgement.

'Go right,' Sarah instructed.

Twin tracks appeared, disappearing into the depths of the forest and Bowman bounced the wheels onto the rutted corridor, then selected third gear. The Panther accelerated up to thirty miles an hour and he relaxed the tension in his arms. The handling was good, and he found the suspension surprisingly compliant.

Mike Bowman focused on the way ahead and pressed on. Time was short.

Lieutenant Boris Tsegler walked cautiously south-west at the forefront of his squad. The expected sighting of a narrow stream meandering north to south across their path caused him to hesitate. For the elite formation of Spetsnaz it was but a small obstacle, a shallow trickle.

Tsegler spoke through his throat mike. 'Watch me across then join me, right flank first.'

He heard the acknowledgements and moved towards the short, steep bank. Beyond the stream the forest thickened, dark and threatening, a cause for concern. He felt the eyes of the men watching, waiting for him to lead the way. He crouched, rifle balanced chest high, and surged forward. The flying jump took him well clear and he sprinted for the nearest tree. Down on one knee, he paused, scanning the nearby forest floor. His earphone clicked. 'All is still.'

He turned to look back across the stream. 'Right flank, go!'

The two men came sprinting, weapons high, and jumped. They landed in unison, veered to their right and vanished into the trees.

'Left flank, go!'

Out from concealment came the last pair, running hard, landing long over the hazard, and swiftly to safety.

Tsegler breathed out and pushed to his feet. All was quiet. The British troops must be well south. A quick data check of the Glonass-K gave him a good fix. Nine kilometres ahead lay the prize; the Uncle's house and the young woman named Anna Kuznetsova.

'Onwards,' he ordered, and followed his men into the darkness. One more hour and Boris Tsegler would be in charge of a hostage.

Anna heard a noise. She tensed and lowered herself into the shallow gulley. The pulse of her heartbeat sounded loud in her ears and her breathing quickened. Slowly raising her eyes above the pine needles she searched frantically for any sign of life.

The sound came again, a soft rustling noise, but from where? It was difficult to pinpoint the direction. Forcing herself to breathe slowly, she squirmed round to look over her shoulder. Only the serried ranks of never ending tree trunks met her gaze and she sank down to the ground. Weak with fear, she shivered. The distinctive squeak of a wooden board creaking underfoot sounded loud in the silent forest. She risked lifting her head, focused on the distant grey of the hut and waited, transfixed by the unknown.

'Anna.' So soft she only just heard it. Her heart raced.

'Anna!' Louder this time. It was the deep baritone of Uncle Medris and she came up on her knees.

'Here Uncle, I'm here.'

And from round the corner of the hut, the tall, broad shouldered bear of a man made his appearance. For all his size and heavy stature, Uncle Medris was surprisingly light on his feet.

Anna managed to stand and stumble towards him. She fell into his all encompassing embrace, sobbing into his chest. He squeezed her close.

'Easy child . . . , easy. It's alright.'

His deep, warm voice resonated through his chest and Anna looked up at the big bearded, grinning face.

'I was so worried when you didn't come.'

He relaxed his arms from around her, held her away by the shoulders. 'I chose to leave the car behind. Better to walk, but I must walk with caution, who knows what men are nearby. Took longer than I thought.'

Wiping away the residue of tears, Anna smiled, a tentative half fearful smile. 'Have you heard from the British, Uncle?'

'Nothing yet, child. But they will come and when they do, we'll be waiting. Come, I have food and a hot flask.'

Anna allowed herself to be led to the hut, comforted by her Uncle's unflappable presence. He was such a big man, a good man, and Anna recovered some of her courage. Around the corner, on the steps of the rotting veranda, a brown backpack lay open, the top of a flask protruding from a flap.

Then Anna stopped in mid-stride. An old hunting rifle stood propped against the door jamb, a telescopic sight mounted along the breach.

'Uncle!' She pointed in disbelief.

He chuckled stroking his beard, raised one eyebrow. 'What?' he asked, all innocence.

'Why the gun?'

'Rabbits, child. You never know when you'll see a fine rabbit for the pot.'

Anna gave him the most disdainful glance that she could conjure up and shook her head. 'I think not, Uncle. I think that is for hunting men and we are in more danger than you admit to.'

'Nonsense,' he grumbled. 'Now sit yourself down and we'll breakfast.' He fumbled inside the backpack and brought out a linen wrapped packet. 'Look, cold ham rolls and hot coffee in the flask. A wonderful picnic.' He beamed and unwrapped the rolls. 'Tuck in, there's more if you want.'

Anna realised just how hungry she felt and took a first mouthful. She chewed, savouring the salty tang and watched him pour coffee. For a short while, she forgot her worries, pretended it really was a picnic and remembered her childhood spent running free, chasing rabbits.

The sun climbed high above the canopy, lighting the forest floor, and a gust of wind came and shook the branches. A few pine needles dropped and the wind died away, down to a gentle breeze, as if the gust had never been. And she and Uncle Medris relaxed with their coffee and ham sandwiches.

The Panther ploughed into a length of muddy standing water and threw a sheet of filthy spray in the air. Bowman grimaced as a wet fleck landed on his cheek.

'Nice,' he muttered savagely. The steering tugged in his hands and the front wheels sank into the quagmire. He shifted into a lower gear, gave it some more revs and the Panther hauled itself out the other end.

'How much further, Angel?' he demanded.

'About a mile. There's a hard right before the end.'

Bowman nodded, concentrating on the twin tracks. The corridor narrowed, tree trunks encroaching on the limited space. The bend in the trail came into view and he slowed. It was tight, but the agile handling took them round first time, and there in front lay a hollow of cleared ground. He brought the Panther around in a clockwise circle before manoeuvring into the trees, leaving himself an easy line of withdrawal. Killing the engine he leaned over to study the map.

Sarah tapped it. 'We're here.' She moved her finger. 'That's the Uncle's house there.'

'Right,' he said, 'weapons.'

They selected their choice. She strapped on an ammunition belt with a holstered Glock attached and reached for the M4 assault rifle. Bowman took the Sharpshooter rifle and picked out five spare magazines. He too belted a Glock 9mm round his waist and shrugged into a bullet proof vest. The helmet needed some adjustment before he was satisfied and he clipped a water bottle to the belt. When he looked up, Sarah waited with a smile on her face. 'Anytime you're ready, Mike.'

'I'll let base know we're here,' he said, and reached in for the radio, toggling the switch.

'Hello Zero, this is Alpha-Foxtrot, over.'

The Sigs NCO was on the ball. 'Hello Alpha-Foxtrot, this is Zero. Send, over.'

'Alpha-Foxtrot, commencing operation, over.'

'Ahh . . . , this is Zero: Roger, out.'

Sarah tilted her head to one side. 'Don't waste words do they.'

Bowman nodded in agreement. 'True, even though it's scrambled, keep it short.' He stood back and glanced around. 'GPS and map?' he asked her.

She held up the GPS then patted her thigh pocket.

'Okay, but go easy, Angel. We don't have a clue what we'll find and it might well be the opposition. Keep it quiet and stay in sight.' He took a long look at her. Helmet, camouflage uniform, assault rifle and hand gun; she certainly gave the impression of a professional. The comforting thought was that she knew how to handle herself. A check on the time and he moved away from the Panther. They separated and walked purposefully into the trees. Time was critical.

8
Contact

Lieutenant Boris Tsegler planted one foot carefully in front of the other and then scoured the dense woodland ahead. Something different caught his eye, a subtle change in colouration. Finally it dawned on him. The house blended cleverly with the surrounding environment, painted a neutral powder grey.

'I have it,' he said into the throat mike. 'Twelve o'clock, three-hundred metres.' He ventured forward another ten paces improving his view. Timber construction, two storeys high and with a steep corrugated roof, and looking directly at the back door.

'Left flank,' he called up, raising a hand. The two men looked round almost hidden against the background. 'Hold where you are.' They nodded and knelt out of sight.

'Right flank . . . , go long, round to the front.'

Their acknowledgements came through his ear and he began to edge slowly forward, giving them time to relocate. He waved up the left flank and they advanced, spread wide, heads up watching the house. Where the trees gave way to a cultivated plot of land he stopped. A weathered picket fence ran along the perimeter of the garden and a small timber shed faced back to the house. Tsegler could just make out the rear of a car parked out front. He again raised a hand and the left flank halted. He waited.

His earphone came to life. 'In position.'

Swinging the rifle to his shoulder he flicked a button and lit up the telescopic sight. The upstairs windows showed no signs of movement, ground floor the same. He queried the men out front. 'Anything?'

'Looks deserted.'

Tsegler thought the same and lowered his rifle. For a moment longer he waited, allowing his mind to run through the alternatives. 'On my command go in fast, front and rear. I remind you, we want them alive.' He looked left and got a thumbs up from the sniper, an affirmative in his right ear.

'Move!'

They went in hard, zigzagging their way to the back of the house. Tsegler held off, rifle up to cover, and watched them race to the back wall. They spun round either side of the door, alert. He loped forward and gave the order. 'Go!'

Simultaneously, front and back door burst inwards and the men dived inside.

Tsegler brushed past the crouching figures and made for the stairs. Rifle pointing, he bounded up two at a time. On the landing he threw himself sideways, down to one knee. Silence. He crept towards the nearest door, the master bedroom, empty. Bathroom, empty; and lastly the second bedroom, empty. But he saw that the single bed had been slept in, the covers were half pulled back and the pillow still bore the indent of someone's head. He touched the sheet, cold. The silence from downstairs confirmed his worst fears; the house was but a shell, the girl could be anywhere.

He cursed and head butted the wall. With an effort he controlled his anger and crossed to a small window that overlooked the front garden. Down below sat two vehicles; a dark green Ford flatbed, and a pale blue Lada saloon. His lips tightened into a thin smile, that car belonged to the girl. Of that much he was certain.

Tsegler made his way back downstairs and found the men in the kitchen.

'Search the surrounding area, her car's in the drive. They're on foot, can't be far away.'

Leaving the half squad of Spetsnaz to get on with it, he took a close look at the two vehicles. The flatbed revealed little of interest and he moved to the Lada. Without thinking he tried the driver's door and it swung open. A few CDs lay on the back seat, a box of tissues on the dashboard. He opened the glovebox and found an empty buff coloured envelope and a pencil. On a shelf under the dashboard behind the steering console he found a red lipstick and a squashed polystyrene cup. An adaptor for a mobile phone stuck out of the cigarette lighter. Exasperated, he jumped out and opened the boot. Under a red tartan picnic blanket he found an old map and half a dozen carrier bags. The map showed the local area, unmarked by any annotations. He threw it back in and slammed the boot. Leaning against the back of the saloon he stared at the house. Maybe he ought to give it another search for clues.

Then Tsegler stiffened to a voice in his ear.

'I think we've struck lucky. I'm two-hundred metres south.'

He found the man standing with his feet apart, arms folded and staring down at the ground.

'Well?' he asked.

'Look at the pine needles, recently scuffed,' he explained. 'And over there, and here. They are not from us, we came in from the north.'

Tsegler looked up as the others drifted in. Once pointed out the markings were obvious, not to be ignored.

'Can you follow them?'

'Of course.' He sounded offended by the question.

'Then you take point. I'll take your place on the right flank and we'll spread out in line, out of sight. Use voice procedure.' Their personal radios had a range of seven-hundred metres, a little less in the forest, but more than enough for this job.

'Go now,' Tsegler ordered, and the five men of the Special Forces again began to stalk their quarry. This time they pushed on with more certainty. The trail was fresh.

Anna Kuznetsova gathered together the mugs and wrappers and returned them to the backpack. Uncle Gvido sat on the top step and she wondered if he felt as confident as he appeared. Did he really believe the British would find them? That was the trouble with her Uncle, you never really knew what he was thinking, always the jovial smile.

'Will they come today, Uncle?'

He looked round lazily and scratched his beard, gave her his most disarming smile.

'Of course, child, stop your worrying. They have soldiers to the south, you will be in safe hands.'

He stood and stamped his feet, settling them into his boots. He ambled over to confront her and took hold of her hands.

'You know,' he said seriously, 'what you are doing is very brave. And also, I am not a clever man, I do not pretend to understand the world of political things. But I think it is not easy for the English. All this must be done in secret. You did not wish to speak with our people, and the British understand why, so they must be careful not to upset our leaders in Riga.'

He paused and she waited. She'd never heard him talk this way.

He frowned. 'But once the British come you will be in their embassy, and there I believe you will be safe.'

She lifted one of his hands and kissed it. 'I'm sorry I brought all this trouble to your door, Uncle, but I had no one else.'

He laughed, one of those deep rumbling laughs that shook his belly. 'Do not give it a thought, child. This is the most excitement I've had for months.'

Fifteen minutes after the Spetsnaz went hunting, Sarah Campbell spotted the house.

'Mike!' she hissed. They were still well within the trees and she waited while he came to join her. She let the assault rifle hang from her shoulder and pulled out the Glock. A press of the release button and the magazine dropped from the butt into the palm of her hand. She checked the loading and slipped it back inside.

Bowman came and squatted on his haunches.

She felt his eyes on her and met them. 'What?' she asked, mildly annoyed.

He shrugged his shoulders, a flicker of a smile. 'Nothing,' he said casually, 'just wondered where the battle is.'

She tossed her head and refrained from answering, and instead pointed to the house. 'Do we just knock on the front door?'

'Let's get a bit closer, see what we think.'

Sarah took the lead and stealthily approached the edge of the pine trees. Bowman crept up behind her, she could feel his presence.

They studied the house together and she could see two vehicles in the drive but no sign of the occupants. Quiet, but not threatening.

Bowman spoke from behind. 'I'll go and knock on the door. Stay here and cover me.'

She sensed his caution. 'Something wrong?'

'Not particularly, but I thought someone might be looking from a window.' He walked out from cover and she watched him up the drive. As he reached a pale blue saloon she changed position, making a short fast run to the gatepost. He glanced round, pistol raised, nodded, and approached the front door. Sarah saw him lift a fist to knock and then pause, changing the fist to an open palm and pushing the door. It swung inwards and he stepped inside, hidden from view.

She ran for the flatbed and knelt behind the rear wheel, focusing on the house. After what seemed an eternity he reappeared and shook his head.

'Front and back doors have been forced and there's no one around. I think the Russians got here first.'

Sarah lowered the assault rifle and joined him on the porch.

Bowman slumped down to sit with his back to the wall and eased his helmet. 'Now it's a needle in a haystack, and a Brigadier waiting to call in NATO.' He found a cigarette and flicked his lighter.

Sarah knelt and took a sip from her bottle. She could sense his frustration, no need for words.

'What a bleedin' mess,' he muttered, flicking ash. 'No girl, a squad of bloody Russians nosing about and we're stuck in the middle.'

She ignored his rant, thinking instead of their proximity to the border, and whether the Russians *had* managed to kidnap the girl. Surely it was worth having a go at finding them.

'Mike, if that squad of Russkies walked across the border at dawn, add on the time it took to get here, they can't be that far away.'

He looked up, eyes narrowed in thought. 'Mmm . . . ,' he sighed. 'Alright I'll buy it. They'll be hiking back north-east. Slim chance but we've nothing to lose.' He climbed to his feet, mumbling. 'No peace for the wicked, worse than being married.'

Sarah smiled to herself. Let him whine all he liked, especially when he was big enough to accept advice, and particularly advice from a 'girl'. She hurried to catch him and rubbed shoulders.

'Thank you, Mike Bowman.'

'For what?' he grunted.

'Nothing,' she grinned, 'just thank you.'

He frowned, gave her an old fashioned look, and shook his head, bewildered. 'Women,' she heard him grumble, and then let him quicken the pace.

The sun tipped beyond the zenith, half a day of light left.

In Gloucestershire, Carol Hearsden patched through a call to the Commander's office.

'Fraser speaking.'

The Military Attaché at Riga's British Embassy came on the line. 'This is Baxter, sir.'

'So where are we?'

'Not quite where we'd like. A small team of Spetsnaz came over the border early this morning, Putting two and two together, they're most likely looking for the girl. Mike and Sarah are out there now. The biggest problem is the Brigadier, wants to alert NATO.'

Fraser took that bit of news with a frown. If only the Latvians could be trusted then all these shenanigans would be over with. As for the Brigadier, he probably just wanted to make a name for himself: the man who faced down the Russians.

'Now listen. Remind the Brigadier that this has been sanctioned by Joint Intelligence. Until he has proof otherwise this mission stands. No NATO interference, understand?'

A prolonged silence followed before Baxter answered.

'I can try, sir.'

'Not good enough, use your authority. In the meantime I'll inform the Joint Chiefs of Staff, get them to apply pressure.'

Another lengthy silence and Fraser found himself getting annoyed. 'For Christ's sake, you're supposed to be the Military Attaché. Get in there and sort him out.'

There was a hesitant; 'Yes, sir,' and Fraser took a more conciliatory line. 'Good, I'm sure your powers of persuasion will prevail. There has to be some common sense applied. Four or five Russians straying over the border does not make for a bloody invasion.'

'No, sir, I'll tell him.'

'Very well. Anything else?'

'No,' Baxter said, 'not at the moment.'

'In that case, I'll let you get on.' He replaced the receiver and came to his feet. 'Carol!' he called. 'Put me through to Whitehall.' If only he had the vaguest notion of what information the girl possessed.

The phone rang. 'You're through, sir.'

Fraser lounged into his chair and swung one foot onto the desk. 'Hello? Get me Sir Hillary Montague. Tell him it's Fraser, urgent.'

A young woman replied. 'Yes, sir. Sir Hillary Montague, one moment, please.'

Fraser made himself comfortable. This would take some explaining.

Anna Kuznetsova sat relaxing on the steps, happy to watch her Uncle playing solitaire with an old set of playing cards. She turned her face to the warmth of the sun, squinting against the brightness glaring down on the open clearing.

Uncle Gvido let out a triumphant 'Ha!' and gathered up the cards. 'I do not beat the cards very often, child,' he said gruffly, 'but sometimes the Gods smile on me.'

She smiled at his good fortune and lay back on the veranda, cradling her head in her arms. With her eyes closed the sun turned blood red through her eyelids, enhancing the lazy passing of the hours.

'Anna!'

She sat bolt upright. He seldom used her name and never in such an urgently harsh way. When she looked he held a finger to his lips, the hunting rifle across his lap. He gestured with his beard.

'Inside,' he whispered, and drew back the rifle bolt.

Tiptoeing through the skewed door she heard the bolt click as he loaded a bullet into the chamber. Not daring to make a noise she backed into the room and sat on the cot, her breath coming in shallow gasps. She caught a glimpse of Uncle Gvido silently passing the half-open door, butt of the rifle in his shoulder, the barrel pointing down.

What had he heard? Anna waited, wanting to be sick.

Boris Tsegler spoke into his throat mike. 'Hold.' He sensed them all stop, dropping to their knees, or finding the trunk of a tree. The man on point held his pose, one arm raised in warning. Slowly he turned his head and indicated towards eleven o'clock. The hand changed to one finger and Tsegler nodded. One-hundred metres. Bending at the waist he moved cautiously up behind him.

Without looking at Tsegler, the man whispered. 'There's a hut, and the trail leads straight for it.'

Tsegler peered through the trees and picked out the old timbers and holes in the roof. Instinct kicked in, that indefinable something that warned of danger.

'Back up,' he ordered via the radio, and retraced his footsteps. When he judged they were well enough clear he signalled for them to join him.

'We'll do this by the book. I want the four of you to come in from the far side, well spread. You hold inside the trees, stay hidden. I'll come in from this side so mark your targets well. We don't know who's there but I'll call if I need you. Clear?'

'Clear,' they chorused, helmets wagging.

He made a circling motion with his hand and they peeled away, rapidly merging with the trees. He again picked up the original path and halted behind a thicker trunk. He could see the right rear corner of the dwelling and just make out what appeared to be a veranda running across the front. He brought up the scope and examined what he could see in greater detail, but only a peaceful sun-bathed clearing revealed itself.

His earphone crackled and three reports came in. He waited and a moment later the last position was reached. He slung the rifle over his left shoulder and pulled the pistol; this would likely be close range.

Tsegler stalked left, bringing the back wall of the hut to his front, and approached with care.

His right ear came alive. 'Male target with rifle to your three o'clock on veranda.'

'Leave,' he said. 'My mark.'

A few steps and he shouldered up to the right rear corner, glanced around. Shuffling quietly along the side wall he stopped a metre short of the raised planking. This was the moment he went into full fighting mode, cold eyes focused, grim faced with anticipation. He took another pace forward, hesitated, and then lunged to his right, into the open and down on one knee.

A big, bearded man swung towards him, raising a lethal looking rifle.

'Stay very still,' he ordered, pistol pointing at his chest.

The man's eyes blazed with anger but he paused.

Tsegler stared at him. 'I will not fire if you put the gun down.'

But the man seemed hell bent on suicide and slid a finger inside the trigger guard. Tsegler reacted. The pistol spat, twice. The first bullet hit left centre, thumping through the fabric. The second hit his hand, smashing the fingers to a pulp, ricocheting off the steel breech. Blood sprayed from the stumps. But Uncle Gvido Medris triggered one shot, an involuntary spasm contracting a finger. The hunting rifle's blast echoed out into the woodland and Tsegler cursed. The man staggered, took a wild step backwards, somehow staying on his feet. The blazing eyes softened, glazed, and he took an involuntary step forward. The impact of a high velocity round smacked into the side of his head, and as the blood spurted he fell to his knees, and crashed to the deck.

And then came a scream, a high pitched animal cry that carried forever.

Tsegler bounded up the steps, jumped the body and burst through the door. Her mouth twisted open, the young woman's scream died on her lips and she covered her eyes, head shaking.

Angered by the noise, Tsegler nonetheless allowed himself a grim smile of satisfaction. The Spetsnaz had triumphed yet again; he might even be rewarded with a promotion.

'Move in,' he said to the throat-mike.

The girl removed her hands, obviously petrified, and he lowered the pistol.

'You are Anna Kuznetsova?'

She nodded.

Tsegler stood aside. 'Out,' he barked.

Cowed by his aggression, the girl slid her feet to the floor and stumbled towards the exit. He made a move to follow but she stopped, staring at the threatening presence of a sniper blocking the door.

'Leave her,' Tsegler demanded. 'Just watch she doesn't run.'

The soldier grunted and stood menacingly to one side, the barrel of his rifle following her faltering footsteps.

Tsegler glanced round the ruined hut. It was empty of anything useful and he strode out to join the squad.

9
Decisions

Mike Bowman flinched at the sound of a gunshot. The haunting scream that followed reverberated in the still air, reached a crescendo, and fell away.

Sarah's eyes locked on his, a meaningful but obvious query. To answer, Bowman stepped closer. 'From the right?' He sought confirmation.

'Yes, and not far off.'

'Mmm . . . ,' he said, thinking fast. 'We'll hold our original heading and then swing east, try to get in front.' He lifted the rifle and slid the selector to the fire position.

Sarah's teeth worried her bottom lip and she followed his example. She felt for a spare magazine and he watched from the corner of his eye. This would be a different sort of contact from what she'd been used to. These guys were professionals, not amateur hooligans showing off with badly maintained hand guns. But she wore that determined expression which convinced him of her courage and he felt guilty for doubting her.

'Good to go?'

Sarah loosened the Glock for speed of use and gave him that familiar smile. 'I'm all yours.'

He grinned at the innuendo and turned away. There'd been no further sounds, and as the gunshot had come from the east, his decision to go north away from immediate engagement tempted him to push on, gain some real distance before cutting right across what he hoped would be their line of travel. If the girl was still alive, she might help impede their progress.

For fifteen minutes he strode out as fast as he dared, mixing speed with caution, Sarah following close in his footsteps. When he judged the distance to be safe they veered right and slowed. Here the forest thickened, sturdier tree trunks, a greater accumulation. Bowman studied the area with care. If the

101

Spetsnaz had chosen this route, it might be the best chance of an ambush.

'Angel,' he said softly. 'I think this is about right. Pick a tree.'

She didn't hesitate and walked a few paces to where two smaller pines stood close together. He nodded his approval, she'd chosen well, the more obvious place being a heavier tree trunk close by, but which would have been all the more suspect to a keen eyed special forces operative.

He joined her. 'I'm taking a line directly east,' he said, pointing straight across the enemy's possible route.

'I want us to stay in visual contact so I'll check back to make sure I still have you in sight. Chances are if we're far enough apart they'll be between us . . . , if we're lucky.' He reached out and touched her arm. 'Intel reported five Spetsnaz. My guess is that they'll have a man on point, and a Tail-end-Charlie.' He was thinking it through as he spoke. 'At least one with the girl, maybe two, and a commander.' He paused looking down into her dark eyes. 'It'll be me to take out whoever's got the girl. As soon as I fire you open up on the lead man and anybody who's clear of the girl.' He squeezed her arm to make his point.

'This won't be easy, Angel. These men will be veterans, elite Special Forces. The first few seconds are vital, that's when we even up the odds. After that we play it by ear. And don't forget, they'll be wearing body armour too, so head and leg shots first. Don't be squeamish about finishing them off.' He stared at her for a moment, knowing what he said was necessary. 'If I go down, you leave me. If the girl dies, save yourself. Won't be much of an operation if she's dead.' He felt he was being heartless but it came with the territory, no good throwing away lives for the hell of it.

Sarah eased her arm out from his finger grip and tilted her head to one side, dark eyes scanning his face.

'Stop fretting,' she said, 'and get on with it.'

He pursed his lips and nodded, then smiled faintly. 'You're right,' he said, and turned to go.

Sarah stopped him with a hand on his gun arm. She stretched up and kissed him on the cheek.

'Good luck, Mike Bowman,' she said softly.

He swallowed, embarrassed. 'And you, Angel. Take care,' and he walked away.

Eventually, after much trial and error, he managed to find a convenient spot that still allowed him to have her in line of sight. He made himself comfortable. Whether it was a long wait, or short, they could only hang it out and trust to luck.

Lieutenant Boris Tsegler had ordered his men into single file, at least ten paces between each man. Grigori led the way, using his sixth sense to warn him of danger, assault rifle poised, and Yuri loped along watching his back. Third in line, Alik towed Anna Kuznetsova with a short length of webbing. The young woman had offered little resistance, too shocked by the killing of her Uncle, and had quickly succumbed to Alik's menacing threats. Bound by her hands and gagged to prevent her crying out, he managed to keep her moving at a reasonable pace.

Tsegler himself slotted in behind the pair, keeping his distance; and the eagle-eyed Stepan brought up the rear, most of his time spent looking back down the trail. As for himself, Tsegler reckoned the least he could expect was a weekend on leave in Pskov. A good meal in the Hotel Kayanashki, and evenings of vodka and dance. Plenty of willing girls on offer, it would be good to let his hair down.

He grinned, pleased with their progress. Not far ahead lay the narrow stream, and once over that it was but a short hike to the border. Looking to the front of the line he could see Grigori pushing on, then checked behind to see Stepan momentarily walking backwards as he watched their tail.

Tsegler's grin faded, reminding himself not to get over-optimistic, this was not the place to relax, not yet.

Bowman heard a faint sound, squinted into the middle distance, and saw them coming. He glanced through the trees at Sarah and he saw the nod of her helmet, the assault rifle lifting to her shoulder.

He turned his attention back to the Russians. As he predicted, they were strung out in single file, disciplined, the girl being pulled along by the third man in line. It looked as if an officer followed them, and Bowman slowly raised his telescopic sight. He would take the soldier pulling the girl first, and then the officer. Sarah should be able to deal with the first two, it would be in the lap of the Gods as to what happened with Tail-end-Charlie.

He concentrated through the 'scope. The soldier's sweat stained face swam into the lens. Bowman's finger caressed the trigger, took first pressure. He equalised his breathing, the man' face centred. And squeeze.

The rifle crashed, recoiled against his shoulder, and the man's face pulped with blood.

Change target, found the officer, eyes wide with surprise.

He fired again, at the chest, bigger target. The 7.62mm round smacked into the man's combats and the bullet proof vest.

From Bowman's right, Sarah's M4 hammered into action. A short burst, followed by another. No time to look. The officer had gone down but moved, raising a lethal looking rifle.

Bowman focused, found a face distorted with pain, and thumped two rounds at the target. He cursed, over exited he'd snatched at the trigger. But a bullet slammed into the man's shoulder, driving deep into the body. Blood pumped and the head sagged.

More gunfire, the M4 cracking another burst at the Spetsnaz. He lowered the rifle to take stock, spotted Tail-end-Charlie returning fire. No real noise and he realised a suppressor muffled the sound. The girl lay on the ground, tugged to one side when Bowman's bullet ended her captor's life. Stepping out from the cover of the tree, Bowman went to a kneeling position and picked out Tail-end-Charlie through the 'scope.

A searing blast of pain slammed his left shoulder. He grunted with the agony, knocked backwards by the force, dropping the rifle. Teeth gritted, he closed his eyes to the stabbing burn. Disorientated, he fumbled for his pistol and found the butt in his right hand. He came up on knees and good arm, shielding the pistol from the dirt. What had he missed, where had the bullet come from? He half-fell behind the tree. Sarah was holding her own, the M4 firing in short bursts. He nervously put his head round the trunk, and jerked it back. But he'd seen enough. The third soldier lay prone, a sniper rifle supported on his elbows.

Bowman steeled himself. He had to finish this with the pistol. Safety catch off, he struggled into a crouch and prepared to charge.

Launching himself into the open he ducked left and sprinted to close the gap. The rifleman fired hurriedly and he felt the wind of the bullet slap past his cheek. His left arm flapped at his side, useless. Closing to thirty feet, he straightened his pistol arm and opened fire, pumping 9mm shells at the man's head and torso.

He saw the bullets strike home and the soldier slumped over the stock of his rifle. More bullets whipped by his head; Tail-end-Charlie had Bowman in his sights. But that change of target was enough for Sarah. A dozen rounds caught the man and threw him back like a rag doll. He lay still, broken and unmoving.

Bowman faltered, collapsed to his knees, head down in pain. Blood seeped freely from his arm. Vaguely, as if from a great distance he heard the girl whimper.

Boris Tsegler blinked one eye open. His blurred vision showed only a carpet of pine needles. His breath came in ragged gasps, harsh whistling, unable to fill his lungs. He would have cursed, but that was wasted effort. His life blood drained away, pumping with every feeble pulse of his heart. A coldness crept over his limbs. He thought of the Hotel Kayanashki and the dancing, and the girls; of the promotion that might have been. A fleeting memory of a dozen firefights and living to tell the tale. Now this, caught unawares, having not fired a shot in return. The irony of losing out to a stupid slip of a girl, a pathetic end to a famous career. His shallow breathing became laboured, a gurgling rattle in his throat and the blood frothed on his lips.

Lieutenant Boris Tsegler gave up the uneven struggle and slipped away, and a once fierce Mongolian wind ceased to blow.

In the unearthly silence that followed, Sarah changed magazines. She moved from cover towards the aftermath of bloody carnage. She could see Bowman was hurt, down on his knees, the only movement coming from the girl struggling to gain her feet.

With the M4 clamped to her shoulder, Sarah advanced warily, eyes on the twisted bodies lying haphazardly around the trees. She reached the first soldier, her primary target, and kicked his shin. No reaction. Walking past Bowman's dejected figure she glanced at the sniper he'd shot to pieces. No one could survive that many hits with a 9mm.

The whimpering girl held out her hands to be freed but Sarah shook her head; not until she finished checking.

Skirting wide of the officer she looked down at Bowman's first target. What remained of the man's face stared grotesquely at the sky, mouth open, a blood filled socket where his left eye had been.

She went back to the officer, his face half buried in pine needles. Holding her rifle aimed at the back of his head she kicked his weapon clear and then shoved the sole of her boot at his contorted shoulder. The body rolled over, no sign of life.

Finally, Sarah made a careful check of the soldier who'd kept her pinned down. She counted seven hits, not bad at that range. Then a muffled whine made her turn to the girl, arms still held out to be freed.

But the adrenalin fuelled action caught up with her body and she trembled, weak limbed. She lowered the rifle and took some deep breaths, desperate to control the bile rising in her throat. She fumbled for the knife tucked in her belt scabbard and cut the webbing from the young woman's hands, then deftly sliced away the gag. A vivid red weal showed up against the girl's pale skin and she spat cloth from her mouth.

Sarah rejected the pleading eyes and went instead to Bowman's slumped figure. Bending over his lowered head she called quietly.

'Mike?'

There was no response.

'Mike?' she called, louder.

He stirred, lifting his face to squint up into hers. He groaned and then grinned through his pain. 'Hi, Angel. Did you see 'em off?'

'All dead. The girl's unharmed, just shocked.'

Bowman glanced down at his blood soaked arm. 'One of those bastards got me,' he said, sounding surprised.

'Let's take a look,' she insisted and removed his Kevlar helmet.

He did his best to help, more of a hindrance at times, but after a few minutes of careful work she managed to clean him up and bandage the wound. The bullet had passed through his deltoid muscle without hitting bone and bled clean. Some antiseptic, a clean field bandage and he was on his feet, still in some pain, but it would do for now.

She made him drink and studied him closely. 'Can you manage?'

A bit of the old Mike Bowman returned. 'Of course I can manage, just a flesh wound. Let's see to the girl.'

Reluctantly, Sarah agreed and they walked slowly to the young woman. She was massaging bruised wrists.

Sarah spoke gently. 'Anna?'

The young woman looked up through tear stained eyes and nodded.

'Do you speak English?'

'A little, speak slowly, no?'

Bowman intervened, patiently. 'We are British. We came because you asked to speak with us. Do you understand?'

Tentatively, she nodded.

Sarah reached out and rubbed Anna's arm. 'Are you hurt?'

'No, only my . . . ,' she held up her hands revealing deep bruises on the wrists.

'We have a big car,' Sarah explained. 'We must walk first.'

107

Anna wrinkled her nose and raised a delicate eyebrow. 'How long to walk?'

Bowman tried a smile. 'Not too long, two or three kilometre. Then we drive.' He mimicked turning a steering wheel.

She stared at him, and then switched her gaze to Sarah. She reached for Sarah's hands and held them. 'My Uncle,' she pleaded. 'He is dead. I must go for him.'

Sarah looked at Bowman and he shook his head. The girl spotted the negative movement.

'I *will* go to him, you *must* help me.'

Bowman sucked air through his clenched teeth. What did she expect them to do, carry the body through the forest? He didn't have the strength and he was sure the girl couldn't. But he supposed it wouldn't harm to go along with it for now. Once she accepted the futility of the situation they could get on.

He inclined his head and forced a smile. 'Okay. Can you show us where?'

Anna's face lit up and she wiped her eyes. 'Come,' she said. 'I show.'

Bowman winked at Sarah and turned back for his rifle. He scooped up his helmet, found the discarded weapon and slung it from his good shoulder. The pain in his left shoulder had dissipated, to leave an occasional burning ache. When he turned to join them, Anna had almost disappeared through the trees. Sarah hovered, not wanting to leave him.

'Go on,' he called, 'I'll manage.'

She smiled briefly and strode after the girl.

Bowman followed, walked a few paces and then stopped to take a last look at the carnage. Five Russian bodies, no disguising the fact they were on Latvian territory. Keeping the lid on this lot might be difficult and Major Holliman would be busy, like it or not.

They found Gvido Medris lying where he'd fallen, his head almost shredded by the impact of a bullet. Anna appeared inconsolable, desolated by the death of her Uncle. Bowman felt helpless and turned to Sarah for inspiration. Woman to woman there was a natural empathy and the comforting presence of

108

Sarah's calming influence gradually brought the girl to her senses.

Bowman looked on, wondering how to resolve the problem of moving the body, well aware that time slipped by. The Brigadier would be champing at the bit, eager to discharge his responsibilities with NATO's high command. He lit a cigarette and walked away from the women's mournful chatter. Behind the hut he studied the relatively sparse woodland. The more he looked, the more he favoured the idea of bringing up the Panther and recovering the body. It might be awkward, fraught with difficulties, but it had to be worth a try. And the girl would be forever grateful; might help smooth the way for what lay ahead.

He wandered back to the women. Anna seemed calmer now, sat away from the body, Sarah hugging her close and talking quietly.

'Angel, got a minute?'

She looked up, disentangled herself from the girl, and came close.

'I think we could get the Panther up here. Not sure how much help I can give you moving the body, think you could manage?'

Sarah glanced round at the bulk of the man's weight and pursed her lips. 'One way or the other, yes, we'll manage.'

'Right, tell the girl I'll give it a go. The GPS,' he suggested, holding out a hand.

She passed it over and went to the young woman.

Bowman waited while Sarah talked, saw Anna glance over. Eventually she nodded and stood up. She walked to Bowman, straight backed, head up.

'Thank you,' she said simply. 'Thank you for my Uncle.'

He shrugged. 'I will try. You wait with Sarah.'

She nodded with the beginnings of a tremulous smile.

Bowman looked beyond her to Sarah, raised a finger in recognition, and moved off. Initially headed west, he activated the GPS, waited for it to find the satellites, and altered his route a few degrees south. Keeping a watchful eye on the undulating woodland, he logged the easiest route to memory, and pushed on.

Forcing the pace and ignoring the pain from his shoulder, he made it to the Panther after thirty minutes of hard going. Shadows lengthened as the afternoon wore on and his first priority was to make contact with Holliman. He powered up the radio and grabbed the handset.

'Hello Zero, this is Alpha-Foxtrot, over.'

He waited, nothing.

'Hello Zero, this is Alpha-Foxtrot, over.'

Still nothing and he frowned at the aerial. Bad signal? Then the radio hissed, crackled, and the Sigs NCO came through loud and clear. 'Hello Alpha-Foxtrot, this is Zero. Send, over.'

Bowman breathed out, relieved to hear his voice.

'Zero . . . Alpha-Foxtrot. Package is secure. I say again, package is secure, over.'

'This is Zero . . . , wait out.'

Bowman took some water, fresh blood seeping down his arm.

'Hello Alpha-Foxtrot, this is Zero, Sunray speaking: what news on uninvited guests? Over.'

Bowman hesitated. Callsign 'Sunray' would be Major Holliman.

'Ah . . , this is Alpha-Foxtrot.' He had to make this clear, unmistakeable, regardless of eavesdropping. 'Eradicated, over.'

This time the wait stretched on.

'Hello Alpha-Foxtrot, this is Zero. What is your ETA with us? Over.'

He was back with the Sigs NCO and he glanced at the time.

'Zero, Alpha-Foxtrot; 20.00hrs Zulu, over.' That should give him ample time to make camp.

'This is Zero . . . Roger your last, 20.00hrs. Out.'

Bowman snapped the handset back and supported his weight on the driver's seat. That was a full acknowledgement of his transmission. They'd understood the incursion had been eliminated. Now he could concentrate on the hard bit, getting this lump of metal to the girls at the hut.

He dragged out the GPS, secured it in the bracket below the dashboard, where it remained visible, and fired up the engine. He trundled slowly down the trail, found the first line of least resistance, and turned into the forest. Wrestling the wheels along his chosen route, Bowman weaved carefully between the solid trunks. Blood dripped on the floor.

10
Hard Truth

In Ross-on-Wye, Anatoly Pushkin sat uncomfortably on the hard concrete floor and pieced together another part of the mechanical jigsaw. Satisfied with the alignment he fumbled in a small plastic box and extracted a tiny Kevlar bolt. He slipped it through the predrilled hole and then fitted the even smaller nut on the protruding thread. Running it down finger tight he checked again that the two components matched correctly and then applied a miniscule spanner to finish the job.

Pushkin fidgeted to ease the pins and needles in his right foot and held up the assembled structure. So far so good. He placed it gently to one side, glanced at the instruction manual and found the next part of the intricate jigsaw. Offering up the new piece to the ongoing construction, he repeated the painstaking process. Having securely tightened two more bolts, Pushkin scratched his head and took a deep breath. Three times he had practised this engineering task, all done in the training facility at Russia's Technical Laboratory for Covert Operations, and the Chief Scientist had personally congratulated him on his expertise.

Even so, Anatoly Pushkin applied his training with care. There would be no second chances, everything depended on the machine working first time, straight out of the box. He located the next component and concentrated on attaching it to the growing assembly.

The intricately designed engineering masterpiece began to take shape and he paused to admire its sleek efficiency. Moscow's scientific elite had surpassed themselves with this innovation. Operation Lightning could not fail to achieve a great coup.

At five past three, Miranda Atkinson met Chris and Tina at the school gates and drove home. She listened to them teasing one another over who was better at playing Minecraft and whether Harry Potter was the best magician ever.

Preoccupied with the heavy traffic of the school run, Miranda approached the turning for the narrow lane. She vaguely noticed a white van parked in the lay-by next to a fresh set of road works.

'Always pecking up something,' she muttered, and flicked the indicator to turn left. Driving slowly down the lane she made the hard right into their driveway, parked up and sighed. It had been a busy day, exciting and hectic. The new clients were on board and she could expect a big fat bonus at the end of the month.

With the kids out of the car and chasing each other noisily round the drive she unlocked the front door. There was the usual accumulation of junk mail piled on the mat with only one envelope of any relevance, a bank statement.

In the kitchen Miranda poured the children fresh orange juice, selected two chocolate digestives apiece and left them to it. Before she got halfway upstairs the sound of CBBC filled the living room, Christopher's raised voice telling Tina what channel to watch.

Changing out of her office clothes she pulled on a pair of stretch jeans and a loose fitting tee-shirt, scraped her hair back and fixed it with a crocodile clip. Comfortable and casual she thought, catching a glimpse of herself in the full length mirror, and made her way back downstairs. From the wine rack she uncapped a bottle of Jacob's Creek and allowed herself a small glass of the burgundy liquid. The day had gone well, she deserved a little celebration, and then she would set about preparing supper. Her favourite cushioned wicker chair waited in the corner by the sun bathed French doors, and with Delia Smith's recipe book on her lap, wine to her lips, Miranda Atkinson relaxed in the comforting privacy of her own home.

In the white van parked in the lay-by on the A40, the man wearing the headphones adjusted the volume and screwed up his eyes in concentration. He heard the clink of bottle on glass from the kitchen, and he thought the almost undetectable squeak revealed she'd sat in a chair. And by the sounds coming out of the lounge the kids were watching TV. He wriggled in the seat to make himself more comfortable. Patience was a virtue.

Dusk was fast approaching the forests of Latvia when Mike Bowman eventually arrived at the abandoned hut. He'd fought the Panther to within a hundred paces of the clearing and then the dense circle of pine trees defeated him. He gave up and switched off.

The girls stood waiting anxiously, but he brushed past to the man's body. In his absence the two women had managed to turn the corpse onto his back, straightening the body before the full effects of rigor mortis set in. Bowman kneaded his injured arm and winced, assessing his ability to lift with his good arm.

'Angel, if you can take his left arm and the girl takes his feet, I can use my good arm to lift under his right armpit.'

Sarah nodded without argument and they gathered round for the lift. Uncle Gvido Medris weighed heavy and Anna struggled to lift her share. It became an undignified wobbling procession and they were forced to rest more than once. Finally the three of them hauled him unceremoniously into the left front seat, and staggered back to recover from their exertions.

Bowman felt his good arm being tugged.

Anna stood looking up at him. 'We go to my Uncle's house now?' she pleaded.

He met her eyes, frowning.

'We must . . . ,' she fought for the right word. 'How you say, we must dig,' and she mimed shovelling dirt.

Bowman stared at her dishevelled, pretty face, puzzled. It dawned on him that she wanted to bury her Uncle, and he took pity.

'Yes, we must bury him.'

Her face broke into a tremulous smile. 'Bury him, yes, that is the word.'

He glanced at Sarah who put her hands together as if praying. 'Thank you,' she mouthed silently.

114

He shrugged; it was neither here nor there to him. Once the body was underground, it'd be one less complication to explain away.

'Get yourselves aboard, I'll have a quick look round the hut.' Leaving them to it, he walked back to the hut. The backpack and hunting rifle lay unattended and he slung them over his uninjured shoulder. Inside the hut, bare floorboards and an empty cot met his careful scrutiny, scuffed footprints in the dust.

Outside, he took a slow walk round the clearing. His keen eyes found one 9mm shell case at the end of the raised platform. Then something caught his attention, something out of place. He allowed his gaze to trawl the cabin and near the crudely fashioned window, a fresh scar in the wooden panel. Buried in the jagged splinters he prised out the misshapen end of a 7.62mm bullet. A few dried spots of blood had sprayed the panels and he realised this was the round that had probably passed through the old man's head. He tucked away both bits of metal, took a last look about the perimeter, and strode back to the Panther.

Sarah stood in the mid-upper gun turret. 'When you're ready,' she prompted.

Bowman managed to smile. 'How's Anna?'

'Shocked, threw up before she got in. It's caught up with her.'

He nodded, not surprised. That amount of violence was enough to upset anyone, especially a young woman like her.

'Can you take these?' he asked, offering up the rifle and backpack.

Sarah reached down, scooped them from his grasp, and stowed them down the hatch.

Bowman pulled himself into the driver's seat, started up and released the handbrake. He reversed and thumped noisily into a tree, cursed, shunted the Panther backwards and forwards and finally had it facing the right way. A sudden weakness coursed through his body, leaving him light headed. He gulped air until it passed, stretching the fingers of his left hand. The shoulder muscle protested, jabbing him with a white hot spasm. He

115

screwed up his eyes against the intense wave of pain, hanging onto the steering wheel.

'You all right?' It was Sarah, concerned.

'Yeah,' he said, gritting his teeth. 'Just a bit sore.' A few more revs and the vehicle eased forward and Bowman focused on driving. Next stop, the Uncle's house.

Fresh blood oozed from the exit wound and trickled down his shoulder blade. He was too engrossed in driving to feel it.

Five-hundred metres beyond Latvia's border, the driver of the Russian APC waited for Lieutenant Tsegler to make an appearance. As yet he wasn't unduly alarmed. A while ago he thought he'd heard the sound of gunshots but couldn't be sure. He'd been listening to 'heavy metal' on his Samsung Galaxy. In the end he thought it was probably the drummer.

He checked the time and lit an untipped cigarette. Watching the sun dip below the tops of the trees he spat a strand of tobacco and leant back with his eyes closed. Starting tomorrow, he'd been granted two weeks leave in Moscow and he hoped the operation went smoothly.

The anvil grey light of sunset descended on the forest.

They buried Uncle Gvido Medris at the back of the vegetable plot close to the open fronted shed. The digging of his grave took place under the bright glow of headlights, and the two women worked side by side until the sad hole in the ground became deep enough to take a body. A strong linen bed sheet sufficed to lower him into the grave, a second sheet becoming an improvised shroud.

They came together then, by the grave, Bowman and Sarah standing either side of the girl.

And Anna Kuznetsova spoke a simple eulogy in her own language, a mournful epitaph to a courageous man. In the sombre silence that followed, Sarah picked up her shovel and hesitated. Anna took her cue and taking a handful of the rich soil sprinkled a few grains onto the white linen sheet.

Tears ran freely down the girl's cheeks and Bowman placed a comforting arm round her shoulder. She laid her head against his chest and he felt her shaking with grief. Sarah scooped the mound of soil back over the body and Anna shook herself free of Bowman's arm. She walked into the shed, busying herself by the light of the headlamps

In a few minutes, with Bowman helping the best he could, Sarah had covered the grave and then with the back of her shovel patted the earth into a gentle mound.

When Anna returned it was to place a crudely fashioned piece of wood as a marker.

Bowman backed away and dimmed the headlights, and Sarah joined him, reaching for his hand. They stood for a while as the girl said her goodbyes, a forlorn figure standing alone, the dark circle of trees standing as a permanent reminder. Bowman cleared a lump in his throat. Eventually, against his better judgement, he told Sarah to bring the girl away.

They were all here for a reason, and time was of the essence.

In England, as night fell over the Herefordshire countryside a man with dual-purpose, day-night vision binoculars, settled himself in the comfort of an oak tree's low hanging branch. In addition to the standard setup, an uprated image intensifier completed the watcher's equipment. He focused on the French doors at the back of the Atkinson home, brightly lit in the darkness.

The woman came into the kitchen-diner and carefully put her wine glass on the side. She began loading dirty plates and cutlery into the dishwasher and he could see her positioning them in the basket trays, adjusting the cups as she saw fit. The watcher rotated a lever and increased magnification, refocused on the woman's face. Satisfied with the amount of detail, he backed off on the zoom and spoke quietly into his throat communicator, giving his initial report.

Raising the glasses he checked on the master bedroom, a faint light through the door to the landing revealing the curtains still drawn back to the sides of both windows. He flicked a button and switched to night vision. Panning between windows he picked out the floor to ceiling built in units, an overhead modern chandelier, and an ornate headboard up against the left hand wall. Traversing to the right, above the French doors, a small pane of frosted privacy glass indicated the presence of the bathroom, the mottled outline of a yellow duck sitting on the window shelf.

Flicking back to day vision, he brought the focus down to the kitchen. The husband had entered, was in the process of selecting a bottle from the drinks cabinet. The watcher zoomed in on a clear liquid and read the label, Smirnoff Vodka. The husband poured himself a good slug and added a slice of orange. The wife, wine glass in hand, sauntered suggestively over to join him and slid an arm round his neck. They toasted one another and he turned his head for a lingering kiss. When they parted the watcher could see she was laughing. Arms entwined around their waists they turned their backs to the French doors and wandered out through the far door.

The watcher gave a quiet update on their movements and rested the binoculars. It was a calm, mild night, making this sort of surveillance all the easier. A pair of headlights swept up the lane, the sound of the engine receding into the distance. He shifted position and found a bar of chocolate, broke a piece off and shifted his weight.

Everything was going according to plan.

The arrival of Bowman's Panther coincided with a Royal Engineer reconnaissance patrol returning to camp from the southern sector of British deployment. Two Panthers and a Foxhound trundled in along the eastern shore of the lake and an impromptu briefing diverted the majority of camp personnel down to the water's edge.

With Anna Kuznetsova safely hidden inside, Bowman drove in from the north and came to a halt within a few paces of the isolated park from where they'd departed. He killed the lights and switched off. The journey had taken its toll. Weak from the loss of blood he let his head slump forward onto the steering wheel, exhausted. Sarah identified herself in the moonlight and clarified their position with the two patrolling Sappers, who reported to HQ.

Bowman felt Sarah haul him upright. 'Mike! What is it?' But he knew she'd felt the sticky residue under her right hand, the question answered. 'God, Mike, you need a doctor. Why didn't you tell me?'

Major Vince Holliman arrived and took control. 'You have the girl?'

Bowman managed a feeble reply. 'In the back.'

'Good, tell her to stay there. Let's get you in the other seat and I'll drive us to the tent.'

Bowman struggled out and across to Sarah's position.

Holliman looked at Sarah. 'Tell the girl to stay in the back until you call her. Baxter's on his way to smuggle her out. The less she's exposed the better.'

Bowman lifted his head to what Holliman had said, inadvertently or otherwise. 'That's a hard truth, Major. Hope we can keep the lid on all this.'

The Major tilted his head round, squinting in the pale moonlight. 'You have my word on it . . . , Captain.' He started the engine and Sarah called Anna to stay put, then jumped down to the ground.

Bowman closed his eyes. For all their sakes, he hoped Baxter didn't take too long.

In London, Helena Goreya walked into Paddington Station at eight-thirty in the evening. Where possible she made a concerted effort to avoid all the surveillance cameras, and where they couldn't be avoided, lowered her face and hid under the brim of the fashionably floppy hat. She bought a one way ticket to Gloucester, grabbed a Costa Coffee and a muffin, and found a seat in the front carriage. There was a scheduled change at Swindon and she expected to arrive at Gloucester Station at 22.46 hours. She carried no luggage, just a large black plastic handbag with a long shoulder strap.

Goreya wore the same clothes with which she'd escaped the naïve British surveillance earlier that afternoon, the only addition was the hat, purchased from Monsoon in Praed Street outside the mainline station.

Helena Goreya sat back and sipped the scalding coffee. She was thirty-two, looked a lot younger, and specialised in military engineering, specifically the technical requirements associated with integrated software systems. Proficient in the English language, she'd studied computer science at Cambridge University before returning to St Petersburg with a PhD. Sitting there waiting for the train to depart, she remembered the first time she'd been approached at the Scientific Research Establishment by a man from Moscow Central. It had all been very hush-hush, sworn to secrecy on penalty of her life, and taken to the weapons research facility east of Moscow. During the next three years, she'd not only proved her worth as an exceptionally gifted software programmer, but had also been inducted into the secret world of covert operations. She'd become highly proficient in the use of small arms and found her unarmed combat to be the equivalent of many men.

Three months ago she'd been chosen as the technical scientist for a major operation. In the next few hours she would be reunited with the man who had taught her the unarmed combat. Alexander Markoff had been deployed on this mission ever since she'd passed her training. There had been rumours that Markoff could be difficult on a mission, too wrapped up in his own worth. She wondered if they would make a good partnership. Then, when the time was right, they would join Anatoly Pushkin.

Goreya Helena allowed herself a rare moment of smug satisfaction, this was the culmination of all that effort.

In Russia, the listening stations spread their radio waves, bouncing off the ionosphere to capture even the smallest of transmissions. And in the nothingness of space a satellite locked onto a new geostationary orbit.

11
Wanted

In Major Vince Holliman's tent, an army Doctor worked on Bowman's shoulder. After a dose of morphine and a thorough cleaning, the medical man had tidied up the ragged exit wound and applied a few sutures. With a fresh dressing and the application of a sling, he warned Bowman not to overexert himself, certainly for the next week.

Bowman, suffering the effects of the morphine, volunteered his thanks and when the man left the tent, tried to stand. He wobbled and Sarah stepped in to support him, taking his weight from beneath his right shoulder.

He looked at her and grinned feebly. 'Sorry, Angel. My legs feel like they don't belong.'

She glanced up at him, eyes full of worry. 'I don't think you should be on your feet, let the morphine wear off.'

He straightened slightly, carrying his own weight. 'Any bloody coffee?' he asked in an undertone.

Sarah half-grinned. Cantankerous as ever, although this time she could excuse it. 'If you'll just sit back down I'll get some.'

He shook his head and made for the tent flap. 'No, I want fresh air and a smoke, provided of course, you have no objections?'

She sighed, resenting his tone. 'Whatever, it's your life.'

He walked out and she turned to the nearest soldier, an officer. 'Is there any coffee?'

The lieutenant seemed very young and stammered a reply. 'Yes . . . , yes, of course. Give me a minute.' He scuttled outside and she heard him calling.

Through the tent flap, darkness appeared complete and she made her way out, let her eyes adjust, wondering how far Mike had walked. The faint glow of his cigarette caught her eye and she found him leaning with his back to a tree. 'Coffee's coming.'

'Feels better out here,' he said. 'Sorry if I spoke out of turn.'

Sarah reached out a hand to his good arm. 'Forget it, I'm just glad you're up and about.' She let her body lean into his, a moment of sharing.

He leaned a little, turned his face and kissed her lips, a fleeting intimacy.

'What was that for?' she asked, inwardly pleased by his warmth.

'For being an Angel.' Then he changed tack, all business. 'Where's the girl?'

Sarah pointed. 'Sleeping in the back of the Panther. Worn out, poor thing.' The vehicle had been parked at the side of the marquee, a soldier standing guard.

'Good. Where the hell's Baxter got to?'

Before she could reply, a head poked out from the tent flap. 'Coffee, Ma'am?'

'Thank you, yes,' and she walked across and took the hot drinks. Careful not to spill any she moved to Bowman, handed him the coffee. He sipped in silence and pinched out the cigarette, gazing out across the lake's dark water.

'You manage to get anything out of her?' he asked.

Sarah thought for a moment, remembering a brief conversation, about the hotel Anna worked at. It had been something about Russian officers at a party, but Sarah hadn't pushed her, and in the end the girl had closed her eyes, drifting off.

'Nothing worth a mention.'

'You think she's for real?'

Sarah tried to imagine going through what the girl had, having to watch her Uncle die, the shock of violent gunfire and more blood. 'I think she's certainly got something significant, important enough to risk her life, and family.'

'Mmm,' Bowman mumbled, pushed himself away from the tree and handed her his empty mug. 'I'll be down by the lake.'

She let him go, strolling steadily towards the water's edge, without stumbling, stronger.

Major Holliman appeared out of the darkness. 'Baxter'll be here in fifteen.'

Sarah breathed a sigh of relief. 'Soon be out of your hair, Major.'

'And pleasant as it's been to have you here, young lady, it won't be a moment too soon,' he said, and she caught the white of his teeth, grinning.

She gave a slight nod. 'I'll wake the girl.' She passed over the two empty mugs and moved off before he could protest, leaving him to his thoughts. At the side of the marquee, the Panther gleamed, a dull glint in the moon's light, and she tugged open the nearside rear door. Anna lay breathing quietly and stirred under Sarah's hand. 'We'll be leaving soon.'

The young woman sat up and leaned back, rubbing a hand over her face.

There was a polite cough behind Sarah's shoulder. It was the Major. 'If you wish to freshen up, there are ablutions for the officers, over there.' He pointed into the trees behind the tent. 'No one will disturb you, I'll see to that.'

'Thank you, Major,' she said, and turned back to Anna. She cowered against the far door.

'It's okay, he's a friend.'

Slowly, Anna slid nearer and reached for Sarah's outstretched hand.

'Come, we can wash.' She mimed cleaning her face.

Hesitantly, the girl allowed herself be led out and Sarah found a way over to the toilet tent. A single strip of bright LEDs lit the interior. They made use of the facilities and then cleaned up the best they could, under a tap of cold water.

Sarah heard the sound of a car approaching and turned to the girl. 'Ready?'

Anna breathed in and lifted her chin, a wavering smile on her face.

'Yes, I am ready now.' There was a fierce pride in her straight shoulders.

Bowman called and Sarah pushed out through the canvas flap, waited for the girl, and the pair of them strode purposefully towards the twin headlights. She could see

Baxter's tall shadow waiting by the open back door and after ushering Anna into the car, squeezed in alongside her. Bowman climbed in the passenger seat and Baxter got behind the wheel.

Holliman stuck his head in. 'Good luck people. Give my regards to England.' He grinned, touched his forehead in salute, and Baxter found the accelerator. The car swept round in a wide circle and Sarah closed her eyes. At last they were on their way.

On the apron at Riga International Airport an unscheduled RAF Airbus A330 waited for three passengers. A Mercedes belonging to the British Embassy pulled discreetly into the parking lot for VIPs, and the passengers, all now bearing diplomatic immunity, were escorted through the terminal. The two women and one man made their way across to the boarding steps, climbed quickly to the top and ducked inside. The man, entering last, took a final look out across the tarmac and adjoining buildings.

Mike Bowman's eyes glinted in the lights of the concourse and he smiled. Latvia, he mused, had proved more exiting then first envisaged, and he bore the scars to prove it. He stepped aboard and nodded to the flight attendant who began overseeing the ramp's clearance from the entry port. Bowman looked up the length of the near empty cabin and turned back.

'Is this it?' he asked.

The attendant checked, surveying the cabin. 'Three of you,' he nodded. 'We weren't told of anyone else.'

Bowman bit his tongue. Funny how money was no option when the chips were down. 'Right,' he said, and found a seat with ample leg room.

Time for some shut eye.

In the airport's departure lounge a woman cleaner emptied a bin next to Baltic Air's main boarding gate and made a mental note of what she'd seen. It was all a bit suspicious. A Mercedes parked in an isolated area of the VIP car park, the hurried throughput of three 'diplomats' ushered airside with minimal checks. And it was very unusual for the RAF to fly out at this time of night. As far as she remembered there had been no soldiers waiting to board the aircraft.

Certain this was what Stefan Illyic would pay good money to hear about, the woman scurried off with the rubbish and disposed of it in a crusher. She was due to finish her shift in half an hour, then would she pass on all that had taken place.

Hugh Atkinson studied the latest batch of GCHQ intercepts and selected three voice comms that had been earmarked for further investigation. Extracting the recordings he filed them for individual examination and loaded the first into the visual spectrum analyser. A quick inspection confirmed the frequency waveform of an O2 managed iPhone relayed from a Croydon antenna mast. Pushing the signal through the oscilloscope gave him an expected correlation and he passed it through the speaker.

The words spoken were in a language he couldn't understand, so he asked the programme for translation and brought it on screen.

The read out was instant:

hello?

hello

do you package have?

yes

good soon will visit

Atkinson rubbed his chin. The literal translation was understandable but he wondered from what language. He touched F10 and got his answer. It was classified as Buryat, part of the Mongolic family of Eastern Siberia in the Russian Federation. It wasn't that rare but it was obscure enough to cause issues when translated. It was a piece of tradecraft that went back through centuries, the earliest form of code, an obscure language.

He loaded the second transmission. Same iPhone located in Croydon, this time a woman answering:

hello

hi

package delivered

when will you check?
tomorrow
let me know

He frowned, analysing it in his mind. Fractionally more information. The man was now subordinate, reporting to a higher authority, in this case a woman. Superior by intonation and instruction, finally with an order.

He pulled the third message and repeated the procedure:
hello
yes
package confirmed
proceed as instructed

Hugh Atkinson stared at the screen, oblivious to the wording. What exactly had he learnt? He had an iPhone number from the sender, initiating contact. Two recipients on separate smartphones. GCHQ could trace those, gain access by hacking the phone, track their whereabouts, and with a greater degree of accuracy than the provider could ever dream of. What concerned Atkinson, why he stared blindly at the screen, was the small but significant problem of convincing Commander Fraser to instruct GCHQ to open proceedings.

On the one hand, all he had was the gut instinct that told him this was a genuine threat, the stuff he thrived on, what got him up in the morning. On the other hand, the facts. A tenuous link between three phone calls, all in a Russian derivative about a mysterious package using what was, on the face of it, a blatant piece of tradecraft. Not to be outdone he moved to the remote station and keyed-in to his programming software.

Within a few short minutes he designed a new algorithm to enable the 'prime emitter' to be married up with both Voice Recognition and Language parameters. The need for rock solid evidence would be paramount to his presentation.

He uploaded to the IBM mainframe and the digital surveillance hummed into action.

Hugh Atkinson went to his master terminal and re-jigged the GCHQ intercepts. His hidden world of observation had come alive, initially with an unexpected two second short-wave 'instruction' signal, and now with a set of smartphone messages. If nothing else, they were interesting developments.

Colonel Ilya Bayalin of the 12th Directorate listened to the driver's report and cursed. He had warned General Zherlenko of the consequences of Lieutenant Tsegler tangling with the British. Not that the driver was certain, but he thought he'd heard gunshots, maybe a machine-gun. More to the point, the Spetsnaz might've lost five highly experienced men, all to satisfy Zherlenko's arrogant pride.

The immediate question was how to establish the truth. Had they really been caught or were they in hiding, unable to wriggle out of the trap? And what of the girl, dead or alive?

Suppressing his anger, he dismissed the driver and checked the time. He looked at the phone, knowing he ought to inform Zherlenko but loath to give him bad news, especially without something more tangible to report.

'Lieutenant!' he snapped at the outer office.

The man's face appeared at the door. 'Sir?'

'Get me a driver and a wireless operator. A GAZ Tigr will do. See to it.'

He disappeared and Bayalin crossed to his locker and pulled out his combat uniform. The Tigr reconnaissance vehicle had all the voice comms necessary for his purposes, could contact General Zherlenko direct if needed. He changed uniforms and strapped on his belt and pistol, not that he expected to use it, more of a habit that went with the combat jacket.

There was a sharp rap on the door and the Lieutenant looked in. 'Driver and signals operator reporting, sir.'

Bayalin performed a final check of his equipment and turned to leave. 'I will be away for a while and you will be in charge until I return. Tell the Signals Office I will be on air and that he must be ready should I call. Got that?'

'Yes, Colonel. I'm in charge and Signals must be ready.'

'Good. If I'm not back by dawn, hand over to Major Rabinovich. Understood?'

'Yes, sir.'

Bayalin settled his belt and strode out into the night. The GAZ Tigr grumbled, ticking over in the park, and he took the passenger seat. 'Follow my directions,' he ordered, and with the headlamps on full beam, the vehicle exited the main gate, drove north on the main road, and then turned west for the Latvian border. Soon, thought Bayalin, this matter would be resolved.

From the quiet suburbs of Riga, a man called Stephan Illyic put through a scrambled call to SFB's headquarters located near the towering minarets of Red Square in Moscow. In answer to the clipped tones of the man he'd met only once, he repeated all that the woman cleaner had told him about the strange happenings at the airport. He was thanked for his information, urged to keep up the good work, and promised a healthy bonus.

Stephan Illyic terminated the call and celebrated by opening a fresh can of beer. Sprawled out on his oversize sofa he turned on the latest in Samsung's flat screen televisions and flicked through the channels to find a film. By any standards, Illyic couldn't claim to be rich, but with the money accrued from Moscow's coffers, life had indeed become very comfortable. He found a movie on the film channel and settled back to watch 'The Vikings'. He raised the glass to his lips and sipped the froth off his beer.

In England, Alexander Nikolai Markoff, with rain beating against the windows, had turned in early, shortly after the ten o'clock news. A persistent ringing of the doorbell forced him awake and he reached for his pistol. Cursing, he rolled out of bed, shrugged into his robe, and hidden in darkness, tiptoed downstairs. Gun outstretched, he edged silently forward and peered through the wide-angle door viewer. An automatic outside light showed him what appeared to be a woman in a soaking floppy hat. He waited, wary. Another ring of the door chime and a pair of eyes looked up. Through a fish-eye lens, distortion made for a poor image but he thought there was a familiarity in those eyes. He remained silent, watching. Then the woman moved her face and he stiffened. His unannounced visitor was Helena Goreya.

Markoff opened up and stood aside, feigning pleasure at her appearance. 'Helena, you of all people.'

She stepped inside and removed her sodden hat. 'Your mission is almost complete, Alexander. I am here to assist. Pushkin is here.'

'Where?' he asked, closed the door and switched on a hall light.

'Not far . . . , Ross-on-Wye, you know it? We are to join him for Operation Lightning.'

Markoff nodded, distracted, looking at her in disbelief, wondering already how much of a problem she would be. His voice betrayed none of his thoughts. 'You look well, Helena, strong. I think stronger than when I taught you.'

'Yes, I am. I never forgot your training, I work exercises every day.'

He grinned, but not with his eyes. 'That is good. Come, you can dry off and bring me up to date.'

They moved through to the kitchen and Markoff made a chair available. 'When do we start? How did you get here?' He had many questions, and he listened intently to her answers. Polite curiosity cost nothing, he pumped her for information and they talked long into the night.

RAF Brize Norton's landing lights blazed brightly in the rain swept darkness as the A320 began a slow descent to the airstrip. The flight attendant had warned Bowman and the girls that final approach had commenced and they were upright in their seats and belted up for landing. He heard the landing gear drop, flaps deploy, and estimated they'd flown over the Outer Marker.

The aircraft touched down with a squeal of tyres hitting tarmac, the rubber spinning up from no revolutions to a landing of 150 knots of indicated airspeed. The noise of the engines lifted as the pilot applied reverse thrust and then eased on down the taxiway to flight arrivals.

When the door swung in and the attendant waved them forward, three men in RAF raincoats entered and advanced up the aisle. Behind them came a man in a glistening wet overcoat.

Anna shrank back in confusion, reaching for the comfort of Sarah's arm.

Bowman realised how this might look and held up a hand.

'No need for the strong arm stuff, she'll be happy to come with my colleague.'

The RAF types hesitated, turning to the other man for guidance, and he nodded. 'Stand down for now.'

They stood aside and Bowman beckoned the girls to follow. Slowly, fearfully, Anna allowed Sarah to escort her to the door.

Bowman stopped next to the man in the wet coat. 'Who're you?'

'Thought you might ask. Name's Gilmore, Brian Gilmore, NDSO. Been sent to make sure there's no problems.'

'Since when have you been NDSO?'

'About six months before we sent you on this mission.'

Bowman blinked. 'How come we haven't met?'

Gilmore glanced at the girl leaving the aircraft. 'I'm London based. I think we ought to go now.'

Outside on the steps the wind whistled in from the west, rain driving sideways, a penetrating wetness. Gilmore pushed his way forward, leading them towards a long-wheelbase Range Rover Discovery. There was ample room for Bowman, Gilmore and the girls to find a seat, and the driver took them north, before turning west on a spray soaked A40.

Twelve-hundred miles east, on Latvia's border with Russia, Colonel Ilya Bayalin ordered his soldiers to wait and crossed into NATO territory. He wore a helmet and a throat microphone tuned to Tsegler's frequency. If he approached near enough to find a signal, if even one man could communicate, then he may well find answers to the mystery. Only the poor light of a fading moon lit his path and he swore, cursing in frustration. The men's destination had been the Uncle's house and Bayalin's Global tracker indicated he moved in the right direction. Now and then he stopped to call on the squad frequency, to be met by a prolonged silence. After walking for a lengthy period he inadvertently stumbled headlong into a narrow stream, scrambled up a steep bank and shook water from his uniform. He squelched on, listening for any sound, but finally came to a halt, defeated at last. Colonel Ilya Bayalin turned back, dejected. He would have to report bad news.

Unknown to the Colonel, less than six-hundred metres from where he gave up the hunt, five unmarked graves hid the remains of Tsegler's Spetsnaz command.

In the hour after midnight, sworn to secrecy, a section of British Royal Engineers had descended on a field of battle and removed all the evidence.

Major Vince Holliman had kept to his promise.

12
Revelations

The gates to the grounds of Salerton Hall loomed out of the darkness and Mike Bowman counted four armed guards standing in the rain. One approached, identified the driver and waved to the gatehouse. Only then did the big spiked gates swing open.

At the circular driveway fronting the Hall, Bowman ducked out into the rain and Sarah led Anna Kuznetsova inside. Gilmore traipsed in last and hung his coat, waited for Bowman to climb the stairs.

In Fraser's office, Carol Hearsden fussed over the girl and brought coffee and something to alleviate the pangs of hunger, thick-cut wholemeal sandwiches of ham and cheese.

Bowman smelt the tang of coffee and poured himself a mug, laced it with Demerara sugar. He felt a painful twinge in his shoulder and rotated the arm, easing the spasm. He stiffened as the Old Man walked in with Brian Gilmore at his elbow. Fraser smiled gently at the girl and Sarah made the introductions.

'This is Robert Fraser,' she said, and he offered his hand.

Anna remained still, peering hard at his face.

Sarah tried again. 'It's okay, Anna. He is like me, a friend.'

Tentatively the girl reached out and shook hands, briefly, snatching her fingers from his grasp.

The Old Man backed away to his desk. 'How's the shoulder, Mike?'

'I'll live, sir,' he said, and watched Sarah settle the girl, helping her adjust to her new surroundings. Her patient kindness worked magic and Anna smiled, relaxing to the room.

Fraser stood behind his desk, fidgeting uncomfortably, an occasional weak smile directed at the girl.

Bowman sympathised, understood his concerns; he wanted information, an imperative given all that had transpired. He noticed Brian Gilmore take up a position by the door, arms folded, one hand cupping his chin.

Anna nibbled on a sandwich, sipped coffee and munched some more.

The Old Man coughed, agitated.

Sarah looked round and flashed him a look of annoyance. He frowned and gestured with his chin.

Sarah took the hint. 'Anna, you are safe here in England.' She chose her words carefully, spoke slowly. 'What did you want to tell us?'

Bowman watched the girl take one more mouthful of coffee and deliberately replace the mug.

'Will I be staying in England? Is that what you mean?'

Sarah nodded and reached for the young woman's hands. 'Yes, Anna, we *will* look after you. No more Latvia, no more Russian GRU. Maybe a small house of your own in the country, or somewhere near a city. Would you like that?'

Anna smiled a little, wanting to believe every word. Her eyes settled on the Old Man and his weather-beaten face broke into an encouraging grin.

Bowman could detect her uncertainty. So much had happened to her once gentle way of life. With Uncle Gvido murdered in front of her eyes, her last living relative had passed away. Blood and brutal death had visited and she had every right to feel afraid.

She refocused her big eyes on Sarah's face. 'Yes, I would like that. I take you for your word, so I will tell you what I know. I worked in the Kayanashki Hotel, it is a big hotel, in Pskov. Always there are parties for the military. The soldiers came from a training camp in the south, weekends for sure.'

Fraser pulled out his chair and sat.

It was an interruption and her eyes strayed from Sarah to Fraser and back again.

'I tell you I work for the Russians. It is true, but I hate them. The money is better than in Latvia so I go over the border, but I hate them.' There was a bitter vehemence in her voice.

Bowman saw tears welling in her eyes.

'My Mama and Papa, they were killed by the Russians. On orders from Moscow. My Papa, he made marches with many others, always protesting against Soviet rule. Mama . . . , she ran a local newspaper. She was warned not to say political things but she ignored them. They had an old boat for holidays and the police said it was an accident. They thought it was a fuel leak and it . . . ,' she hesitated searching for the right word. 'It exploded.' The tears came freely now and Bowman looked away.

Through the tears she said: 'A friend of the family, a government man, he told me it was ordered by the Kremlin.' She sat and cried quietly, her cheeks glistening. She caught her breath and wiped her face, looked up, eyes blazing. 'This night in the hotel was not the same. Officers came, twelve officers, celebrating someone's promotion. They came with women.' She pulled a face at Sarah. 'They are not like us, they do not wear their dresses properly, very short, you know?'

Sarah nodded.

'I am just a waitress and I served many drinks, more and more vodka. One of the officers, a man they called Major Shinsky, he got very drunk. He took three women to a side room, with a lieutenant, it was not nice.' She shook her head, remembering. 'I was told to wait in the room, if case they wanted more drinks or to clear away empty glasses. Shinsky talked much, about Moscow and how he worked with Generals making big plans.' She paused to brush a stray hair from the corner of her mouth.

'The lieutenant laughed at the Major, and said for him to prove it. Shinsky got angry, said the British were going to pay for making rich Russians poor, no money from British banks.' She looked down at her hands, twisting them in her lap. 'One of the women tried to calm him but it made him more angry. He pushed her and slapped her face, yelling. He shouted that it was a big mission, Operation Lightning, and they would strike British security, and the lieutenant should wait and see.' Anna stopped and looked imploringly around the room.

Sarah glanced over her shoulder at Fraser and he nodded, urging her to continue the questions. She touched the young woman's shoulder.

'What else?'

'He said a name.' She spoke in such a subdued whisper Bowman had trouble hearing the words. 'Anatoly Pushkin.'

From the corner of his eye Bowman saw the Old Man grimace.

Sarah again reached for a hand, held it in both her own. 'Is there more?'

Anna looked at the floor, head tilted to the side, took a deep breath and raised her eyes to the Old Man.

'He told the lieutenant another thing, a strange name. He said the top man must be killed, and the lieutenant asked what top man, and Shinsky said, Bullseye.'

Bowman wondered if he'd heard right. That wasn't a name as such, more like a nickname, a nom de guerre, could relate to anything. He felt exasperated. Surely she had something more important to tell. He looked over at the Old Man. There was something in his expression that caught Bowman's attention. He was looking at Gilmore, shaking his head with a frown, a sort of warning. For his part, Gilmore appeared stunned, open mouthed with surprise. There must be a significance to Anna's words that escaped Bowman.

Sarah pressed her, questioning. 'Is that all?'

Anna shrugged. 'Yes,' she said, crestfallen by the reaction. 'The lieutenant stopped laughing and the Major stopped shouting. A new officer came in, also a major, I think. He talked with Shinsky, in his ear. The last thing I heard was from Shinsky, he said, 'special operations'. Then they all stared at me and Shinsky told me to get out.'

Bowman thought rapidly. The Old Man had been very cagey, a secretive glance between Gilmore and himself, nothing said. And then those two other words, 'special operations'. A man might read more into that; he felt uncomfortable.

Sarah turned to Fraser who hesitated and held up a hand.

'That's enough for now, let her rest. We'll talk more tomorrow.'

135

Gilmore had recovered his poise. 'Yes, it's been a long night, we could all do with some sleep.'

Fraser called, raising his voice. 'Carol?'

She looked in from her office.

'Anna's tired now. Perhaps you'd show her to a room, see she has everything.'

Carol nodded and helped Anna to her feet, a protective arm round her shoulders. 'Come on then, Pet, we'll find you a nice bed.'

Sarah closed the door behind them and the Old Man sat drumming his fingers. Bowman reflected on what he'd heard, there was a lot he didn't understand, made him feel a bit sidelined. Fraser and Gilmore had reacted almost guiltily to Anna's revelations, particularly Gilmore.

'So, what do you make of this Bullseye stuff, sir?'

Fraser stopped drumming his fingers and glowered from under his eyebrows. Gilmore looked away, shuffled his feet awkwardly. Sarah frowned, becoming aware of an undercurrent, something amiss.

Bowman changed tack, less diplomatic. 'Gilmore?'

The man appeared thoroughly uncomfortable, his eyes appealing to Fraser.

The Old Man got to his feet and ambled past Bowman to the window, staring at the darkness through the rain speckled glass. 'All right, Brian, fill 'em in.'

Gilmore rubbed his forehead and sighed, stammered out an explanation. 'Well . . . , it's a long story, but briefly, Bullseye was a name given to Commander Fraser years ago, when we were in training on the Brecon Beacons.'

It was Bowman's turn to be taken unawares. This directly impacted NDSO, the head man of a supposedly anonymous organisation.

'So that bit Anna said about, 'special operations', that's probably specific to us, not a generalisation?'

Gilmore nodded sullenly. 'Afraid so.'

Pain lanced Bowman's shoulder and he again exercised the arm. He turned to look at the Old Man's back. Somehow, somewhere, NDSO's security had been breached and Fraser had become a target. The thoughts kept coming; not only the Commander, but any of them might be compromised. His eyes went back to Brian Gilmore, late to the party, made a man wonder.

'I take it the girl's telling the truth then?' he asked, conscious of a chill in the atmosphere. 'Not something she could've conjured out of the blue. And we don't have a time span on this.' He looked at the Old Man, still stood staring into space, and deliberately provoked him. 'Do we, sir?'

The reaction was unexpected. Fraser turned from the window and chuckled, eyes smiling, no hint of a crisis. 'Now don't go jumping in at the deep end. Assumptions don't get us anywhere, we deal in probability, so called 'facts', as a matter of routine. These allegations happen to be aimed at us . . . me, if you like. We need to be objective, find the reality. Mind you, sounds like the financial sanctions on top officials is working.'

Bowman looked at Sarah. A miniscule frown flickered across her brow and she stuck out her bottom lip. He dropped his gaze and focused on Gilmore, seeing him in a new light, slack jawed, caught in the moment. Bowman scratched his forehead, needing to hear something more definite, wanting Fraser to be more positive. And what was Sarah's problem? Enough, he thought, and walked up to the Old Man. Raindrops streamed down the glass, pushed sideways by the wind. 'With all due respect, sir, we must put precautions in place. At the very least, you have to increase your personal protection.'

Fraser shook his head. 'You're tired, Mike. We're all tired. Let's get some rest, sleep on it, and see what we come up with tomorrow.'

Anatoly Pushkin put the finishing touches to his engineering jigsaw and stood back, arms folded in satisfaction. As an exercise in modern methods of mechanical assembly it was a masterpiece. He walked round the garage and surveyed his handiwork. Pleased with his efforts he switched off the light, nipped through the drizzle and headed indoors.

He took the stairs two at a time and then climbed the ladder to the loft. He flicked a switch and by the light of a single, naked bulb, crouched over a large holdall. A British assault rifle nestled inside. Next to that lay a kilogramme package of PE-4 explosives, a British variant; the detonators were safely housed downstairs, also British. He grinned at the deceit, confusion to your enemies. Pushkin lifted the gun, checked it was unloaded and squeezed the trigger to a reassuring click. He repeated the process, smiled, and replaced the weapon.

He sat back on his haunches and looked at the time. The woman should be here tomorrow. She would be pleased. Over his head the constant patter on the roof tiles ceased. It had stopped raining.

In the Russian borderland south of Pskov, Colonel Ilya Bayalin of the 12th Directorate put through a radio transmission to General Viktor Leonid Zherlenko and waited nervously to be connected. Eventually the strident tones of the Deputy Commander rang in his ear.

'Speak to me, Bayalin.'

'Bad news, General. Lieutenant Tsegler and his men are missing and we are unable to make contact. His driver returned alone.'

Silence greeted his words and he wondered if Zherlenko had heard him.

'What,' the General demanded, 'have you done to find them?'

Bayalin smirked into the mouthpiece, having deliberately pre-empted the question by his actions. 'I personally made the decision to search the area and entered enemy territory. I searched for three hours, found nothing. Combat radio remained silent, it was as if they had never existed. I called it off and I'm calling from the Latvian border.'

A longer silence followed.

Bayalin pressed transmit. 'General?'

'You will return to camp, Colonel Bayalin. This matter must not be mentioned. If anyone asks, they are operating a planned deep reconnaissance. Do not talk to anyone off base and inform all personnel they are not permitted to spread rumours. Do I make myself clear?'

'Yes, General, perfectly clear.'

'Good,' said the General. ' I will let you know when to speak of this, in the future.'

The call disconnected and Bayalin found himself soaked with perspiration. More than a little relieved he clipped the microphone back on the bracket.

'Take us back to camp,' he said, and wiped his face. His prospects of promotion had survived.

Mike Bowman had furnished his cottage with, amongst other bare necessities, a single bed. Guests were a rarity and on the odd occasion when it was needed, his oversize couch served as a more than adequate put-me-up.

'No,' he insisted, when he and Sarah entered the house, 'I'll be happy enough downstairs.'

'Not with that shoulder of yours you won't,' she said, and dropped the takeaway on the kitchen table.

Bowman lobbed his keys on the worktop and gave her a superior grin. 'My house, my rules. The lady sleeps upstairs.'

Sarah tossed her head in resignation and went in search of spoons and forks.

'Wine?' he asked, 'or there's coffee, or something stronger if you fancy?'

She looked over, thought seriously and nodded. 'Wine's good, a Merlot . . . or Shiraz maybe.'

'Just for you,' he said, and pulled a gold topped bottle from his home made wooden rack. A chink of glass on glass, the pleasant gurgle of pouring liquid, and he offered her the stem.

She accepted it between thumb and forefinger, swilled it round and swallowed a large mouthful. She gritted her teeth, narrowed one eye, and arched a delicate brow. 'Phew . . . nice. Won't need too much of that on an empty stomach.'

They sat on opposite sides of the table and opened the bag, then solemnly removed the lids. It was a takeaway for two, Chinese set meal of Pancake Rolls, Sweet and Sour chicken balls, Beef, Mushroom and Chicken Chop Suey and a large portion of Egg fried rice. For a long moment they looked at each other, then Bowman laughed.

'Dig in, Angel.' He wanted her to eat first, anticipated her enjoyment.

She speared a sweet and sour chicken ball, put it to her lips, and with a wicked glint in her eyes, teased it into her mouth.. The eyes smiled and she swallowed. 'That,' she said, pointing with the fork, 'is absolutely delicious.'

'Good, thought you'd like it,' and Bowman went for a pancake roll and fried rice. It was all tasty, hot and filling, and for a while the food took centre stage. He finished first and pushed the tray to one side. 'Magic,' he smiled, and took a mouthful of wine.

Sarah came up with a spoonful of chop suey, and then stopped with it poised halfway to her mouth, frowning. 'Do you really think we have a leak?'

Bowman had long since made up his mind on that one.

'Absolutely,' he said, nodding over the rim of the glass. 'The proverbial 'mole' in our midst.'

'What will Fraser do?'

'Haven't a clue, and I don't intend losing any sleep over it.

Sarah took a last mouthful and reached for the wine bottle, held it inquiringly above his glass.

Bowman nodded for the refill.

She replaced the bottle and raised her glass in a toast. 'To us then.'

Bowman clinked rims and they drank.

Sarah tilted her head provocatively, white teeth nibbling at her bottom lip, eyes twinkling. 'You take a lot for granted, Mister Bowman.'

Now what, he thought. 'Meaning?'

'That I'll be sleeping in your bed alone.'

He leaned back and studied her face, flushed now from the hot food and wine. She really was beautiful, it would be too easy to get drawn into something more. He dismissed the thought and came back on firmer ground. 'Not really, Angel. You always have the option of going home.'

She pouted, disgruntled. 'Not likely, somebody's got to nurse the wounded.' she said, and began clearing the rubbish. 'It's time to get some rest. You sure you'll be alright on the sofa?'

At 05.30 am, London Transport Police placed an emergency call to Army Logistics Bomb Disposal. A suspect package had been discovered at the gates to Victoria Main Line Station and armed police arrived under a flashing blue. The station was evacuated, trains halted, and the public cordoned off. A two hundred metre security zone kept the press at bay. Fourteen minutes elapsed between the emergency call and the Bomb Disposal squad deploying to the front of the station. The entrance to the turnstiles came under heavy scrutiny and Warrant Officer Dan Middleton RE., walked forward to carry out an initial reconnaissance.

After a rapid but thorough visual inspection he returned and reported his findings. Within minutes a remote controlled bomb disposal robot descended the lorry ramp and headed for the station foyer. Using its onboard camera, Dan Middleton sat with his glorified 'games controller' and guided it forward. An order was issued for all personnel in the vicinity to take hard cover. Sophisticated analysis of the suspect package provided no definitive answers and the decision was taken to initiate a controlled explosion.

Ten minutes later, a small explosion echoed through adjoining streets, and a dozen television crews reappeared from cover. In the interests of public safety, it took nine hours of detailed searching before the area was declared safe enough for Victoria Main Line Station to reopen for business. Warrant Officer Dan Middleton went back to training his latest batch of recruits.

A press conference later revealed what little the Security Services chose to make public, and a furore of media speculation ensured it all made headline news.

In Moscow, Colonel-General Viktor Leonid Zherlenko, alerted to breaking news on the BBC, watched with pleasure as ex security experts came on and voiced their opinions on who could have been behind the latest terror inspired incident.

Zherlenko chuckled at the transmission. Operation Lightning had only just begun.

13
Danger

In Europe, three more incidents alerted Brussels to the latest in a wave of attacks, and Germany and France suffered four deaths and a number of civilian casualties.

In London, the Prime Minister convened an emergency meeting of COBRA which resulted in Britain's threat level being temporarily raised to 'critical', the highest available. Authorisation was given for GCHQ and MI5 to conduct intrusive surveillance and disregard any laws on privacy. MI6, primarily concerned with foreign intervention, already had their hands full.

Commander Robert Fraser, on behalf of NDSO, personally acknowledged the Government's directive to remain on standby and await further orders. Fraser reminded himself where his priorities lay even though he had issues closer to home.

He hadn't slept, hadn't even left the office, too much to think about. His mind went back over the years, grappling with the personal history of those under his command. It was such a tight knit unit, security had never been an issue. Twenty-two people, and he knew everyone by first name, vetted them himself. Each person had sat here and subjected themselves to the same exhausting process of cross questioning. All had previously served in either the Forces or the Security Services, all at senior level, beyond reproach.

And yet, within NDSO, the finger now pointed at only one of three possible suspects. The most obvious choice, almost too obvious, was Brian Gilmore. Recently seconded from MI5 on the recommendation of Sir Hillary Montague, who was himself beyond any form of suspicion, Gilmore was the only man Fraser had not interviewed. When his name first came up in conversation, Fraser knew all about him, remembered him for a lot more than just that day on the Brecon Beacons. He'd become a name to be reckoned with; Special Boat Squadron, covert missions in the Middle East, transferred to 'close protection' of government officials, and then selected for a senior post in the Home Office. Yes, they'd had a conversation over a meal at Sir Montague's club in Mayfair, a casual reappraisal of Gilmore's current situation, and Fraser felt justified in taking him on.

So, to his way of thinking, that left only two other vague possibilities, and he was loath to admit that he could be naïve enough to have been fooled. He leaned back in the chair and stared at the elaborately frescoed ceiling, hands clasped over his stomach, debating the pros and cons. One of those men had also trained alongside Fraser in the Brecon Beacons, not that he'd made his acquaintance, he'd been just another volunteer hoping to pass the rigorous regime that enabled a man to join the elite forces.

Fraser had not heard of the man again until eleven years ago, and then it was Fraser who had made the first approach, eventually managing to squirrel him away from his well remunerated employment. It had taken a lot of persuasion. And until now Commander Robert Fraser had been convinced of the man's loyalty.

Lastly he focused on his Assistant Director for Operational Deployment, Angus 'Jock' Monroe. West Berlin had been so much a part of Monroe's career. Could he have been 'turned' during his prolonged detachment; Fraser had his doubts, Jock had no hidden agenda, he was first and foremost a loyal servant of the British people.

He heard Carol enter her office, early as usual, and came to his feet. When he opened the door she started in surprise.

'Sorry, Carol, but I didn't go home. Would you tell Despatch to get hold of Bowman, I want him, soonest.'

She nodded, fully composed. 'Yes, sir. Of course,' and she reached for the phone.

Fraser went back to his desk and delved into the computer's personnel file. He pulled up an image and stared at a man's face. Could that really be the picture of a traitor? He wasn't convinced, didn't want to believe, but he'd spent too many years in the Service to ignore the possibility.

144

He looked at the time. He could wait.

Bowman finished shaving and checked the dressing covering the wound, thankful for no sign of blood. Down in the kitchen, about to boil the kettle, his radio squawked and he answered the call from Despatch. The Old Man wanted him, urgently. He made for the stairs and went up trying to be quiet, without much success. Every tread creaked underfoot and by the time he reached the landing he could hear Sarah awake. Tapping on the door he poked his head round. She lay with the duvet tucked under her chin, one eye open. 'Yes?'

'Sorry to disturb but Fraser wants me. I need some clothes.'

'If you must.' A petulant dismissal of his intrusion.

He grinned and crossed to the wardrobe, dug out a freshly laundered pair of black jeans, a shirt that had drip-dried on the hanger, and from the bottom drawer, socks and underwear. He turned for the door, felt her eyes on him and gestured with his chin. 'How was my bed?'

'Lumpy,' she said, and turned over with her back to him.

Bowman flashed her a grin, grabbed the foot of the duvet, and tugged hard. It dropped to the floor, exposing her naked bottom and shapely waist, and with a wicked laugh he flew out the door. A squeal of annoyance followed him down the stairs.

He made it to the living room and dressed, listening with amusement to the occasional shouted obscenity emanating from the bedroom. He considered wearing the shoulder holster, attempted to fit the harness and thought better of it. In the hall he lifted his well worn, soft leather jacket from its hook, and slipped his wounded arm inside the sleeve. As he'd imagined, it settled comfortably over his shoulders, no significant irritation to the wound. He eyed his Sig, slid it inside his left waistband and searched for his keys, found them where he lobbed them, on the worktop.

Upstairs, all was quiet. 'Angel?' he called. 'I'm off now.'

Sarah appeared wearing his robe, loosely tied at the waist, and came down to stand close, fixing him with her liquid gaze. 'And what if I don't want you to go?'

Bowman swallowed. 'It's urgent,' he said, wishing it wasn't.

She ran her fingers up his chest and slid her hands behind his neck, interlocking them, pulling his face down to hers. He put his hands on her waist, accidentally dislodged the belt and the robe fell open, revealing her breasts. He slipped his hands round the small of her waist, drew her closer, and her full moist lips parted, lingering softly.

He broke off, with an effort, denying himself the opportunity. 'I can't,' he said, avoiding her eyes. 'I have to go.'

Sarah released her hold from round his neck and traced a lazy finger along his lower lip. When she spoke it was with a silky softness, a woman's intuitive knowledge of seduction. 'I might not let you.'

Bowman struggled with his emotions, knowing how easy it would be to crumble, allow his natural instincts to take over. But he shook his head, firmly. 'Later, Angel, right now I *have* to report to the Old Man.'

She took a step back, put on a disappointed face and tilted her head. Dropping her hands to her waist, she eased back the robe to reveal her body, no hint of shyness. She raised an eyebrow and gave him a provocative smile. 'Sure?'

Mike Bowman took a slow lungful of air. Here was this beautiful, exquisite woman, willingly giving herself, and he couldn't reciprocate. Fraser's need came first, and the call to answer his demands overruled all else. Full of apology he took a step towards her, transfixed by what he could see.

Sarah shrieked with delight, wrapped the robe back in place, and ran laughing up the stairs. On the landing, she stopped, spun round and poked out her tongue.

'That'll teach you to take liberties with my duvet,' she giggled, and swept into the bedroom.

Bowman stood, amazed by her reaction, and then allowed an embarrassed smile to creep across his face, he'd been well and truly done. He walked out to the Land Rover and laughed.

The occasional large puddle lingered from the overnight rain, glinting in the late morning sun. Bowman brought the Land Rover to a halt at the entrance to Salerton Hall and stuck his head out of the driver's window. The visibly menacing guards of the previous night had disappeared but in the gatehouse Jim had company. Allenby and one other hovered in the background.

'Morning, Jim,' he volunteered.

'Good morning, Mr Bowman. Despatch said you'd be along.'

'Any news?'

Jim reached sideways to press the button for the gates. 'That Gilmore character left an hour ago,' he said, and Bowman detected a distinct lack of respect in his phrasing. 'Other than that, seems pretty quiet.'

The gates had swung inwards.

Bowman grinned easily. 'And the missus?'

Jim chuckled and winked. 'Same as ever, still the boss.'

Bowman withdrew his head and drove in, holding the Land Rover in low gear, content to cruise towards the old mansion, pondering on all that had transpired. Outwardly, the Old Man had put up a brave face, making light of a direct threat to his life, the head of NDSO. For his part, Bowman understood the need for a professional response, they all lived under the shadow of imminent termination, no good getting excited by a threat. The more important aspect was the corruption of NDSO's capacity to operate in complete secrecy, a vital component of their 'deniability'. It gave him an odd feeling. He determined to get it sorted, at the first opportunity.

Bowman parked away from the Hall and crunched noisily across the gravel. A 'gardener' with a wheelbarrow tended the rose bed, and he looked up and nodded. A man in a chauffeur's cap polished the Jaguar's gleaming black paintwork.

In the marbled hall he took the sweeping staircase up to Carol's outer office and peeked in.

'You're late,' she said brusquely, and ushered him through.

The Old Man had his feet up resting on the corner of his desk, ankles crossed, leaning back in his chair. He waved airily. 'Come in, Mike. Have a seat.'

Bowman sat, and Fraser rubbed his chin engrossed in thought, then ran his hand back through the iron-grey head of hair. 'How's the shoulder?'

'Better than it was, sir.'

'Good . . . , good,' he said absentmindedly. 'I'll take it for granted you understand the gravity of the situation?'

'Yes, sir,' Bowman said, keen to show his involvement.

'Mmm, then you'll also appreciate I've been giving it a great deal of thought.' He dropped his feet to the floor and sat forward in the chair, eyes gleaming. 'Now I know you're not happy with Brian Gilmore, new boy on the block and all that, but take it from me, he's not our man.'

Bowman had opened his mouth to protest but Fraser held up a hand.

'It's okay, I'd have thought the same in your shoes.' He stroked the bridge of his nose. 'No, I believe we're looking at an entirely different proposition, someone I would have staked my life on, but in retrospect someone who's the absolute epitome of clandestine assignments.'

Bowman waited patiently, letting him talk it through.

The Old Man shifted in his chair, leaning forward on his elbows. 'It was what Anna said about Bullseye. Brian Gilmore wasn't the only person in NDSO that knew I had that nickname.' He paused, staring into mid-air, his mind briefly elsewhere, in the distant past. He rubbed his forehead in frustration, brought himself back to the present.

'I believe it might be Ian Webster, but I want to be damned sure before I make a move. So I need you to become his shadow. I want to know where he goes, who he sees, when and why.'

Bowman looked away, avoiding Fraser's eyes. Covert operations were one thing, part of what he'd trained for, was good at. But this was altogether different. This is what MI6 were for, or MI5 at the Home Office. The NDSO fell under an entirely different remit, a specialised unit of last resort. Yes, it was all a subsidiary of the secret services, but ferreting about for ill-defined, clandestine information felt like a hiding to nothing. And in one aspect Ian Webster was a colleague and Bowman didn't like the idea of watching one of your own, morally unethical, it didn't sit well. Against that he'd been brought up to respect the old fashioned traits of, duty, honour,

148

patriotism even. It wasn't something he made a song and dance about, just a quiet recognition that the flag flying above Buckingham Palace had become part of his very being.

He met the Old Man's gaze, not flinching from the probing query. 'In other words, sir, to put it in plain language, you want me to be . . . a spy?'

Fraser held his eyes, and Bowman waited for sentencing.

'In all but name, yes.'

He stood and shoved his hands in his pockets. 'When do I start?'

'Yesterday?'

'I'll need someone with me.'

Fraser raised an eyebrow. 'And who do you suggest?'

'Sarah Campbell.'

The Old Man hesitated. 'You sure?'

'Positive,' Bowman said. 'She's as good as they come.'

'Alright, that's settled.'

Bowman walked round and leaned on the back of the seat. 'Do we know his current whereabouts?'

Fraser nodded. 'Working from home right now. You know where that is?'

Bowman gave him a tight lipped smile. 'I know where everyone lives, it's my business.'

'Oh yes, of course,' Fraser said, dripping with sarcasm, 'a bit like a spy.'

'True,' Bowman conceded, and grinned.

The Old Man leant back in the chair and pointed a warning finger. 'Until I say otherwise, you report direct to me. Everyone else is out of the loop. Do I make myself clear?'

'Yes, sir. I take it that means we're off the radar?'

'That is exactly what I had in mind.'

Bowman straightened, thinking of Anna's story, remembering another name involved. 'And what about this Pushkin, sir?'

'You let me worry about that, you just concentrate on your own job.'

Bowman turned for the door.

'And, Mike . . . , anything happens to me, take your findings to Sir Hillary Montague.'

He glanced back over his shoulder at Fraser's commanding presence, an indomitable force. 'Sir Hillary Montague,' he acknowledged.

The Old Man turned to his desk and nodded. 'Good luck.'

Bowman pursed his lips in thought and walked into Carol's office. She raised her eyes from the screen and he smiled.

'Won't be around for a while,' he said. 'How's the girl?'

Carol glanced back at her screen. 'A lot happier than she was. She's agreed another interview with Commander Fraser, to answer more questions.'

Bowman laughed softly. 'I'm sure she'll love that,' he said, and opened the door. 'See you later.'

From behind her screen, Carol's northern dialect carried quietly. 'Aye, mind how you go, Pet.'

He grinned to himself, clicked the door behind him and found his keys. Taking the staircase down he exited the building and strode purposefully out to the Land Rover. There was work to be done and he needed Sarah on board, quickly.

Commander Robert Fraser stood gazing down from his window and watched Bowman walk across the gravel. He saw him rub his shoulder and flex the arm, and winced in sympathy. He watched him clamber into the Rover, start up and drive toward the gatehouse, at the same time wondering where this would all end. If he'd called it wrong, two of his best agents would be off line when they were most needed.

The Land Rover receded into the distance and he turned from the window to his desk. Given the choice his preference would have been an outside agency to handle Webster but resources were stretched too thin. Relationships with Russia had deteriorated to a low ebb. America had expelled diplomats, the middle east was in a state of flux, Russia had threatened retaliation, and the Baltic states, along with Ukraine and Georgia eyed their neighbours with genuine concern. MI6 were up to their eyeballs in a covert battle for supremacy and MI5 battled to stay ahead of home grown threats.

Fraser contemplated the empty room and tugged an earlobe. This office symbolised his command of the NDSO and his legitimate pursuit of 'deniable' assignments. He lifted his chin and called aloud.

'Carol!'

The door opened. 'Yes, sir?'

'Time to interview Anna Kuznetsova, we could do with a few more answers.'

She bobbed her head and Fraser walked slowly to his chair, this might be somewhat protracted.

Helena Goreya completed fifteen squat thrusts and dropped onto her belly for thirty push-ups. After twenty her biceps ached but she forced herself to take the pain. Ten more and sweat dripped off her face. At the limit of endurance she managed two more and called it quits, collapsing onto her back to catch her breath.

She looked over at Alexander Nokolai Markoff standing by the door and he clapped in appreciation, and then tossed her a towel. 'Here, dry your face.'

She managed a smile and sat up, still breathing hard. 'Will we have more information today?' she asked of his impassive expression.

A momentary frown and he shrugged, non-committal. 'I must look for the signal, then there will be a drop.'

Helena nodded, towelling the perspiration from her face and arms. The 'deadletter drop' was crucial. The entire operation hinged on the information it should contain, if all was well. No reason they should think otherwise but she felt apprehensive, couldn't shake her misgivings.

'When will you check?'

'Soon,' he snapped, and she heard the impatience with her questions.

She let it go and changed the subject. 'Pushkin must be ready now. The package arrived on time.'

Markoff grunted, not wanting to be drawn. 'Well, he'll have to wait.' He glanced at his watch. 'I will leave within the hour and be back by late afternoon. Then I will take you to the drop.'

There was no arguing the finality in his tone and until her expertise could be translated into action, Markoff held sway. 'Of course,' she nodded, and climbed to her feet. 'I will shower and rest until you return.'

He muttered something unintelligible, which she ignored, and made her way upstairs. If he wanted to sulk, so be it.

In General Zherlenko's office on the outskirts of Moscow, the clock on the wall ticked off the hours.

14
Signpost

Mike Bowman returned to his home and abandoned the Land Rover outside. Sarah met him in the kitchen, concern on her face.

He grabbed her by the arms and met her gaze. 'The Old Man's given us a job. Not something I'd have volunteered for, but there was no choice. I did get a say in who comes with me and you're it. We're on surveillance so get your gear, and make sure the pistol's loaded.'

Without a word, Sarah made for the stairs and Bowman went in search of his camera. He found the bag in the cupboard under the stairs, made certain the batteries held a charge, and selected his prime telephoto lens. If spying was to be his new role then he'd go properly equipped. He zipped the bag, retrieved a camouflaged waterproof smock and strode outside to the garage. Hidden under the workshop bench his personal backpack contained enough emergency rations to sustain a man for a week. Importantly, ten spare magazines for his Sig and a second transmitter-receiver for emergencies. After topping up the water bottle, he deposited the bags on the floor of the Land Rover, and returned to the cottage.

Sarah called from upstairs. 'Do we have a duration?'

'No, but I'm hoping no more than two or three days.'

'Are you going to tell me who we're watching?'

He heard her descending the stairs and waited until she came into the kitchen. He gave her a long look. 'Hold on to your hat . . . , it's Ian Webster.'

'No!' she said, 'never!'

'The Old Man seems pretty convinced,' he added, 'but needs to be sure before he acts. We have to find the evidence.'

Sarah shook her head in disbelief, and bent to tie her boots.

He smiled to himself; she certainly looked the part. Black hooded waterproof with deep flap pockets and a pair of tough combats. Her own equipment bag waited in the hall. 'Gun?' he asked.

She nodded. 'Glock. Ready when you are.'

'Whose wheels, Mike?'

There was no hesitation. 'Mine, there's more room in the Defender, makes more sense being as we're working together.' He flashed her a broad grin, and locked the cottage door.

Sarah Campbell took a deep breath and pulled out the keys to the Land Rover. Bowman had again accepted they could work as a team. No hesitation, no excuses, just let it slip out in conversation. And yet she knew most men would have baulked at the idea, especially when faced with the recant loss of a female operative.

That was another thing that attracted her to Bowman. He made up his mind and let you know where you stood.

She opened the cab door and climbed in. He took the passenger seat and checked the gun. She frowned. 'Is that really necessary?'

He nodded, tight lipped. 'You just never know, Angel . . . , you just never know.'

She found first gear and turned for the bumpy lane. This was where the Defender came into its own. She hit the accelerator and launched the four wheel drive over the uneven surface. From the corner of her eye she saw him reach for the grab handle.

Sarah Campbell smiled at his discomfort and headed for a large pothole. This would be fun.

Deputy Chief of Russian Military Intelligence, Colonel-General Viktor Leonid Zherlenko, entered his Operational Command Centre and paused just inside the door. The men and women of Communication Intelligence rose to their feet and stood stiff backed in salute.

He touched a finger to the peak of his cap.

'Carry on,' he said abruptly.

They sat, and all around the workstations glowing computer screens lit the faces of their users. Keyboards and printers added a subdued clatter to the hum of voices, messengers striding between desks and delivering urgent pieces of information.

Zherlenko had taken the time to come and see an image that hung on the far wall. Dominating the workspace, it had been taken by satellite exactly four weeks ago to the day, and a unit from Digital Enhancement had printed out the large copy for all to see. To those involved in Operation Lightning it served as a permanent reminder that the building featured in the picture, nestled in the heart of the English countryside, was their prime focus. He advanced closer until he stood below, allowing his eyes to roam freely across the detail. Salerton Hall itself was but a small part of the detail, isolated in the middle of a large estate. And it was that assumption of isolated invulnerability that would be NDSO's undoing. They might have the most comprehensive electronic surveillance in the world guarding the grounds, but Zherlenko had found the Achilles heel, and he intend to exploit that weakness to the full.

A cruel smile twisted his heavy jowls and he thought of the secretive corridors in Britain's Intelligence community, how those in command would reel to the destructive power of Russia's Special Forces. The famous British stiff upper lip might well wobble.

A Colonel of the GRU detached himself from a console and marched across to the General.

'Seventy-two hours is the time frame, sir. Beyond that it would mean a delay of one month.'

Zherlenko eyed the man with disdain. 'Delay,' he said loudly, ' you talk to me of delay? Take it from me, Colonel, there will be no delay. This has been too long in the planning, there will be no delay. Do you understand?'

'Of course, General, but if . . .'

Zherlenko snapped, losing patience. 'No buts, I will not tolerate any hold ups to this mission.'

The Colonel paled under the verbal onslaught. 'As you say, General. No delays.'

'Good . . . , good, then all is well,' Zherlenko relented. 'The Kremlin expects the operation to proceed as planned.'

The Colonel stepped back respectfully. 'Thank you, sir,' he said, bowing his head.

Zherlenko dismissed him with a casual wave and swaggered back to the entrance. A junior officer stepped quickly across and held the door, but Zherlenko paused to glance over his shoulder.

Salerton Hall blended seamlessly into the bigger picture, exactly as the General had intended. With a grim smile, directed at the young officer's eager expression, he walked out into the corridor and took the lift to the ground floor.

The Kremlin's hierarchy would be pleased.

Alexander Markoff, head down, hands in pockets, walked nonchalantly up the village lane and passed the Blue Lion Inn to his right,. Outside the ivy clad walls a young family sat eating at a wooden table, beer and lemonade on display. The high pitched excitement of the two small girls carried clearly on the still air.

A tall privet hedge marked the boundary between the pub car park and the next dwelling, a large four bed-roomed, mock Tudor affair, with a red tiled roof. Beyond that, on the other side of the road and barely glimpsed through a screen of yew hedging, a chalet-bungalow basked in the afternoon sun. A saw-toothed brick edged driveway led to a detached garage where a rambling mess of hawthorns hemmed in a large meadow.

Markoff cleared the garage and moved up alongside the prickly hedge. A hundred paces further on a BT telegraph pole stood braced with wires, cables hanging in sweeps to the next pole ahead. Blackbirds teetered on the lines, silhouetted against the blue. He slowed as he approached the pole, looking carefully to find a sign. He was disappointed and double checked in case his eyes deceived him. For a long moment he hesitated, almost breaking his stride, and then forced himself to walk on. He cursed with annoyance and wondered how many more times before the signal came. Kicking out at an old tin can he tightened his jaw and pushed on, a bitter pill to swallow.

A crooked smile came and went. Helena Goreya would just have to wait.

Before sunrise the next day, from a dense thicket on the edge of a small copse, Mike Bowman aimed the telephoto lens at Ian Webster's house and congratulated himself on finding a fairly half-decent location. Lying comfortably prone, elbows supporting his upper torso, he could watch both front and back of the property. If Webster departed, Bowman's vantage point covered both doors. It also allowed him visual access to three windows on this end of the house. They consisted of a downstairs hallway, upstairs landing, and a dual-aspect window centred on a bedroom.

Sarah lay to his right, a pair of binoculars clamped to her eyes. Less than a stone's throw to their rear, the Land Rover sat facing a farm track which gave them immediate access to the main road through the village. If Webster drove out they could tail him from a discreet distance. The sun lifted above the horizon and bathed the valley in warm sunlight.

'Odd,' Sarah said, 'watching a colleague.'

'My thoughts exactly,' he answered, refocusing the lens on a pair of Blue Tits flitting round the branches of a bush. Behind them, Webster's coveted silver Porsche Carrera GT had been reversed up to the front porch.

The day wore on. They drank water, chewed vitamin bars and passed the time as only they knew how; with a patience born of unswerving dedication. Bowman photographed the birds for want of anything better and spent time enhancing the images with the inbuilt features.

It was late morning when Sarah uttered a warning.

'Mike, he's leaving.'

Bowman traversed his lens from the back garden and picked up Webster in the act of locking his front door. A dog appeared at his side, a Cocker Spaniel, and Bowman remembered the distinctive name, 'Churchill'. It tugged at the lead tail wagging, and sniffed the ground, eager to walk. Webster led the dog to his Porsche and the animal jumped up onto the passenger seat. He walked round behind the car, bent into the cockpit and strapped himself in behind the wheel. The car eased out to the road and turned left downhill towards the school.

'Grab your gear,' Bowman said. Collecting their packs they backed out of the tangled undergrowth, ran to the Land Rover, and jumped in.

Bowman fired life into the engine. He made a point of staring sideways at Sarah and she turned her head, her eyes alight with excitement, and he grinned. 'Hang on, Angel.'

The Defender snarled under his foot and he snatched a gear, hauling it round to bounce down the potholed track. With hardly a pause at the main road, he whipped out between two cars and slewed hard left down the hill. He hung back, slowing to allow cars to overtake. When four vehicles hid the Defender from the Porsche he picked up speed. The road twisted out through the end of the village and followed the undulating sweep of ancient landscape.

At a busy junction the Porsche turned right into heavy traffic, sandwiched between a National Express coach and a foreign plated juggernaut.

Bowman waited for his moment and dabbed the accelerator, nipping across the oncoming vehicles to slot in behind a car transporter. Six gleaming BMWs filled the ramps. Three miles along the carriageway the Porsche Carrera stopped to turn right, waited for a gap, and peeled off into the lush canopy of the Forest of Dean. Bowman queued for his chance and swung right down into the tree lined road. He slowed to a crawl, wary of what lay ahead.

Sarah, peering through the windscreen, pointed to their left. 'There's a car park.'

Through the screen of trees, Bowman watched the Porsche drive in amongst the twenty or so parked vehicles and then pick a remote spot at the far side. On the right, a large chalet style log cabin served as a café, a few customers sitting out at the rough hewn wooden tables.

Bowman pulled off the tarmac onto the verge and paused in neutral, ticking over.

'We'll wait, see where he goes.'

Below them, Webster brought the dog out on the lead. He crossed the uneven ground with the Spaniel pulling him on, skirted the café, and disappeared up a bank into the forest.

Bowman gunned the Land Rover down the slope, manoeuvred into the park and aimed for a space between a VW campervan and a big Hyundai Tucson. The Defender slotted in perfectly, almost hidden from view. They jumped out and headed for the cabin, moved to the left, and pushed up into the shade of the trees. Initially unsighted under the dense foliage, Bowman clipped his left shoulder into a tree trunk and grimaced. A sharp pain bit him, and then subsided, leaving a persistent ache. He glanced round. Sarah hadn't noticed and he forged ahead, willing the pain away. They were on a narrow trail, worn by constant footsteps, winding around the woodland floor. There was no sign of Webster or the dog and Bowman picked up the pace. They couldn't afford to lose him now.

The trail meandered left through a stand of Silver Birch, then right into heavy oaks. A carpet of ferns dragged at their legs, brambles scratching exposed skin.

Sarah took a left fork and they separated, continued to move apart, and Bowman frowned. Losing Jessica was still raw in his mind, he didn't want a repeat performance, especially not with Sarah. He cut diagonally across, disregarding the brambles, and came up behind her. At a convenient point he squeezed past, two or three paces ahead. His shoulder gave him a sharp reminder.

A thinning of the trees made them cautious, and they trod with care, guarded. A thought crossed Bowman's mind. Once again he found himself in trees, what had happened to the cities? Where were all the skyscrapers and the congested streets? How come he'd ended up as a nursemaid, again? Partly his own fault for suggesting her, but he hadn't reckoned on this sort of exercise.

A firebreak came into view, crossing their path at right angles. What was Webster up to? Meeting someone, or really just here to walk his dog?

Sarah came alongside. 'Now where, left or right?'

Bowman looked both ways, and the firebreak curved out of sight within a hundred paces. 'Something tells me left,' he said. 'You?'

'Good a guess as any,' she agreed, and made a move to step into the open.

Bowman grabbed her arm, dragged her backwards.

'No!' he whispered harshly. 'For Christ's sake stay in the trees.'

Sarah tore her arm free and gave him a withering look, but nodded in submission. He pushed past, aware of the resentment, knowing he'd acted in good faith. Better safe than sorry.

And then he heard the muffled sound of a dog's bark, not the throaty call of a big dog, but the higher yelp of a smaller breed. He glanced round at Sarah and she nodded, no animosity, professional.

'Somewhere over there,' she said, gesturing ahead with her chin.

The firebreak curved gently to the right, so Bowman went wide to the left, deeper into the trees, but giving them a better view around the bend. A dozen paces further on he halted, hand raised. Sarah came up to his ear. 'What?'

He pointed. Away in the distance, where the firebreak turned from view, the Cocker Spaniel trotted back towards them. He was running free, no longer on the lead. Bowman froze searching for Webster. He wouldn't be far from the dog.

Sarah found him first. 'To the right, edge of the trees.'

He was walking away from them, in the opposite direction to the dog. They heard a low whistle and the animal stopped, looked towards Webster, then turned and loped after him.

Bowman needed to keep Webster in sight but that dog could cause all sorts of problems. That sense of smell might be their undoing.

Sarah waited at his elbow and he nodded, and they pushed forward staying well within the trees. For ten minutes Bowman moved on holding the dog in sight, the odd fleeting glimpse of Webster.

Then nothing. No dog, no Webster, nothing.

Bowman went down on one knee, staring hard at shades of green, alternating brown trunks, dark branches and shimmering leaves. He forced himself to be patient, one way or the other he felt sure that Spaniel would reappear, or yelp, something.

Sarah didn't speak, held her peace. Good girl, he thought, wait it out.

After five minutes he began to doubt his judgement. Webster might be talking to someone right now, out of sight. And if seen with a stranger he could plead it was just an innocent encounter, passing the time of day. But deep down, Bowman didn't believe it. If the Old Man suspected Webster he'd have had good reason, and this walk had taken Webster well away from the usual trails.

'Sarah,' he whispered. 'We'll move on, but quiet now. I want to see if he's meeting with anyone. If there is someone, I'll stay with that new target. You go back to the car park and wait till I get there.'

She nodded.

Bowman rose to a crouch and pressed on, careful with his feet, making absolutely certain he wasn't treading on dead wood.

But then he stopped in surprise. Webster stepped out from the trees on the far side of the firebreak, the dog on the lead, blatantly walking along without a care in the world.

Bowman held position, moving only his eyes. So much for the best laid plans; if he had spoken with someone they missed it. He slowly sank into the knee high ferns and prayed the dog wouldn't smell them.

As Webster drew level the Spaniel swivelled his head, poised, with a paw in the air. It let out a low whine, nose probing, twitching ears. But Webster tugged at the lead, ignoring the dog's posture, impatient to move on. With no option, and with his head and eyes still searching in Bowman's direction, the dog succumbed to the inevitable and allowed himself to be dragged away. It trotted up alongside Webster's feet.

Bowman breathed out, caught Sarah's eye and gave her a sickly smile. He waited for Webster to move out of sight.

'Well, if he met anyone, we're none the wiser now, but I want to take a look up ahead, see what's what.'

With a final glance back along the firebreak, he stepped into the open and crossed to the far side. Together they walked slowly along the cleared track, peering at every conceivable oddity, hoping to identify something out of the ordinary. Then Bowman had a thought. What if Webster had never intended to meet anybody, what if he'd been delivering a message instead? This would be an ideal location for a 'drop'.

'Sarah,' he called softly.

She ambled over.

'There's a chance he wasn't meeting with anyone. I think he may have been delivering a message, old fashioned 'tradecraft', a deadletter drop.'

Sarah jammed her hands on her hips and made an exaggerated search, turning her head in all directions. When she looked at him, it was with a pessimistic smile. 'Needle in a haystack springs to mind.'

He shook his head. 'Not really. If there is a 'drop' there'll be a signpost, an obvious marker you could pick out in the dark.'

'Well I don't see one,' she insisted, all sarcasm.

He swallowed his irritation not wanting to sound patronising. 'You have to think outside the box,' he said patiently, 'from a new perspective. It might be near one of those triangular fire warnings, or a fallen tree, anything out of the ordinary. Try to think like the man who set it up. Where would you put it?'

She held her tongue and flounced off, and he smiled at the shake of her head. But he could see her working it out, thinking it through.

They covered more ground, searching. The ancient woodland mocked their efforts, an indeterminate sea of leaves and branches, fallen twigs and waving ferns; even the trees appeared indistinguishable from one another.

'Mike!'

Bowman looked ahead, twenty paces up the firebreak. She was pointing. 'That tree,' she called, unable to disguise her excitement.

He stepped to his left, allowing for a clear view down the right side of the track. A grotesquely misshapen oak tree leaned precariously, old and craggy, branches spread like bony fingers. No-one could miss that silhouette, not even at night. He looked at Sarah, grinning, and hurried to join her. Maybe his hunch was about to pay off.

'Well done, Angel, that is one enormous signpost. At least we know where to start.'

They walked over together until the entire tree stood before them. Bowman touched her arm. 'It won't be the tree itself, too obvious. Be somewhere in the vicinity, well hidden, if I'm right.'

Sarah pouted. 'Of course you're right. This is exactly where I'd have chosen.'

He couldn't argue the logic. 'Then let's get on with it, might take some time.' And they began to search. In the high canopy overhead the breeze stirred the leaves.

From Moscow to London, and in the heart of the English countryside, the Russians played their deadly game.

15
Deception

At Salerton House, Hugh Atkinson sat back from his workstation and made a decision. He'd accumulated enough data to make a serious presentation to the old man. Copious amounts of SigIntel were filed in chronological order and he'd meticulously trawled through reams of analysis in an attempt to refine his conclusions. The open document waited for the upload to the USB hard drive.

He rang Carol Hearsden. 'Is the Old Man free? I need to have words.'

'Hang on, Hugh, I'll check.'

Atkinson waited nervously, removed his glasses and gave them a polish, settled them back on his nose. It wasn't everyday that the backroom staff called on the head of NDSO.

Carol came back to him. 'He says he'll make time.'

'Cheers, be down in a minute.' He hitched up his trousers, tugged his jacket into place, and hit 'return' on the keyboard. The data completed transfer and he unplugged. Making his way downstairs, he tapped on Carol's door and tentatively looked in.

She looked up with a smile. 'He's waiting, go right through.'

Atkinson nodded weakly, crossed her room, and with a good deal of apprehension, entered Commander Fraser's office.

The Old Man glanced up from his desk, pre-occupied by his laptop.

'What's up, Hugh?'

He seemed in a sour mood but Atkinson persevered and held out the hard drive. 'I think you ought to see this,' he said nervously.

'Why?'

'Because I think it links to Anna's warning. I believe this proves a Russian team is on our doorstep. I've been accumulating this data since the report came in from Dover

164

Coastguard. There's both SigsIntel and voice traffic.' He felt more certain of his findings, talking of that which he handled on a daily basis, his own comfort zone.

The Old Man gave an exasperated sigh and logged out from the laptop, turning it towards Atkinson. 'All yours,' he said, and sat back.

Leaning over with the hard drive, Atkinson plugged in the USB, opened the encrypted document and brought up the first file. He turned the screen for Fraser's benefit and began to studiously present each piece of data in the order they'd been acquired. For almost thirty minutes, Atkinson explained his findings, occasionally interrupted by the Old Man needing further clarification on the detail. Confidence restored, he rattled off the remaining specifics and finally pointed at the satellite image of a house in Ross- on-Wye.

'That's where the last transmission came from.'

The Old Man rubbed his forehead, staring hard at the screen, assimilating all that he'd been shown. Atkinson held his breath.

'I think,' Fraser said slowly, 'I think you're onto something.'

Atkinson managed a relieved, 'thank you, sir,' and pushed his glasses back on his nose.

'I would go further,' Fraser continued. 'Indeed, I would go so far as to say some kind of intervention is required. Is that what you propose I should do?'

Atkinson met the Old Man's eyes and thought he saw a glint of amusement.

'Yes, sir, that's why I'm here.'

'Thought as much,' Fraser growled, and hauled himself to his feet, braced his hands on the desk. Atkinson felt the full force of an inquisitive gaze, and then the Old Man smiled, an unexpected warmth between boss and underling.

'Nice work, Hugh. Can you dig up any more?'

Atkinson stood straighter, to his full height, pleased that his efforts had been recognised. 'Yes, sir. I'll get on with it.' He disconnected the USB and turned to leave.

Fraser stopped him. 'Hugh?'

'Sir?'

Fraser frowned. 'How long have you been with us?'

'Almost five years now, sir.'

'Well you should remember you're my senior intelligence officer. I trust your judgement. Don't worry about what others might think. You have a unique perception of covert espionage, an intellect that outperforms all of us. Don't be shy. If you do find anything, anything you think significant, come and see me. Don't bother with an appointment, just knock the door.'

Atkinson nodded, a touch embarrassed, gave the Old Man a half hearted smile. 'Yes, sir. I'll bear that in mind.' And with that he slipped from the room.

Robert Fraser massaged his eyes with a thumb and forefinger. Atkinson was a genius. When it came to computers and data, and all that complex algorithms and machine code, there was no one to touch him. But more to the point, his naturally inquisitive ability to process obscure, ephemeral bits of streaming electronic data was unsurpassed. Beware the commander who ignored such a gifted talent.

But Fraser's concern centred on NDSO's ability to mount a meaningful follow up to Atkinson's revelations. With his two best operatives already engaged on a covert mission, and off limits until they contacted him, his problem was one of resources. Or rather the lack of them. He leaned forward and booted up the laptop. Clicking on 'Current Operations', he browsed through his list of active personnel. He had a pair in Hong Kong, following up on a suspected North Korean operation. Two more had individual assignments assisting the CIA in Syria. Based in Jordan they waited for the right opportunity to dispose of a high ranking Syrian official, a distant relative of Assad.

Lastly, in answer to a personal request from Number Ten, one of NDSO's agents stalked a drugs Lord in South America. Sentenced in his absence but never caught by the authorities, it was deemed necessary to expedite his demise. And that was it, seven primary personnel in the field on 'live' undertakings.

But there was a further possibility, one he was loathe to implement because of the man's erratic past behaviour. Geoff Allenby had pleaded for his 'active' role in the Directorate's operations to be reinstated. Since his one and only disastrous foray into 'deniable' territory, Fraser had suspended his status until deemed appropriate. Thus far he'd been usefully employed as a general dogsbody, it might be time to reintroduce his licence.

'Carol!' he barked.

She swept in, notebook at the ready, all high end efficiency. 'Sir?'

'Would you please get Despatch to locate Geoff Allenby and have him report to me.'

She raised an eyebrow, reminding Fraser of her misgivings.

'I know,' he said, disarmingly, 'needs must.'

She allowed him a critical frown. 'As you wish, sir,' she said, and retreated to her office.

Fraser settled back to wait, chin resting pensively on a pyramid of fingers, and pondered his decision.

In the Forest of Dean, beneath the splayed branches of the old gnarled tree, Bowman paused in his search, to stand back and take stock. He walked away to the cleared firebreak and took a long look around the ancient trunk. Sarah busied herself to the left where a number of entwined branches had been cleared into a tidy stack. It was a possibility but Bowman thought otherwise. The pile of branches might be disturbed, or added to, not very permanent. His keen eyes lingered on the tree; he wondered if there might be a particular branch that signalled direction, pointing to a particular area. His only answer came in the shape of a lower limb, sturdy enough not to break any time soon, but pointing directly at him. Between his feet and the tree only trampled ferns met his gaze, not a place to hide anything. And then, slowly, he swivelled until he faced in the opposite direction, and checked the trees on the far side of the firebreak.

A vague smile flickered across his face. Not ten paces from where he stood, a flat granite rock, rising from left to right and no more than knee high, emerged from the carpet of ferns. He'd been so taken with the obvious he'd missed the important.

Without a word to Sarah, he walked over to the rock and sat on the high end, feeling down behind him in the damp crevices.

He leaned slightly backwards, searching lower with his fingers, and where granite met earth he found a hollow pocket. His fingers found something circular, man made by the feel and he carefully withdrew the object. It turned out to be a small, translucent plastic bottle with a screw top. Inside, protected from the elements, lay a capless Microsoft 32GB Flash Drive, and Bowman grinned. He'd just discovered a modern evolution of the deadletter drop. 'Gotcha,' he said to himself, and closed his fist around the bottle.

Careful not to attract her attention, he wandered aimlessly back to the tree and scuffed leaves with his boot, and then let out an exasperated oath. 'Sod this for a game of soldiers,' he said, and walked miserably over to the stack of branches and slumped to the ground.

'Oh, you make yourself comfortable,' Sarah said pointedly, delving in amongst the ferns. 'Don't worry about me ruining my nail varnish.' She flashed him a withering glance and swept away more leaves.

Bowman held his silence, grinning all over his face.

Eventually she looked up, saw the laughter and exploded. 'What's so damned funny?'

Gradually, little by little, Bowman held out his fist, turned it face up and slowly unfurled his fingers, the small bottle plain to see.

Sarah screwed up her face, peering intently at his open palm. As it dawned on her that he'd found the offending article she took a pace closer and raised a finger at his nose. 'You bastard!' she said, not able to hide a smile. 'Where?'

He pointed. 'That rock, behind the far side.'

She came closer and reached out. 'May I?'

He gave it to her and found his cigarettes, lit one.

Sarah peered inside the tube, nodded without speaking and handed it back. 'Now what?'

'We have a choice,' he said, struggling with his thoughts. 'We can either take this to the Old Man and tell him what we know, or go back and watch Webster again.'

'What good would we do at Webster's place?'

Bowman drew on the cigarette, blew smoke. 'There's a chance we might find who this is for.'

'How?'

'This is only part of the story. Whoever is due to pick this up might not yet know, still waiting for the signal.'

She thought about that, nibbling her bottom lip. 'And?'

'And,' he said, choosing his words with care, 'Webster is the supplier, this USB is intended for the agent, and in this case the agent might also be the handler. It all leads to the same end game; a Russian operation to take out the Old Man. We identify this agent and we'll have the assassin . . . , maybe.'

Sarah shook her head. 'We can't prove Webster hid it here, we're assuming. We didn't actually see him do it.'

Bowman agreed. 'True, circumstantial evidence, but the contents might be damning.'

'Mmm . . . , fingerprints?'

Bowman heard the ex policewomen. 'Doubt it, he'd be too aware. Nope, our best bet is to go back and watch.'

She wrinkled her nose. 'Oh what joy.'

He grinned and got to his feet. 'Nothing quite like being on surveillance.'

They made a final check on their surroundings and moved off, and the patch of forest returned to its slumber, surrounded by a thousand trees.

As evening came and the sun dropped towards the western horizon, Bowman settled down in the observation hide expecting a long wait. Sarah had her head down in the Defender, snatching a few hours sleep before she relieved him for the next watch.

Darkness came to the woodland thicket. The lights came on in Webster's downstairs windows, and now and then his shadow flitted past. At midnight, Sarah took Bowman's place and he got his head down, pillowing his head in his arms on the Land Rover's floor.

Commander Robert Fraser looked up to the knock on his door and swivelled in his chair, hands placed palms down on the desk. 'Come!' he barked.

The door swung open to reveal Geoff Allenby's anxious face, brown eyes narrowed in concern. He stepped in and hesitated, door ajar.

'Close the door and sit,' Fraser ordered, reminding himself to be less severe and more accommodating.

Allenby sat without a word and stared expectantly across the desk.

'How are you, Geoff? Good to go?' Fraser asked.

Allenby looked somewhat disconcerted, surprised by the question. 'I'm fine, sir,' he blurted out.

Fraser stared for a moment, considering the man he was about to reinstate. 'I'm putting you back in harness,' he began. 'We're in receipt of fresh information, traffic analysis of recent transmissions. It all points to a house in Ross-on-Wye.'

Allenby nodded, thin lipped, attentive, enough response for Fraser to continue.

'As yet, that material is sketchy, but Hugh Atkinson feels there's enough to go on and I agree with his findings. I need you to find out who's in that house and I want you over there today. Atkinson will brief you.'

Allenby's mouth turned down at the corners, and Fraser knew enough to know Hugh Atkinson wasn't on Allenby's Christmas list. Nonetheless he received a resentful, 'Yes, sir.'

Fraser took note, mindful of Carol's unspoken warning. 'When you're done,' he went on, 'get kitted up with comms from Despatch. We want a running commentary, any and everything you find.'

Allenby remained stony faced and Fraser fixed him with a glare. 'This is important, Geoff, it's vital we find out what's going on.' He caught the first real glimmer of interest cross Allenby's features.

'Our main concern is the whereabouts of these two men.' He pushed a file over the desk. 'Mug shots, take a look.'

Allenby opened the folder and glanced at the photographs, holding them side by side.

Fraser elaborated. 'Russian Special Forces.' And now he had the man's attention, a flicker of emotion.

'The one on the left is Pushkin, Anatoly Pushkin, and we're almost certain he's in that house. The other one is Alexander Markoff. We don't know if he's active or not. What we do know is that he and Pushkin work as a team, professional killers.'

Allenby nodded. 'I've heard of Markoff, supposed to be good at his job.'

'Is,' Fraser emphasised, 'not supposedly. So make damn sure you abide by the rules. Stay out of harm's way but do everything you can to establish their identities. Do I make myself clear?'

Allenby's pale eyes latched onto his own and the man gave him a lopsided smile. 'Absolutely, sir. Surveillance only, I understand.'

For a moment Fraser rubbed his chin in thought, questioning his own judgement. In terms of experience, *real* experience in the field, Allenby was a beginner. But what choice was there? None, NDSO had run out of options, time for the man to stand up and be counted.

'In that case, make a move.'

Allenby pushed the dossier across the desk and stood. 'Right, sir,' he said, and walked out. As the door began to close, Fraser raised his voice, just enough.

'And don't cock it up,' he called.

The door shut with a solid click.

In the pre-dawn light of another day Mike Bowman was up and about, made coffee on a camp stove and took one to Sarah.

She sat up and cupped the heat in her palms, took a sip and smiled. 'My hero.'

He lay down beside her, camera at the ready, and glanced at her elfin face. 'I know,' he said with a grin. 'Good, aren't I?'

She gave him a clip to the side of his face and chuckled into the mug.

Bowman turned onto his stomach and lifted the lens. The sun broke above the eastern hills.

At two minutes to eight, Webster opened the front door with the Cocker Spaniel at his feet. They watched as he strode down the short drive and turned right up the slope. He let the dog pull him along, wandering amiably up the pathway.

Bowman tensed as he lost sight of them, the green leaves of a nearby oak tree blocking his view. The Spaniel reappeared as they came out the far side, Webster shortening the lead as he stepped onto the road. The pair crossed to the left and walked on, passing the Blue Lion Inn on their right.

Bowman moved his elbows to stabilise the camera, took three or four images in quick succession. The dog stopped to look back at his master, tongue out, tail wagging faster. Webster waved a hand forward and the Spaniel ran on until the lead stretched taut.

Sarah changed position, up on one knee, but still concealed by the foliage.

In Bowman's lens, an old telegraph pole swam into view and he watched as the dog cocked a leg. Webster approached slowly and the animal finished it's business and trotted over to the thorny hedge, sniffing at the roots. Webster made a point of guardedly looking behind him, then cautiously glanced around. Satisfied all was well he leaned casually against the post.

'What's that in his hand?' Sarah asked.

Bowman steadied the lens, took a dozen or so quick-fire photos and then zoomed in with a half turn of the speed lever.

'A small blade by the look of it,' he answered. 'Hard to tell.'

The dog pawed at the dirt, digging a hole, and Webster stepped away from the telegraph pole towards the road. The Spaniel pricked his ears and loped back towards his master, but on the opposite side of the pole. The lead wrapped around the base of the upright and Webster moved back to untangle it.

Bowman caught a movement of the man's free hand, and hit the button on the camera, captured more pictures.

Webster's hand came up level with his chest and he pushed at the wood with a twisting motion of his wrist. It was swift, deliberate, and only then did he walk round the pole to free the dog's lead.

'Did you get that?' Sarah queried.

'Yep, I'm sure that was a knife.'

Webster tugged the dog away from the verge and turned for the village, retraced his original footsteps and crossed the road near the Blue Lion. A little old lady came out of a big house on the right and Webster stopped and chatted as she stroked the dog's ears. The old lady waved goodbye and went on her way, and Webster ambled the last few yards to his house. Two minutes later he and the dog disappeared inside.

'Keep an eye out,' Bowman said, and twisted round to view the saved images. He scrolled back and chose a clear shot. Enlarging it in the viewfinder he closed in on Webster's hand and sure enough the point of a knife scarred the dark wood.

'Got it,' he said, and turned the camera for Sarah to see.

She nodded briefly. 'Am I seeing what I think I'm seeing?'

Bowman pressed a button and returned the camera to readiness. 'If we're right, we've just seen one of the oldest bits of tradecraft in the book. They can use all sorts. Chalk marks, bricks turned in a dry-stone wall, a curtain drawn in a window, washing hanging on a line; there's a multitude of ways. And they all indicate the same thing, a deadletter waiting for collection.'

'And?' She tilted her head.

'Sit tight for now. Someone's going to come for a look-see.'

Mid-day came and went, the sun high in a brilliant sky, hot enough to sweat, even in the shade. But they sat tight and watched, hunters waiting for prey.

16
Exposed

At three in the afternoon Webster's village became a bustling street of mothers and children, the primary school disgorging the kids down the bottom of the road. Four-by-fours queued well clear of the gates, push chairs and buggies vying for space on the crowded pavement. An old grey tractor rumbled noisily up the incline, blue smoke curling from the exhaust. The noxious smell from the towed bowser of raw silage tainted the warm air, a reminder of farming life that supported the inhabitants. The once hourly bus for Gloucester came and went, depositing a young woman in a Tesco top to find her way home.

It was then that Bowman spotted a man walking up towards the Blue Lion. He could have passed for anybody but Bowman's intuition went into overdrive, a familiar tingling of his scalp.

He reached over and touched Sarah's arm, warned her.

'This end of the pub.'

He focused the camera, tracked the man's movement. He looked neither left or right, head down, not hurrying but not dawdling, maintaining a steady pace. The man wore a faded red polo shirt, stonewashed jeans and trainers, and the peak of a baseball cap shaded his eyes. It was a classic piece of covert behaviour, anonymity amongst strangers, deflecting attention by the very act of being commonplace. Bowman's gut instinct kicked in, this man didn't belong in these surroundings.

The target shuffled to a halt at the edge of the pavement, and Bowman zoomed in on his head. The cap lifted as the man checked for traffic, glancing left, and Bowman snapped his face beneath the peak. A metallic blue Peugeot drove past and then he stepped into the road and crossed over. Bowman detected a lithe muscular build beneath the casual clothes, an athletic poise to his outwardly nonchalant appearance.

174

Sarah wriggled on her elbows, binoculars steady.

The man drew level with the garage on the left, slowed his walk and raised his head. Nearing the telegraph pole he stepped onto the grass and deliberately stopped to rest, one hand supporting his weight on the post. Bowman could see his fingers splayed out just above the fresh scar in the wood; took more images.

Sarah lowered the binoculars. 'That's pretty conclusive.'

Bowman nodded, holding the image. Having rested for a moment the man pushed himself away, crossed the momentarily empty road, and began to stroll downhill towards the Blue Lion. Bowman zoomed in tight on the target's head and shoulders, waiting for a clear shot of the hidden face. His chance came when a teenager on a bike raced up the hill. The man looked up to avoid a collision and Bowman triggered a rapid sequence of stills.

'Got him,' he said, and relaxed the camera to the crook of his arm. The man quickened his pace, strode past the pub and went by Webster's house without so much as a glance up the drive. And then he moved out of their line of sight heading down to the school.

He felt Sarah's eyes. 'What now?'

Bowman reflected for a moment. Webster wasn't an issue now. He'd served his purpose, twofold, but didn't yet know he'd been compromised, cover blown. He could be picked up anytime. As for this new target, could they afford to let him walk? Out there on a wide open road, with no concealment, it was tantamount to suicide. He wracked his brain for an answer.

'Sarah, the Old Man really needs to know who this is, where he comes from. We have to try and tail him.' He met her solemn gaze, beautiful soft eyes. 'It won't be like working with a team, everyone on radios and the crowd to hide in. It'll be you, me, and the Land Rover. You up for it?'

'After you,' she said with an elegant bow.

He chuckled and made for the Defender. 'You drive and drop me off before the main road.'

Sarah took the wheel and they swayed unevenly down the rutted farm track. She pulled up short of the main carriageway and Bowman checked his gun.

He opened the door and dropped to the ground, hesitated and delved inside his jacket. 'Here,' he said, and passed her the container with its USB. 'Worst comes to the worst, that goes to the Old Man.' He held onto her fingers as she took it. 'And remember, no one else, his eyes only.'

She nodded. 'I know, Mike. I'll make sure.'

'Right,' he grinned, 'you keep this old jalopy out of sight.' He slammed the door and walked the last few paces to the road. He turned out left and immediately glimpsed the distant image of a red polo shirt beyond the school gates. On the opposite side of the road, two middle aged women with shopping bags waited for a bus and an old man in a straw hat stood last in line. He lengthened his stride, picking up the pace.

Bowman hadn't covered more than fifty yards when the red shirt up ahead stopped walking and bent to tie a shoelace. Oldest trick in the book, Bowman thought, the quickest way to check if anyone was following. Without hesitating, he waited for a gap in the traffic and boldly crossed to the bus stop. He joined the loose queue, half hidden at the back.

The man stood and strolled on, hands deep in his pockets and head down. Bowman stayed in the queue, content to remain with the three waiting passengers in the bus shelter. He realised that being on this side of the road gave him a better vantage point, an uninterrupted field of vision. He glanced back for Sarah. The Defender had turned onto the road and pulled into the kerb, stationary.

But when he brought his gaze round for the man in the red shirt, Bowman cursed under his breath. The target was no longer in sight.

Stepping clear of the shelter he took a long look up the road. And in that moment a motorbike barrelled out from behind a privet hedge, bounced off the pavement and accelerated away in a haze of blue exhaust fumes. A black helmet hid the rider's head, but Bowman caught a flash of red beneath a flapping bomber jacket.

176

He swore loudly and one of the women gave him a withering glare. He dashed into the road, waving for Sarah to pick him up. The Land Rover came hammering up the street and skidded to a squealing halt. He tore open the door, fell into the passenger side and shouted. 'Go! He's on a bloody motorbike!'

Sarah slammed into first gear, floored the pedal and laid a long streak of rubber on the highway. The Defender powered down the hill, out past the end of the village and retraced the previous journey through the rolling hills. A brief glimpse of a fast moving motorbike as they crested a hill. Sarah didn't spare the horsepower as she went up through the gears, tearing along the sinuous twists of tarmac. They dropped into a shallow valley, lost sight of the bike, then hit the final stretch of road leading again to the busy junction, but which way? To their right, towards the Forest of Dean, there was no indication of a motorbike weaving amongst the cars. To the left a continual stream of vehicles filled the road, no chance of a visual contact.

'Left,' Bowman ordered, making an educated guess, partly a hunch.

Sarah swerved into line and came down to a crawl, less than thirty, with no possibility of overtaking. She weaved behind the hatchback in front, looking for an opportunity, nosing out beyond the middle of the road, pulling back for an oncoming lorry. Even if they managed an overtake, they'd still be going nowhere in a hurry.

'Give it up, Angel,' Bowman said. 'We'll head for HQ, report to the Old Man.' He checked the time. 'Friday conference at the moment. Should be interesting.' A mirthless smile crossed his lips.

Alexander Markoff throttled the motorbike down to a sedate twenty miles an hour. He rolled quietly through the peaceful village until he reached the house and turned in, killing the engine and drifting up to the front door. He dismounted and pulled the bike on the stand, hung the helmet from the handlebars and wandered inside.

'Helena,' he said. 'We have the signal.'

An initial silence greeted his announcement and he peered into the kitchen. The back door hung open and he walked outside. He found her lying on a bath towel wearing the smallest of white bikinis, eyes hidden by sunglasses, soaking up the sun. She gave no indication of having heard him and he walked quietly over to stare at the exposed flesh. Her skin had an olive hue and glistened in the light, fine beads of perspiration on her upper lip. A small tattoo embellished her left hip, just above the pelvis. He leaned to take a closer look, saw the shaded outline of a tarantula.

He grimaced. From what he'd heard, she was more like a Black Widow spider; eat you up and spit you out. Even so, he enjoyed the view, a beautiful woman in the prime of her life.

'What are you staring at?' she asked suddenly, and he stepped backwards.

'A woman,' he said, blatantly staring at her midriff, not taking his eyes from the supple torso. The two scraps of white cloth did nothing to conceal her shapely body and he continued to leer.

Helena cursed, sat up and removed the sunglasses. He grinned at her discomfort. 'You show it off, I'll enjoy the scenery.'

She got up and modestly wrapped the towel round her waist. He could see the anger in her movements.

'Did you get the signal?' she snapped.

'That's why I came to find you. The drop should be ready.'

'So, am I coming with you?'

He thought about winding her up some more, rejected it. 'Yes, we'll use the van.'

'Good,' she managed between clenched teeth, and he watched in amusement as she strutted into the house, obviously still annoyed by his attitude.

While she went upstairs to dress, Markoff changed out of the red polo and pulled on a dull green sweat shirt. It had seen better days. He slipped the bomber jacket over the top and repositioned his gun.

Her footsteps on the stairs signalled she was ready and he looked round at the boyish outfit, the recent nakedness now hidden under a shapeless pair of baggy jeans and a long sleeved dark top.

'Ready,' he asked politely.

Without a word she brushed past to the front door, stepped outside and waited with folded arms.

He shook his head. 'Stupid bitch,' he muttered to himself, and banged the door shut behind him.

They clambered in and a minute later the white van turned left into the village lane and he headed for the Forest of Dean.

She sat with her back towards him, pointedly staring out of the side window.

He glanced at his watch. Twenty minutes and they'd be in the car park.

17
Cybergizmo

The Defender ground to a halt outside Salerton Hall's entrance porch. Bowman engaged the handbrake and switched off. He looked over at Sarah and gave her a grim smile.

'You ready for this?'

She responded with a firm nod and glanced at her wristwatch. 'The meeting should be in full swing.'

'Yeah,' he said, distracted by her profile. 'If you give the USB to the Old Man, I'll stay close to Webster. I don't expect trouble, but . . .' He let the statement hang in the air.

They dropped down from the Land Rover and made for the entrance, walked through newly installed electronic security and crossed the floor of the atrium. The solid oak doors of the library barred their way and Bowman opened the left side and ushered Sarah into the long room.

Jock Monroe sat to the right, in the middle of a speech, but drifted into silence as all eyes swivelled to latch on to the newcomers. Winslow 'Tubby' Palmer and Webster sat facing Monroe, and at the head of the table Fraser straightened in his chair.

Bowman eased left to position himself behind Webster, leaning casually against the book shelves. Sarah walked round Monroe's side of the table, all the way to the Old Man's chair and Bowman watched as she reached into her hip pocket. In total silence she produced the container and placed it very deliberately on the table.

Fraser raised a bushy eyebrow and picked it up, stared hard at the contents, and looked at Sarah. 'And this is what, exactly?' he asked, totally unperturbed by their arrival.

Bowman saw her eyes come to meet his own and nodded, and then straightened up from the bookshelves.

'A Flash drive, sir. It recently belonged to Ian Webster.'

There was a long pause while the Old Man glared down the length of the table. 'Did it indeed?' The words were spoken with restrained anger and Webster visibly shrank in his chair. To forestall anything rash, Bowman placed a hand on his shoulder.

Fraser tapped the plastic cylinder on the table, consciously repetitive. It had a menacing, hollow ring. He stopped and looked at Sarah. 'Would you be so good as to tell Carol that I want Hugh Atkinson down here, sharpish.'

Webster attempted to move in his seat and Bowman leaned on the shoulder, dug his fingers through the jacket. He settled.

Fraser started tapping again, a rhythmic quiet banging.

It seemed like an age, but Atkinson probably only took sixty seconds to show his face. 'You wanted me, sir?' he asked breathlessly from the office door.

'Ah, Hugh, just the man.' Fraser held up the container. 'See what you make of this.'

Atkinson walked over, took the cylinder and held it up as if inspecting the clarity of a diamond. 'A USB, sir.'

The Old Man chuckled, a deep gurgle from his throat. 'Got it in one, my lad. I want you to tell us what's on it.'

Bowman could see Atkinson's brain go into overtime and he swept his eyes round the assembly. 'Where did it come from?'

'Why?' Bowman asked.

Atkinson gave an exasperated sigh and answered slowly, as if explaining to a small child. 'This little thing could infect every computer system we have. You know what a cyberworm is?' He spoke to all of them but his eyes remained fixed on Bowman.

'A Trojan thingy?' he offered.

A glimmer of amusement crossed Atkinson's face. 'Good try,' he said. 'Quite similar in fact, with one major exception . . . if this contains what is now known as a 'cyber weapon', the consequences, unlike your average Trojan, could be catastrophic.'

Bowman attempted to laugh, but it came out as a sheepish grin. He raised an eyebrow. 'Bit of an exaggeration?'

If Atkinson felt maligned he didn't show it. 'Would you please answer my question?'

Bowman looked to the Old Man who nodded. He placed the other hand on Webster's right shoulder and bore down with both. 'We found it at a deadletter drop this afternoon. It was probably put there by this man,' and he dropped his eyes to look at the top of Webster's bald head.

Atkinson bit his bottom lip and turned to Fraser. 'I seem to remember you telling me that Mr Webster had worked in GCHQ?'

The Old Man passed a hand through his iron-grey hair and gave a tentative nod. 'True,' he agreed.

Hugh Atkinson grimaced and sucked air through his teeth. He held up the USB in its pot. 'At the very least, this is probably encrypted. The worst possible scenario is that it also contains a cyberworm, and I gather that somebody,' and he looked meaningfully at Webster, 'might be giving away state secrets.'

The Old Man cleared his throat and straightened in his chair. 'Well we certainly need to know what it contains. Can you manage that?'

'Definitely, sir, but I'll need to pass it through a number of tests, and more specifically, put an air-gap round it.'

Fraser rubbed his forehead, perplexed. 'You've lost me, I think you need to tell us in layman's language.'

Atkinson rubbed his nose and adjusted his glasses, and for a moment, glanced down at his feet, the centre of attention. When he looked up, his eyes were alight with enthusiasm.

'What I'm about to say is highly classified. The Americans won't talk about it, deny they had anything to do with it, but in my field of deep analysis while I served with GCHQ, I had been tasked with helping decode a virus, or, as it later turned out to be, a cyberworm.' He looked down at Fraser for guidance. 'Do you want me to carry on?'

The Old Man squinted up at Atkinson and cocked his head to one side. 'Oh yes, Hugh,' he said evenly. 'Anything the Americans are involved with always intrigues me.'

Atkinson squared his shoulders. 'Have you heard of 'Exsulate' sir?'

Bowman felt Webster twitch, and Fraser slowly shook his head. 'No . . , can't say I have.'

'It is a cleverly put together piece of software, which carries a usable payload, as in 'weapon' payload, and that when activated, can physically destroy enemy hardware. It forms part of what is loosely termed, cyber warfare. Until Exsulate arrived on the scene, our programmers had always used their skills in a defensive capacity.' He paused for effect. 'Unfortunately, this piece of software spread too far, outside the original parameters. A private anti-malware company picked it up, and quickly decided it was so complex, only a nation state had the wherewithal to design it. The cat was out of the bag.'

He looked round the room, daring them to interrupt. 'The Russian Federation now have it, and they understand the mechanism by which it works. And it only takes a USB Flash drive, of which there are millions, to be inserted into a web linked laptop, or desktop, or even an IBM mainframe, for Exsulate to multiply and instigate a targeted explosion. A real world explosion.'

The Old Man rubbed his chin. 'And you think this USB might have that capability?'

'It might, sir. So to make certain sure I know what I'm dealing with, I'll upload into a sacrificial laptop, off-line, thereby maintaining an air-gap. An impenetrable moat if you like.'

'I see,' Fraser ventured. His eyes came up and fastened on Bowman's, and then levelled down on Webster. 'I don't suppose you'd like to add anything to this discussion?'

Webster held his silence, head bowed.

'Didn't think so,' said the Old Man, and stood up and paced the room, both hands in his jacket pockets, and Bowman waited for the outcome.

'Carol?' he called.

She came in, smoothing down her grey skirt.

'Tell Jim to send over the armed patrol. I want Webster under lock and key, not to be left unattended.'

Carol raised an eyebrow and gave Webster an unsympathetic glance. 'Yes, sir,' she said and hurried away.

'Hugh,' Fraser continued, 'Do what you have to but be quick about it. I must know what's on that gizmo.'

Atkinson nodded and scurried off.

Bowman stepped to the side of Webster's chair. 'On your feet,' he demanded, and the man obeyed, pushing back the seat and coming to his full height. He stared straight ahead, avoiding eye contact.

The double doors banged open and three men strode in, all of them with pistols to the fore. Bowman smiled briefly. He recognised the gardener and the chauffeur, the other man he'd seen in the gatehouse. The chauffeur made the first move and came over to Webster's side. 'This way,' he prompted and waved the gun towards the doors.

Webster hesitated, staring at the opposite wall. He turned his eyes on the Old Man.

'I have a request, a favour if you like,' he said.

Fraser rubbed his mouth before answering. 'At this particular moment I can't promise I'll grant it,' he said. His voice came across as extremely measured.

'I wouldn't ask but it's not for me,' Webster said. He cast a pleading glance round the table. 'My dog, there won't be anyone to look after him. Perhaps . . . ?'

Bowman saw Fraser frown, hesitate, and then nod. 'I'll have someone take care of it.'

Webster gave a small smile of thanks and accepted the inevitable. The three men with sidearms escorted him from the room.

'Now, Mike,' said Fraser, when the room had settled, 'you two have a seat and tell me what you know.'

Bowman walked up to the side of the conference table and sat opposite Sarah. After a brief moment to collect his thoughts he launched into an explanation of everything that had taken place.

Commander Robert Fraser listened intently to every word.

In the Forest of Dean, Alexander Markoff dispensed with the known trails and cut west on a roundabout route that would bring them to the drop box from the north. He'd travelled this route in all weathers, day and night, and had no hesitation in guiding Helena through the fern laden forest floor. Now and then he peered ahead for the next marker, a singular specimen of sweet chestnut, or a large beech tree framed against the background of larch. They crossed a trickle of water at the bottom of a dip and Markoff swung east bringing them round to join a well maintained firebreak.

He glanced behind. Helena followed without a murmur, easily maintaining his forced pace. Moving left off the firebreak he headed for a tall Douglas fir, then turned right by a small clearing and stopped. Helena came up alongside.

Markoff pointed south. 'Not far now, five-hundred metres. Let us be quiet.' He led on through the clinging ferns, frequently pausing to listen, and then pointed again.

'See that oak tree? That is the main marker.'

In fits and starts they covered the last few paces and finally stood beneath a strangely deformed oak tree next to the firebreak. He saw Helena searching round, puzzled by her surroundings. For the first time since their argument she spoke to ask a question. 'This is it?'

'Almost,' he answered smugly. 'Watch.' He stepped over to a low hanging branch, lined himself up and strode to the far edge of the cleared break. Finding the granite rock, he bent to the far side and felt for the hidden recess. His fingers scrabbled in the soil, against the hard rock, searched the base, and he cursed. Moving to the rear he bent on one knee and parted the fronds of serrated ferns, desperately hunting for a cylinder that contained the 'letter'. In the end he shook his head in disbelief and stood up. 'It is not here.'

She laughed, ridiculing his efforts. 'Of course it's here, you have mistaken the spot.'

'No,' he said, suppressing an urge to slap her face. 'This is correct but there is no message.'

She giggled, almost hysterical, pointing at him in derision. 'In that case, oh mighty Markoff, what do we do now?'

He advanced towards her, seething at her disdainful mockery, but also worried by the turn of events. The mark on the telegraph pole could not have been anything but the signal. Deep gouged into the wood, neatly above the last cut, exactly as it ought to have been. So what had happened? Had the man been caught in the act?

Markoff refocused his mind, ignored her taunts, this could be more serious than they knew. Even now they might be under surveillance. Espionage was a dangerous game. He pulled his gun, saw her look of concern replace the scorn, a serious frown. Holding up his hand he urged her to back off, and then checked the firebreak, left and right. Not that he expected to find anything, that wasn't the way it worked. They melted into the undergrowth behind the oak tree, while he took a final survey of the site.

It was a setback, no doubt, but the training covered all eventualities, how to cope with all circumstances. Asses the pros and cons and move on, make a decision.

'Come,' he said, 'no good mourning over what's out of our control.'

'But what will we do now?' she worried, as they hurried away.

'We go ahead as planned, as if we had confirmation. Nothing has changed, all that is missing is an exact time. For this we can compensate.'

They came to the dip and the meagre trickle of water. He whispered as they cleared the brook. 'Go to the right, in those bushes. We will see if we're alone.' A full three minutes elapsed before he felt confident enough to move on and then made a bee-line for the car park.

The van was as they'd left it and Markoff gunned the throttle and headed for the house. The woman sat motionless beside him, head down as if asleep. Not that Markoff cared right now, the mission remained his to command and she had become irrelevant. They would link up with Pushkin.

Hugh Atkinson cleared his workstation of all the usual paraphernalia and pulled the table to the centre of the room. He stood back and cast a critical eye over the move, knowing in his heart of hearts it actually made not the slightest difference. It was more a visible separation, a physical air-gap, and he felt better for doing it.

He placed the sacrificial laptop squarely in the middle, retrieved the cylinder from his pocket and withdrew the Flash Drive. Booting up the computer, he keyed in a command for machine-code and attached the USB to a vacant port. The cursor blinked, waiting for the prompt, and he converted to the assembly language of alphanumerics. NDSO's Senior cryptanalyst then took a slow breath and typed in the first line of instruction.

Having compiled his programme, Atkinson hit 'run' and waited for the results. It took the central processing unit just under two minutes to penetrate Webster's encrypted communiqué. The screen flashed up with a myriad columns of binary data and he sat back, quietly elated with his breakthrough.

Now all he needed was a translation of the data stream to understand the underlying message. Fingers hovering over the keyboard, he began to type.

Colonel-General Viktor Leonid Zherlenko strode into the Tactical Operations Centre and took his place at the head of the conference table. Around that table sat some of Russia's most highly regarded members of the Intelligence Services. Into this complex flowed real time world surveillance, watched over and collated by a specialist team of communication analysts. Each morning a Situation Report landed in front of the Assistant Commander in preparation for a daily briefing of current risk probability. In conjunction with the GRU and SVF, ongoing operations received their own dedicated team of officers to ensure Remote Command should the necessity arise.

This particular meeting had been convened by Zherlenko to answer the Kremlin's request for further updates on Operation Lightning.

'What do you have for me?' he asked of the Assistant Commander.

'Nothing more than routine communications from our London Embassy, General. We assume all is running smoothly.'

'What about Markoff, have we had communications?'

'Not for eight days. The last we had was from Goreya before she left the Embassy.'

Zherlenko stared into the middle distance. He considered their findings. No news could be good news but before that Latvian woman had escaped, the Signals Branch had always maintained regular contact with Markoff. Was it coincidence? From Pushkin he expected silence, as it should be; with Markoff and Helena Goreya now active and the Operation coming to a head there should be authenticated signals from Markoff. Even if it were only his station ident, it would've shown a live feed.

He dropped his gaze on the Assistant Commander. 'Can we contact Markoff do you think?'

'Of course, General, but in reality we operate as per mission statement. The countdown has begun, less than seventy-two hours before Lightning strikes. There must be no communications during the final phase, in case we are compromised. Those are the orders.'

Zherlenko buried his head in his hands, yearning for the days before America dominated with their high tech surveillance systems. He blew out his cheeks and eyed the men and women on whom he relied, and shook his head.

'I am not here on a whim, Commander, the Kremlin demand an update. I have to give them something, Can we not risk one call to Markoff?'

The Commander looked dubious and turned to a Major, his senior controller.

The man grimaced, looked down at his laptop, and then met Zherlenko's glare. 'Do you authorise me to do this, General?' the man asked, narrowing his eyes.

Zherlenko hesitated, the man was wise to being manipulated. He knew his orders and wasn't about to be thrown to the wolves, much bigger consequences might follow. But the weight of expectation fell heavily on Zherlenko's shoulders and he felt obliged to break the rules. What added to his troubles was the knowledge he must soon explain the disappearance of Lieutenant Tsegler's unit in Latvia, even though he'd ordered them in with the best of intentions.

'I do,' he agreed. 'You have my full authorisation. Ask only if they are on schedule, nothing more. The answer will be either yes or no, as short as possible. If no, we will have to make decisions, if yes, there is nothing more to say.'

The Major moved his tongue in his cheek and pursed his lips. 'As you command, General,' and he turned to a woman behind him. 'See to it.'

She nodded, keyed in the request, uploaded for Sat-Comms, and transmitted.

The Major caught her brief nod and turned to the General. 'They have it now, sir. Next time they are on air they will see it.'

'When will that be' Zherlenko queried, impatient.

The Major looked at the digital wall displays showing various time zones round the globe. 'In two hours and twenty-seven minutes, sir.'

Colonel-General Viktor Leonid Zherlenko got up from his chair and picked up his cap. 'I will return in two hours and twenty-six minutes precisely. Let us hope all is well and Moscow Central do not have reason to call on us.' He glowered at them and walked out. For all the planning things had become a lot more complicated.

In GCHQ a satellite transmission was intercepted and logged. An auto register flagged the signal for the attention of NDSO's IBM, and Hugh Atkinson's remote terminal began to flash. It would be only a matter of time before he became aware.

18
Deadly Encounter

It took Hugh Atkinson forty-one minutes to unravel Webster's coded information and what it revealed was surprisingly bland. No secret files from NDSO's briefings, no intimate details of names or numbers, and definitely no state secrets. It did contain a map of Salerton Hall; every floor, all the rooms on those floors, the doorways and windows, and the precise placement of major furnishings.

The only other piece of information of possible importance: six numbers, "0904050", isolated from the map and without reference to it. Atkinson felt mildly disappointed, he'd expected some kind of 'Eureka' moment. He scrolled back through the main mass of data to search for a missing clue, a definitive instruction he'd somehow bypassed, all to no avail. He scratched his head in frustration and sat back, deflated.

After a few moments pondering, he finally accepted that the Flash Drive simply contained a map of the building, and a six digit number. It would have to be enough. Across the room his eye was drawn to the IBM's remote monitor, flashing steadily. He walked over and downloaded the transmission, saw that it contained a Russian intercept and filed it for further analysis.

He returned to his workstation, gathered up the laptop, USB attached, and made his way down to the conference room.

In the village of Longbridge, Helena Goreya had good reason to be concerned. Things were not the same between her and Markoff, he had assumed total command and demanded her obedience. No longer a man she might reason with, he made his decisions with no prior warning. And without the anticipated report from the drop, a major part of her authority had gone. A scientific approach to the operation had become largely immaterial.

Helena sighed and moved to the bedroom window, her brow creased with misgivings. Now it would be Markoff unleashed, the bloody assassin free to inflict uncontrolled mayhem. She turned to the bed and cast an eye over her meagre equipment. Of course, she still hoped common sense might prevail. Markoff might yet listen to reason, be persuaded that technology was the key.

She heard his guttural call from below. 'We don't have all day.'

'Coming,' she answered lightly. It did no good to antagonise him, better to humour his mood and pray he would listen. With her bag ready, she went down to the hall and followed him out. Markoff jumped in the back of the van with his own large canvas bag and shoved it up front against the headboard, covered it in dust sheets and dropped a workbench over that. He stacked a heap of brown, uPVC waste water piping over it and then moved some blue tarpaulins onto those. A big chest of tools was strategically placed in the middle to partially hide the sheets and he repositioned two yellow transformers and an electric saw near the back doors. Lastly he dragged over a large cardboard reel of electric cable, grabbed a few pairs of rigger's gloves and two orange helmets, and dropped them haphazardly on the floor. He jumped down, satisfied himself that all looked as it should, and slammed the doors.

'Jump in,' he said, and Helena made for the passenger side. Seat belt on she noticed the clutter strewn on top of the dashboard. Give Markoff his due, he hadn't been idle. The Sun newspaper lay open on page three, there were two empty polystyrene coffee cups, one on its side, and a McDonalds takeaway box perched precariously on a paper wrapper. A half packet of wine gums leaned against the windscreen. He climbed in beside her and saw her looking.

'That's what the British do,' he grinned, and despite herself, Helena had to smile. It was true; if British builders were on a building site, that is what they did. The British had a name for it, 'white van man'.

Markoff started up and drove forward and Helena uttered a warning. 'Seat belt.'

He grimaced and angrily complied, snatching it from the side and banging the buckle into the pod.

She nodded, pleased. Between them, they'd agreed to follow the law. No speeding, no unnecessary overtaking, indicate properly. An unmarked police car might just as easily be driving on the same stretch of road, they didn't need unwarranted attention.

Markoff took them out onto the village road and turned left on the A40 for Ross on Wye, joining the carriageway where it curved past the end of the village, and settled down to fifty miles an hour.

Helena toggled the door switch for the nearside mirror, angled it so she could see behind. The road appeared empty and she leaned back and tried to relax. But her inner concerns over Markoff's behaviour surfaced again and she took a surreptitious glance across. He sat tensed, knuckles white on the steering wheel, jaw clamped in grim determination, eyes unwavering on the road ahead. In Moscow she'd heard rumours about his state of mind, brushed them off, not wanting to believe. Now she wasn't so sure. He'd become agitated, openly talking of killing, an animal intensity lighting his face. It showed a lack of discipline and she hoped his temper could be controlled.

With the late afternoon sun hanging low over the road ahead they cruised through the small village of Lea, past Ryford Hall and on through the sprawling hamlet of Weston under Penyard. A few minutes later they pulled into the outskirts of Ross-on-Wye and she breathed a sigh of relief. For a short period they manoeuvred through the back streets of residential housing before coming to an isolated house that backed on to a large industrial estate. Markoff swung left into a narrow driveway and braked to a halt.

'Pushkin's place,' he announced, and climbed out.

The front door opened and a man stepped out, a broad grin lighting his face.

'Alexander, you swine!' he called.

'Anatoly Pushkin, you son of a whore!' Markoff yelled and she watched them stride towards one another. They met like long lost brothers, laughing and swearing, embracing one

192

another with much slapping of backs. They parted, and then with an arm around each others shoulders, turned towards the van. Markoff said something in Pushkin's ear.

Helena climbed down and closed the van door, waiting to be introduced. They came nearer and the one named Pushkin shrugged free of Markoff and stepped forward.

'Helena Goreya, I've heard good things of you.' He reached out with a hand and she shook it. His grip was strong and he held tight, pulling her closer. His eyes were bright, arrogant. He bowed his head and raised her hand to his lips, a mocking resemblance of gentlemanly conduct. He let go and made an exaggerated show of eyeing her up. 'Beautiful, they said. Not wrong I think.' He glanced round at Markoff. 'Have you tamed her, Alexander?' The lewd laughter came easily and he slapped a thigh. 'How long have you two been working together?' He laughed again, and Markoff chuckled.

'Too long, maybe,' he said.

Helena heard the answer and for the first time began to feel uncomfortable. She felt like a piece of meat at a cattle auction.

Pushkin met her eyes, a twisted grin on his cruel mouth. 'Come, Helena Goreya, you are welcome in my humble abode.' He bowed from the waist and swept a hand in the direction of the front door.

She nodded her thanks and walked past him with a smile, head high, not showing any signs of concern, and followed Markoff inside. Pushkin came in and closed the door with a shoot bolt top and bottom, then went through to the kitchen. He rummaged in a glass fronted wall cabinet and found tumblers and a bottle of Smirnoff. He poured and handed them round, lifted his own in salute.

'A toast,' he suggested. 'To the Motherland.'

'The Motherland,' Markoff joined in, and Helena played along and raised her glass. 'The Motherland.'

Glasses were touched and she swallowed. The burn of the liquor wasn't on a par with what she was accustomed to, but it had a distinct kick. She realised Pushkin was staring at her and met his eyes.

He smiled secretively. 'Would you like to see Lightning?'

Spoken out loud the very word made her shiver. 'Very much,' she nodded. Maybe Markoff would understand the advantage technology could give them.

'Then come, I will show you.' He led them out back and round to a garage, and unlocked the steel up-and-over door. Helena followed him in. The sun had slipped beyond the horizon but there was enough daylight left to see by.

In the middle of the concrete floor a pale dust sheet had been draped over a waist high bulge. Pushkin walked over and carefully lifted it from the object beneath. With a final flourish he wafted the sheet to one side and stood back.

'There,' he said proudly. 'Is it not done well?'

She strolled slowly round the garage viewing it from every angle and had to admit Pushkin had done a remarkable job.

'Yes,' she volunteered, 'it is good work.'

Markoff grunted in the background, loathe to praise a bit of engineering.

Helena moved in and touched the carbon fibre, inspected everything from close up and nodded. 'It appears exactly as those we had in Moscow. General Zherlenko would be most impressed.' She turned to Markoff. 'When do we attack?'

'When I say so,' he snapped, and stalked off to the house.

She shrugged. He wouldn't leave it too long, the killing mood was upon him.

Pushkin replaced the dust sheet, lowered the door and secured it. She wandered back to the rear of the house. In the kitchen Pushkin began to prepare a meal.

'Have you tested the controls? Does it respond to a signal?' she asked.

'It does. I gave it three instructions over two seconds. It recognised each order.'

Helena Goreya smiled. 'I think I'll have more vodka,' she said, and reached for the bottle. All that remained was the final test of her equipment. She drank to that and perched on a stool, watching him chop an onion.

The lights burned bright in Salerton Hall, not yet totally dark outside, but too gloomy to see without them inside. Bowman passed his camera to Tubby Palmer who studied the rear screen, meticulously scrolling through the images.

'I don't think there's much doubt Webster's notifying whoever of a deadletter. There's no other reason for gouging the telegraph pole like that.' He continued his scrolling back, then paused, peering closely at the next picture. Lowering the camera he turned it to Bowman. 'Know who that is?'

Bowman shook his head. 'No, he's the one on the motorbike.'

Palmer nursed the camera for a final look and then handed it to the Old Man. 'That is Alexander Nickolai Markoff.'

Fraser studied it for a moment and slowly nodded. 'Agreed, there's no doubting that face. The 'Butcher of Ukraine', chief executioner bar none. That is Moscow's main man.' He looked up and Bowman felt the full force of his probing glance. 'Not someone to take lightly.'

Jock Monroe leaned for the camera, took one look and curled a lip. 'Confirmation that Pushkin's in the vicinity.'

Sarah spread her hands on the table and looked inquiringly at Bowman. He winked and grinned. 'Enemy at the gates.'

The door to Carol's office barged open and Hugh Atkinson came in walking backwards, protecting the laptop at his waist.

'Ah,' said the Old Man, 'our Maestro, what do we have?'

Atkinson shuffled to the head of the table and gently placed the laptop in front of Fraser.

'Well, sir,' he said awkwardly, 'I'm not sure this is what we expected, but it's all there is.'

The Old Man beckoned to the rest of them, and they gathered to look over his shoulders.

Atkinson waited until they were ready and then opened the file. The plan drawings of the Hall expanded onto the screen, with the six digit number appearing immediately below.

They stared, mesmerised, not saying a word, and Bowman wondered what the significance might be.

Monroe broke the silence. 'If I wanted to infiltrate Salerton Hall, everything I need is in front of me.'

Bowman looked again, trying to reconcile the image with the statement. The floor plan didn't seem to give much

195

information on security. If NDSO wanted to get inside, he'd want to know where the alarm system was, how it worked, armed patrols. At the risk of putting Monroe's nose out of joint he said what he thought.

'No detail on the security systems though. Where to get in, I would have no idea.'

'Mmm,' Monroe muttered, mulling it over.

The Old Man shifted in his chair. 'And what's that number all about? More to this than meets the eye.'

One by one they dispersed and found a seat, leaving Fraser glued to the laptop.

Bowman looked across the table and caught Sarah's eye. She gave him a negligible shake of her head, a faint shrug of the shoulders.

Winslow 'tubby' Palmer leaned forward, scratching his short-curled greying black hair. 'Forgetting the lack of security detail for a minute, that's nonetheless a pretty comprehensive floor plan, from top to bottom. And we've only got this one communication. There must have been others and they might well have included the alarm system and duty rotas.'

'Granted,' Fraser said, and then gazed at Atkinson. 'What do you make of that number?'

'No obvious tie-ins, sir. Could be telephone numbers, sequential file data, radio frequency, any number of possibilities.'

'Nothing to do with the house plan?'

Atkinson hesitated. 'If it is, I can't place it.'

The Old Man pursed his lips. 'Alright, Hugh. We'll let you get on while we try and figure out the implications to all this.'

'Thank you, sir,' Atkinson said, and closed the laptop. He nodded to the table in general and walked out.

When he'd gone, Winslow Palmer stood and dug his hands in his pockets. 'However we look at this, there's a theme running. Anna's information on Bullseye . . , Pushkin, Markoff, the house plan, Webster, and Hugh's SigIntel. Like it or not, the Russians are on a vendetta and we're the target.' He looked over the top of his heavy rimmed glasses. 'What's with the house in Ross?'

Fraser squirmed in his chair. 'Ah, sorry, but I'm on it. Sent Allenby down to investigate.'

Bowman frowned. 'New to me, sir. What house?'

'A bit complicated, Mike. All happened while you were 'off radar'. Electronic surveillance and a Russian voice link up convinced me to act. I gave Allenby another chance.'

'Hope that's justified,' Bowman said, knowing how short tempered he'd been.

The Old Man rubbed his jaw. 'Didn't have much option, told him to keep us regularly updated.' He straightened in his chair and vigorously rubbed his hands. 'Now, what are we going to do about all this, any suggestions?'

Monroe raised a finger. 'I have a proposal. You may or may not like what you hear, but I'll give it a go.'

The Old Man smiled a little. 'Go on then, Jock, give us both barrels.'

Monroe sat forward and began to explain his idea, and Bowman settled back to listen. Jock often liked to hear the sound of his own voice.

The Russians were still on schedule, preparing for the inevitable.

In Ross-on-Wye, night had fallen and few people walked the streets. The summer warmth of the day, bolstered by a soft southerly breeze, had hardly had time to cool. In the suburbs, where the A40 entered town, a shadow floated unseen outside the glow of a street light. Geoff Allenby had spent the day in hiding. He'd seen movement around the house, nothing substantial. Eventually he'd grown frustrated by a lack of activity, irritable with the monotony of tedious observation.

And then the shadow cast caution aside, and under cover of darkness, crept into the garden of the property, determined to find answers.

Helena Goreya wanted fresh air and moved outside. To her disappointment the night air had a sultry feel, a wet heat, damp on the skin. She wandered up the back garden, listless, seeking relief from the oppressive warmth. Perspiration gathered on her forehead and beneath her chin. Lifting the hem of her singlet she wiped her face and neck, and dabbed at the moisture down her cleavage. She let the damp material fall away, then stiffened, alert.

A faint noise caught her attention, from beyond the garage. It came again, a rustling in the overgrown border and she strained to pinpoint the location. Uncertain, she tiptoed towards the back door.

Markoff stood by the kitchen sink crunching crisps, and turned as she entered.

Helena raised a finger to her lips and he froze. She mouthed a whisper. 'Outside by the garage.'

He gently placed the packet on the draining board and came up with his pistol, checked the silencer.

She selected a carving knife from the wooden block and Markoff switched off the light. He came towards the door and whispered in her ear. 'Front or back?'

'Far side rear, I think,' she answered, and stepped out behind him.

In the pale light of a cloud obscured moon, Markoff signalled her to go right, round the front of the garage, and she watched for a second as he flattened his back to slide up the left wall. She took a firm grip of the knife, extended waist high, and strode silently in the opposite direction. The up-and-over door glimmered softly, undisturbed, and she skipped past it to the far wall. Dropping on all fours, and with her head at ground level, she cautiously peered round the corner.

The soft light of a miniature torch met her gaze, with the vague outline of a man in dark clothing staring through the window.

Rising to her feet, Helena paused, gathered herself for action, and stepped round the corner.

The man must have seen her move. The beam of the torch hit her full in the eyes, blinding. She ducked right, rushed forward, tensed to strike with the blade.

Then Markoff bellowed. 'Stand still!' The torch angled down, fixed on the grass. Helena could detect their outlines,

Markoff standing back, pistol aimed at the man's head. She moved into the man's eye line. 'Hands in the air,' she ordered.

He did as she said and Markoff took a step closer. 'Move.'

Helena took a pace backwards to give him room, wary, the point of the knife aimed at his throat.

But he lunged for her legs, smashed into her shins, and they crashed to the ground. She twisted free of his weight, thrust the knife at his body and felt the impact. Steel in flesh, felt the crunch of bone, jolting back through her arm. He grunted and lashed out with a straight-armed chop. The full force caught her throat, but disregarding the pain, she jabbed again. Soft tissue and the heat of blood on her fist, spraying up her arm.

Markoff's gun spat, a silenced blast, and Helena felt the man jerk, gasp for breath, and he lay still. She pulled her legs out from under him and wriggled clear.

'Are you hurt,' Markoff asked.

'No,' she said, breathing hard, and reached for the small torch lying on the ground. She played it over the face; one pale grey eye open, one half closed, his mouth distorted. Markoff went through his pockets, empty. In a professional shoulder holster he found a Sig 9mm handgun, no obvious markings. Markoff cursed and tucked the gun in his belt.

Helena felt the stickiness of blood on her arm, cloying, smelt the metallic odour and gagged.

Markoff hauled her to upright and gave her a push. 'Leave it,' he said. 'Tell Pushkin to check the front. We go in the morning.'

Helena flashed the torch once more over the dead man's bloodless features and walked away.

Geoff Allenby died in the mistaken belief that he could bend the rules, disregard years of training, enter the lion's den and escape unscathed. Impetuous and unreliable, an elementary slip-up had cost him his life, and the 'shadow' perished in the knowledge he'd failed again.

19
Eyes and Ears

Alexander Markoff woke with the pink light of dawn and swung his feet to the floor. He stretched flexing his muscles, arms aloft, tightening and relaxing. At the window he touched the half drawn curtain, thinking of the coming day, the culmination of many months planning. And he'd waited patiently, abiding by Zherlenko's instructions, careful to avoid putting the operation at risk.

But no longer. Yes, he would carry out Operation Lightning and let the woman try her new weapon. Personally he was convinced she would fail. Then it would be his own mission, and no one to stand in his way. Certainly not Helena Goreya, even though she assumed Moscow gave her the ultimate authority. He smiled grimly. Out here on 'covert operations' Markoff was in his element, able to make spur of the moment decisions. Last night's episode proved to him that Helena Goreya had a weakness, slow reactions when it came to the real thing. Not good for the Special Forces.

The brightening sky lifted his spirits, a good omen. He turned from the window and went for a wash and shave. Today he would be smartly turned out, for too long he'd been acting as a peasant in second hand clothing. No longer, time to dress the part. In twenty minutes he was ready and went outside to the van.

From a pocket in the side of the driver's seat he pulled out a Nokia 210 phone and made three calls. Each call was acknowledged by Russian undercover agents. The first reply came from a man with binoculars, the second from the driver of a surveillance van, and the third call asked only, 'when?'

Satisfied with the result, he then sent a simple text to the Russian Embassy. It consisted of a numeric code, six digits: 0904050. Markoff then stripped the Nokia of its Sim card and returned the phone to the seat pocket. He would dispose of it in some hedge once they were on the road. The Sim card he broke in two and trod into the border.

With a derisive smirk he strutted back to the kitchen. Five men and a woman were about to activate Operation Lightning.

Fifty miles to the east, Mike Bowman also awoke to a crimson dawn. He dragged on a pair of jeans, washed and shaved, and ran a comb through his unruly hair. A quick glance in the mirror showed he looked better than he felt and he grinned at the reflection. In the kitchen he got the coffee going and went outside for a smoke. He breathed cool morning air and watched while the sheep across the river nodded their way downhill. A shiver ran through the muscles of his naked chest, a reaction to the chill, and he thought about putting on a tee shirt. Walking back inside he found a crumpled top and slipped into it. The kettle boiled and he poured.

Bowman did all these things without really seeing or thinking of them, his mind elsewhere, churning over the image of Salerton Hall, trying to piece together how the Russians intended to carry out their mission.

'Morning, Mike.'

He turned from the doorway and smiled at Sarah's tousled hair. She wore one of his white shirts, leaning with one hand resting high on the door jamb. The shirt had just enough length to retain a modicum of decency, her shapely bare legs crossed at the ankles.

'Hi, Angel, what would you like?'

She grinned wickedly. 'What's on offer?'

'Muesli, eggs, toast, bacon, whatever you like.' He kept a straight face.

She chuckled quietly and dropped the suggestive pose. 'I'll settle for Muesli.'

It was Bowman's turn to smile. 'As you wish, my lady,' he said, and reached into a cupboard. When he finished preparing they sat and contentedly disposed of the food and Sarah picked up her coffee.

Bowman leaned forward, elbows on the table. 'I'm going to take a look round the grounds of the Hall.'

Her eyes found his over the top of the mug and she lifted a delicate brow. 'Why?'

He rested his chin on a fist. 'I think that land is vulnerable, I want to see for myself.'

Sarah took a sip, eyes glued to his. 'Do I get to come?'

'Wouldn't have anyone else,' he said, and meant every word.

She lowered the mug to the table and ran a finger round the rim, frowning in thought. 'What will we be looking for? There's so many sensors dug into the earth they'd have to be magicians to get anywhere near.'

'If Webster ran that deadletter drop for any length of time, they'll know all that. Special Forces don't go into things half cocked. We know it's a planned operation, question is how? Something's missing.'

'I'm game if you are. When?'

Bowman looked at his watch. 'This morning would be good, before the Old Man thinks up something new.'

Sarah stood and came round behind him and he felt her hand on his shoulder. 'I take it they'll search Webster's house?'

'As we speak,' he said. 'I doubt they'll find much. He wouldn't leave a trail, too professional.'

'I'll get dressed then. Won't be long.'

He glanced behind as she left, the shirt-tail swaying sensually above the back of her thighs. Someday, he thought with a warm smile, I'll call her bluff.

Commander Robert Fraser strode into Despatch and pushed through into the 'radio shack'. A dozen UHF wireless/transmitters met his gaze, manned by three signals operators. A mainframe terminal glowed soft green in the far corner, enabling communications access via an Astrium Skynet 5D satellite, and that's where he found the Duty Officer. Fraser wanted a first hand account of when Allenby had stopped calling.

'Last transmission came at 22.00hrs, sir.'

202

'What did he say?'

'No sighting of targets and that he would take a closer look.'

Fraser swore quietly. 'Too close, maybe.'

The Duty Officer inclined his head in deference to the Old Man's position, it wasn't for him to theorise on what may have happened.

'Have you tried contacting him since?'

'On the hour, every hour, sir.'

Fraser rubbed his jaw with a twinge of remorse. In retrospect, 'Don't cock it up' might have been a bit harsh.

The Duty Officer looked round as Skynet came to life. 'Excuse me, sir, I'm wanted.'

'By all means,' Fraser said, 'you carry on.' He lingered awhile watching the almost motionless operators typing or talking quietly into their respective equipment. He pictured Atkinson sat at his console upstairs. Invariably, the majority of his data from GCHQ streamed in through Skynet. Everything might be a lot more sophisticated but the Service had been on this kind of surveillance for eons.

Reluctantly, and with a shake of the iron-grey head, he walked out into the corridor and sauntered back to his office, deep in thought.

Carol interrupted his melancholy. 'Commander Fraser, sir.'

'Yes, Carol?'

'There's an initial report from Webster's house. The search proved inconclusive. They're still working on it.'

'Thank you.' He looked at the time. 'Let's have some coffee, and bring a cup for yourself.'

He saw the quizzical expression flick across her face, but being the obedient secretary, refrained from making a comment and nodded.

Fraser moved behind his desk, and opened the central drawer. He reached into the back and felt the comforting coldness of his pistol and took it out. He hefted the weight in the palm of his hand, remembering when he last used it. The magazine slipped into his other hand and he extracted a 9mm cartridge, a flat nosed Parabellum, great stopping power. For the first time in a long while he thought it might be prudent to have the gun to hand. Clipping the round into the magazine he palmed the mag into the handle and tucked the gun inside his jacket.

Carol came in with a tray and slid it carefully onto the desk.

He nodded his thanks. 'You sit down. I'll be mother.' He took the coffee pot and poured, passed one across the desk and settled in his chair. He could see she was watching carefully, wondering why she was here.

'How's Anna?' he asked.

'Not too bad, considering. I think she's waiting for a house.'

Fraser stirred his coffee. 'You haven't had much holiday this year,' he said casually.

She stiffened, eyes narrowed, on her guard. 'No, sir, not yet.'

He set the spoon down in the saucer and drummed his fingers on the table. 'Any plans?'

'Not specifically, why do you ask, sir?'

Fraser fingered his jaw, uncertain how to broach the subject. 'Don't take this the wrong way, but I'd like you to take some leave, starting immediately.'

She stared at him, slightly open mouthed, her coffee forgotten. 'But what have I done?'

He smiled amicably. 'I told you, don't take it the wrong way. I want you somewhere safe, and I think this would be a perfect time to visit Newcastle.'

Carol set the cup down and frowned. 'Somewhere safe, why?'

Fraser leaned forward, taking her into his confidence. 'Because I think NDSO is about to be attacked and I don't want you in the firing line.' He held up a hand to her pained expression. 'You're too valuable to me, Carol, indispensable. I can't really afford to be without you, and I'm certainly not going to be responsible for your death.'

She looked at him, astonishment in her eyes. 'So it's alright for the 'deniables' to be in danger, but not me. I signed up for this remember, the same as all the other girls and boys. Like Jessica Stewart, and Sarah. What's the difference?' Her eyes glinted with anger.

Now he was on the defensive. 'No, Carol, not like the others. You signed up as my PA, not front line.' He shook his head. 'I'll not knowingly put you at risk.'

Her eyes blazed. 'And if I refuse?'

Fraser sat back in confusion. He hadn't bargained on such a vehement refusal, thinking she might well enjoy the break. He tried a different tack.

'Well I can't force you to go, but you ought to know we've probably lost Geoff Allenby.'

'Probably?'

'No contact since 22.00hrs yesterday.'

Carol looked away, down at the carpet. 'Was he off the radar?'

'No,' Fraser said, 'just the opposite, in regular contact.'

She regained her composure and gave him an old fashioned sideways glance. 'It makes no difference, I'm not going.'

Exasperated, Fraser sighed and reached for his coffee. It was well within his power to insist, put her on a spot of 'gardening leave' but heavy handedness seldom achieved a good outcome. She'd only bear a grudge and that wouldn't bode well for the future. He need her willing co-operation and if it wasn't to be, then maybe he should let it drop.

He gave it one last try. 'Please,' he begged. 'Pretty please?'

She smiled and shook her head, firmly. 'Not even for a pretty please, you're stuck with me.'

'So be it, but don't say I didn't give you fair warning,' and he left it at that.

At the house in Ross-on-Wye, Markoff instructed Anatoly Pushkin to load the van. They opened the garage and backed the vehicle up to touch the raised door, and between the three of them, gently lifted 'Lightning' into the back and replaced the dust sheet. Helena oversaw the loading of the haversacks, checked the payload and then returned to the house for her own specialised piece of equipment. She climbed the stairs to the bedroom and crossed the room to the shabby dressing table. Two items waited for her attention. The pistol she checked and tucked under her loose top at the small of her back. Then she deliberately picked up her black bracelet and carefully snapped it round her left wrist. Raising it in front of her eyes she gave the surface a rigorous inspection and smiled. The embedded Graphene trace glinted as she angled the bracelet to the light, the delicate silver chain an adornment added solely to prevent the Customs security scanners from identifying the encapsulated carbon print.

Helena lowered her arm and shook the bracelet into place, secretly marvelling at the scientific ingenuity behind this advanced design. In the field of microelectronics, with the backing of military muscle, Russian research and innovation was on a par with the best of the Western developers.

Mike Bowman powered the Defender along the final stretch of road, slammed on the brakes, cogged down into second and swerved to a dusty halt outside the gatehouse.

Jim's craggy face appeared at the window. 'In a hurry are we, sir?' he asked dryly.

Bowman grinned at the understated query. 'Is the sensor field on or off, Jim?'

'Off at the moment. Security are on maintenance. The Old Man seems concerned.'

Bowman indicated Sarah in the passenger seat. 'We're taking a look round the grounds, might be an hour or so. We'll let you know when we're done.'

'I'll tell them. Wouldn't want 'em getting too excited, might start shooting.' A broad grin settled on his face, obviously amused by the thought, and hit the button to open the iron gates.

Bowman drove in and turned hard left across the grass, following the line of the fence. After two-hundred metres he stopped and climbed out.

'Coming?' he asked, and began walking.

Sarah hopped out and caught up. 'What are we really looking for?'

'Hard to say, something the security people have missed, I honestly don't know.' He gestured at the ground around them. 'It's alright having all these acoustic sensors below our feet, and the infra-red stuff and the cameras, but technology is only an advantage until someone comes up with something more sophisticated.'

He came to a halt, searching outside the chain link fencing. 'There's an old saying, 'boots on the ground', in our case I'll make that 'human eyes and ears'. He turned to face her. 'I'm trying to look at this from an enemy standpoint, a bit of lateral thinking.'

Sarah held his gaze, and he watched as a faint smile crept across her mouth. 'Us women are good at that, have to be in a man's world.'

He accepted the implied criticism without dissent and turned away, shielding his eyes against the sun's glare. Salerton Hall itself, detached from the surrounding countryside by acres of flat grassland, sat prominently against a distant northern backdrop of low hills. To the west a small hamlet of nine secluded family homes ran in a scattered line parallel with the perimeter fence. To the east, farmland, as far as the eye could see, and behind Bowman the southern boundary with the road, dominated by the old gatehouse. He walked a little further, towards the Hall. There had to be a weak link somewhere, it was just a matter of finding it.

A pair of 20x60 Russian made binoculars slowly traversed the grounds of Salerton Hall. The man holding the powerful glasses stood in plain view on a piece of rising ground, a mile north of NDSO's outer margin. For anyone looking out from the old mansion, he was but a speck in the landscape, and to the casual observer, just one more rambler taking the public footpath through a field of grazing cattle.

He focused on a Land Rover Defender crawling along inside the fence, and on the vehicle's two occupants who every now and then stopped to stand and look around. Lowering the binoculars to hang from the strap he ambled on up the hillside. In less than thirty paces he came to a standstill and scanned the countryside in the opposite direction. And very casually, the man turned through 360°, careful to avoid dwelling on any one direction.

He saw enough to know the Land Rover had moved and stopped again while the man and woman inspected their immediate surroundings. He also caught a movement on the roof of the Hall. An officer with an assault rifle patrolled the castellated façade.

The man peeled the strap from round his neck and slipped the binoculars inside the his backpack. Now it was time to prepare for the rendezvous with Markoff.

This last period of surveillance had been a struggle but he'd achieved all that had been asked of him. He'd discovered the British agent and found where the man lived. The reported electronic defences around Salerton Hall had been exposed, and during that same period, he'd bugged the Atkinson's house while keeping them under observation.

He was certain Markoff would be pleased.

Bowman moved steadily towards the Hall, stopping occasionally to look back at the perimeter fence, studying the ground beyond. He felt an odd sensation of being watched, and not by friendly eyes. Signalling Sarah to fetch the Land Rover, he turned and strode due north, parallel with the west side of the building. Sarah slowed the Defender alongside and he jumped in.

'Take us over there, Angel,' he said, pointing towards a few roof tops, half hidden beyond a wall of trees.

She swung left and headed for the fence almost half a mile distant.

A hundred yards inside the perimeter he said, 'This'll do,' and they rolled to a stop. Bowman sat looking through the windscreen eyes fixed on the nearest house, a tall contemporary build of recent times. Clearly visible were an upstairs set of French doors that opened onto a wide balcony, and what appeared to be a bathroom window on the right. He swivelled in his seat and peered through the back of the Defender at Salerton Hall, at the west face containing the Library.

Sarah turned and also stared at the Hall. 'What?'

It came as an irritable demand and Bowman replied without taking his eyes from the building. 'Not sure, a bit odd that's all. Direct line of sight.'

'So's the church steeple to the north,' she said.

Bowman swung round in the seat, took another look at the balcony. 'You know who's house that is?'

'No, should I?'

'Hugh Atkinson's family.'

Sarah shrugged. 'Not a problem then.'

He wondered why he felt uneasy, couldn't shake it. 'No . . . I guess not,' he finally agreed. 'Lets move on.'

Sarah engaged first gear and they drove slowly along the boundary, north until a sweeping curve took them east below the rising ground of low lying hills. The church steeple sat high on their left, silhouetted against the clear blue sky.

'Hold up,' Bowman said, and took time out to properly inspect this part of the estate. This area overlooked the north wing of Salerton Hall, a row of poplars standing tall this side of the building, a slight lean from the prevailing winds. Open fields led out to the rolling hills, a well scattered herd of black and white Friesian dairy cattle grazing on the lush grass. In general, an uninterrupted view and reluctantly, Bowman nodded.

'Okay, let's do the rest.'

20
Friday

Without fail, on the third Friday of every month, the senior personnel of the National Directorate for Special Operations gathered at an evening meeting in the Library of Salerton Hall. Prior to the event, Carol Hearsden dressed the conference table with notebooks and ball-point pens, coffee cups and iced water. At the rear corner of the room a drinks cabinet held bottles of Vintage Reserve Port and a Hennessy Cognac in readiness for the after meeting drinks. With the press of a button, the master display monitor for video conferencing slid out from behind a wooden panel, and in case they were needed, NDSO's encrypted laptops could be accessed from her office. She warned the kitchen to prepare freshly ground coffee and then checked on a plentiful supply of biscuits. Job done, she returned to her normal duties at the keyboard in her office. She located the Old Man's latest batch of paperwork and proceeded to type the next letter for Whitehall's approval.

Mike Bowman walked into Salerton Hall at twenty minutes past seven and strolled into the Grand Library with Sarah.

Carol heard them enter and popped her head in from the office. 'Should be starting at quarter to eight,' she volunteered, and began straightening the chairs at the table, looking critically along to see they were all in line.

Bowman smiled softly as she carried out her housekeeping duties, worrying over tiny imperfections. He ambled over to one of the tall windows, keen eyes flitting across the open ground, instinctively wary. Behind him Sarah joined in with aligning chairs. 'Anything I can help with, Carol?' she asked.

'No thank you, Pet. It's all under control.'

They nattered on, inconsequential stuff about family life; births, deaths and marriages as Bowman liked to think of it. He was more concerned with timing, who would arrive when. He wandered back to the entrance hall and out onto the gravel drive, moving right for a cigarette. A noise made him look over his shoulder and a close protection officer emerged from round the corner. Dressed in black fatigues, black helmet and bullet proof vest, he carried an MP5 semi-automatic machinegun fitted with a holographic sight.

Bowman nodded and received a discreet blink of the eyes in return. The officer walked past, boots crunching on gravel, and disappeared round the far side of the Hall.

Drawing contentedly on his cigarette, Bowman stood, feet braced apart, and waited.

At half seven the first of NDSO's senior officials began arriving. Angus 'Jock' Munroe's Jaguar sighed to a halt outside the entrance and the chauffeur let him out. He gave Bowman a curt nod as he passed, then stood aside for Sarah to exit. Sir Hillary Montague's Bentley took its turn and he walked inside without acknowledging Bowman's presence. Brian Gilmore arrived with Bernard 'Tubby' Palmer and they went straight in, engrossed in conversation.

Bowman felt Sarah nudge his elbow. 'Anyone else coming?'

'Only Hugh Atkinson, he usually shows up at the end.'

She yawned, stretched and sighed. 'I hope it's not too long winded.'

It was eight fifteen when Markoff drove the van into the lay-by. Half way into the journey he'd hurled the incriminating phone into a waterlogged ditch. At the side of the road a rabbit froze at the sound of the engine, and then darted for the undergrowth. Late evening shadows lengthened from the trees as Markoff switched off. The few cars travelling past took little notice of just another white van parked at the roadside. He glanced across the front seats at Helena, a pensive look on her face as she sat staring out through the windscreen. Pushkin in the middle seat, leaned forward with anticipation.

In the rear, two men sat with their knees up, hunched with their backs against the side of the vehicle. Each man carried a semi-automatic carbine, a pistol and a fighting knife. They had enough ammunition to hold off a small army.

Markoff looked at the time. 'Five minutes and we move. All ready?'

'We're ready,' said those in the rear.

Helena nodded lost in her own thoughts. Anatoly Pushkin uttered a string of obscenities, turned his head and gave Markoff a savage grin. 'More than ready.' He said, and wiped his mouth.

Minutes ticked by and Markoff started up. Easing onto the carriageway he turned left into a narrow lane and drove down beyond Atkinson's house on to a street lamp on the right, braking to a stop when the rear doors drew level with the drive. A bang on the side of the van and a grinning face snatched open the door. It was the man with binoculars and he slapped Markoff's knee.

'Alexander! You bastard, you took your time.'

Markoff grabbed his shoulder, exhilarated. 'We had some issues, but no matter. We're here now. What can you tell us, Vasily?' And he listened while Vasily of the binoculars revealed his secrets, of all that he'd seen and heard. Finally he pointed to Atkinson's house. 'The wife is alone downstairs, the children in bed. She will not be a problem.'

'You've done well, my friend. And what of my other target?'

Vasily unfolded a map and pointed to a small cottage by the River Wye. 'There,' he said, 'in the middle of open ground, but at night, no problem.'

Helena interrupted. 'What other target?' she demanded.

Markoff waved a dismissive hand. 'Nothing that involves you, woman. A little side show for our amusement.'

Pushkin nodded. 'You concentrate on your game, leave men's work to the men.' He laughed at his own wisdom.

Markoff decided it was time. 'We go now. . . , Helena?'

She gave a slight nod and climbed out, and Pushkin shuffled across and followed. The two men inside removed the dustsheet from 'Lightning' and remained hidden.

Markoff led them up the short drive and stood aside for Helena to ring the bell. Pushkin moved left out of sight and

Vasily melted into the shrubbery. The door opened a fraction and the pretty face of a blonde haired young woman appeared.

'Yes?' she asked, head tilted in curiosity.

Markoff made his move. He whipped across and slammed the door inwards. The woman staggered in shocked surprise, a violent intrusion. She opened her mouth as if to scream and Markoff clamped a big hand across her lips.

'No,' he snapped, 'no shouting.' He grabbed a wrist and twisted her arm backwards, shoulder blade high. She whimpered in pain, fear in her wide eyes.

'You will not be harmed if you do as I say.'

Pushkin pushed his way in giving her a menacing glare and Markoff felt her wilt under his grip. He leaned to her ear. 'Will you be still?'

She nodded against the pressure of his hand and he slowly relaxed his grip. Red imprints from his fingers showed on her face and her eyes glistened with tears.

Helena raised a finger. 'Quiet,' she warned. 'the children.'

The woman nodded obediently and sobbed in silence.

Markoff lost patience and pushed her away. 'Bind her,' he ordered, 'and make sure she stays silent.' He turned and followed Pushkin, who headed upstairs. They found the master bedroom and walked through to the balcony.

Pushkin pointed. 'There it is.'

Markoff grunted, surprised by the distance, how far it was in reality, as opposed to the photographs he'd studied. He dropped his gaze to study the balcony, wondering if it would suit their purpose.

Pushkin must have seen his doubts. 'Worry not, Alexander, this will be fine.' He rubbed his hands together, relishing his opportunity.

'Mummy . . . , Mummy?' It was a child's plaintive cry and Markoff crept across the room to check the landing. Helena appeared on the stairs dragging her captive with her.

A young girl stepped from a bedroom rubbing sleep filled eyes, saw Markoff and screamed. He leapt forward and muffled her noise, but she wriggled frantically and then bit his hand. He cursed and slapped her face, the force of it sent her sprawling.

Her mother moaned through the tea towel gag, fighting to go to her aid.

A boy came out from another door and Pushkin seized him, wrenching his arms behind his back, elbows touching.

Markoff hoisted the girl roughly to her feet and threatened her with a finger waved under her nose. 'Silence. No more shouting.'

She looked to her mother who managed to shake her head, her brother did the same. Her bottom lip trembled.

'Helena, tell them to bring your weapon, and get Vasily to tie them up and guard them.' He pulled out his fighting knife and scowled at the mother. 'If they do not behave I will cut your face. Do you understand me?'

A petrified frown creased her forehead and she nodded vigorously.

Helena went in search of Vasily and for a minute or so there was silence on the landing. When Vasily joined them he came armed with cable ties from the van and quickly set about securing their wrists.

Markoff nodded his approval and glanced into their bedrooms. The girl's bed had a headboard made of iron scrollwork. 'Tie the kids to her bed, I will see if the woman has a phone.'

Vasily hauled the children into the bedroom and Markoff stepped towards the mother.

'Hold her,' he said to Pushkin.

Pushkin grabbed her from behind and Markoff closed in holding the knife in his left hand. She turned her face, avoiding the sharp point. He ran his hand over her tight jeans, patting the pockets, and needlessly felt between her legs and then up under her loose top. He squeezed each breast in turn, his hand lingering round the lace of her bra. Slowly, he let his fingers slide down her belly to the waistband of her jeans. She turned fearful eyes to his, and he sniggered.

The front door banged open and Helena edged her way inside with the two men carrying the weapon. Markoff whispered. 'Another time, woman,' and stepped back.

Vasily reappeared and Pushkin released the mother into his safekeeping. Markoff stood watching the men ascend the stairs, allowing Pushkin to guide them through to the balcony.

'They won't go far now,' Vasily said, and Markoff peered into the girl's bedroom. The boy and girl had been secured on opposite sides of the bed head, kneeling on the carpet, the girl crying quietly. Their mother lay with her arms spread-eagled and tied high on the ironwork. The cable ties looked to be painfully tight.

He slapped Vasily on the shoulder. 'Come, my friend, let us join the others.'

A final glance at the family and they walked into the master bedroom. Operation Lightning was about to be mobilized.

Hugh Atkinson busied himself with fine tuning his presentation. It would be shown to the conference at 9pm following reports from outlying operations. He was due to attend the meeting fifteen minutes beforehand in time to sync the main monitor with his laptop. Skimming effortlessly through files and folders he edited the sequence one last time and performed a random check on the list of images.

In accordance with the Old Man's wishes, he'd also refined the evidence linking Webster with Bullseye. That information would be presented as a stand alone section at the conclusion of all other business.

The phone rang. It was Carol. 'Ten minutes, Hugh.'

'Thank you,' he replied automatically, eyes on the screen, reading the final paragraph. He put the phone down and logged out of the programme. It would have to do. To his personal annoyance he'd not managed to link Webster's six digit number with anything. And thus far, all attempts to extract an answer from Webster himself had proved worthless.

Standing up from the workstation, he stretched and wandered over to the window that looked over the grounds to his home. The roof and bedroom window were just visible above the garden trees. He imagined the kids in bed and Miranda curled up peacefully in her kitchen chair. Friday evenings were usually quite special in the Atkinson household, and even when he had to work late, she still conjured up something special for their meal. He glanced at the time and sighed. Better get ready.

He unplugged the laptop and slid it inside his case. Spare mouse and keyboard and the Flash Drive if needed. At the door he glanced back to check he had everything and then made for the staircase.

Atkinson knocked on Carol's door and heard her call. He slipped in and grinned sheepishly. 'Not late am I?'

'No, Pet, it's eight forty-five.'

He smiled his thanks and took a step past her desk and paused, a chill running down his spine. 'Say that again, Carol.'

'Say what . . . , eight forty-five?'

Atkinson breathed in, teeth bared, and repeated her words. 'Eight forty-five,' he said. 'Eight . . four . . five.' He stared at Carol, not seeing her, and changed the words. 'Nine . . four . . five.' He emphasised each digit. 'The numbers in Webster's code, nine forty-five, a time of day.' He swore under his breath. 'A time, and I never spotted it.'

But where? And morning or night? What day? A myriad questions and no quick answers. His eyes were drawn to the library, a conference room full of NDSO's top brass. Nine forty-five, it might mean tonight, in less than an hour.

Carol frowned and he focused on her concern.

'I think,' he said softly, 'we might be in a spot of bother.' He knew it might sound far fetched, might make a fool of himself. He looked for reassurance. 'I have to warn them don't I, even if I'm wrong?'

She stood and laid a comforting hand on his arm. 'Yes Pet, get in there and tell them, they need to know.'

Atkinson swallowed and pushed his glasses up on his nose. He shrugged and put down the laptop. 'Ah well, into the lion's den.'

He turned and opened the interconnecting door, stepped over the threshold and walked uncertainly towards the Old Man.

Sir Hillary Montague was in mid-flow, rattling on about some situation in South America. As Atkinson approached,

Montague's voice diminished in volume and finally stopped half way through a sentence.

Fraser looked up, shrewd eyes narrowed in query. Atkinson hesitated, doubtful.

'Yes, Hugh?'

'Sorry to interrupt but I think we're in danger.'

The Old Man raised a cynical eyebrow and looked round the table with a smile. 'You might have to expand on that theory,' he said, and chuckled.

Atkinson absorbed the criticism but stuck to his guns. 'Those numbers in Webster's Flash Drive, I'm sure I've found an answer.'

Fraser pushed himself upright with the arms of his chair 'Go on.'

'Well sir, if you take away the noughts you're left with three numerals, nine, four and five. Put those numbers together in a different way and say it out loud and it becomes a time of day. Nine forty-five, sir.'

Jock Monroe scribbled on his notepad and nodded. 'True,' he agreed, 'and?'

Atkinson singled him out, made eye contact. 'Third Friday of every month we have this meeting, regular as clockwork. We insist on other departments varying their schedules and yet when it comes to it, we don't take our own advice. So here we are again, third Friday in the month, and what happens at quarter to ten?' He waited for an answer.

Tubby Palmer intervened. 'We make our closing submissions and start 'happy hour'.

'Exactly,' Atkinson said, confident of his theory. He glanced back at the Old Man. 'Respectfully, sir, everyone gets together over at that window with the drinks trolley, and *you* insist on playing the barman. By the time you've poured all the drinks you might be stood there ten or fifteen minutes. More than enough time for who knows what to happen.' He looked at each member of the meeting in turn, challenging them to dismiss his logic.

Brian Gilmore got to his feet and walked to the window. In the gathering darkness of a sun below the horizon he peered

217

through the glass and nodded. 'We are a bit vulnerable, yes,' he said at length. 'But there's nothing out there except fields. Should we cancel the rest of this conference?'

The Old Man rubbed his jaw. 'Sit down, Brian, you're making the place look untidy.' He raised his head and Atkinson saw the twinkle in his eye. 'Relax Hugh, it's a good supposition. Assuming you're right, we'd be foolish not to take precautions.' He thought for a minute, pursing his lips.

'Do what you can to secure your equipment upstairs and take the IBM offline, shut it down. Warn GCHQ, otherwise they'll wonder what's up.'

'Yes, sir,' Atkinson said. 'Will you want my presentation?'

'Anything new to add?'

Atkinson couldn't help his smile. 'Not now, sir.'

The Old Man smiled in return, appreciating the irony. 'In that case, go. Let me know when you're done.'

Atkinson turned away relieved to have had his theory accepted, a lightness to his stride.

'Hugh?' It was the Old Man.

He paused and glanced back.

'Good job.'

Atkinson inclined his head, pleased with the compliment, and walked into Carol's office.

'Well?' she asked.

He reached down for the laptop. 'I didn't make a fool of myself,' he said, grinning broadly. 'And if I were you, I'd back up anything important. There might be trouble.' He left her open mouthed and bolted upstairs.

21
Firebolt

Alexander Markoff heard Helena dismiss the others, and as he reached the balcony, saw her kneel beside Pushkin's toy.

'Turn all the lights off,' he ordered and one by one the ceiling lights in the landing, kitchen and living room went out.

'So, how does this thing work?' he asked, curiosity overriding his reticence.

She glared at him in the dim light. 'You really want to know, or do you mock me?'

He thought it was time to show some respect. 'I am serious, Helena. Tell me.'

She looked at him a moment longer, doubt in her eyes, and then turned to the weapon. Pointing to the sloping square tube braced at 45°from a small base plate she said, 'This is the launcher, designed to give instant ground to air clearance from a stable platform. Inside is Lightning, an Unmanned Aerial Acquisition Module, and capable of phenomenal acceleration.'

Markoff watched as she caressed the tube.

'It is very clever, Alexander. The power comes from lightweight cells specifically designed for this machine. The speed comes from a Graphene Accelerated Impeller, like a miniature jet engine located inside the body. Swing wings deploy when airborne and they combine to produce a paragliding capability.'

'Graphene?' he asked, having never heard the name.

She smiled a secretive smile. 'It derives from carbon, like the graphite in a pencil, only much more refined. Nanotechnology, an atom in thickness. It allows electrical conductivity to flow a hundred and fifty times faster than silicon based copper.'

He shrugged, but smiled in response. Most of that was beyond his comprehension.

'And the explosive?'

'It carries your kilogramme of plastic explosive with a reliable contact detonator.'

Markoff noticed her removing the black bracelet from her wrist and with a deft flick, part the oval into two halves. She disconnected a silver chain and slipped it in her pocket.

Helena stood, holding one semicircular piece in either hand. 'These are Graphene Enhanced Polymer Platforms. One of them slots into Lightning's nose and the other half into my voice activated Electronic Display Controller.'

'How do you guide it?

She pointed to the weapon's nose. 'That is a wide angle, gyro-stabilised camera for flight control. And this one,' she said, pointing beneath the forward section, 'is a multi-spectral targeting system.' She unclipped a soft bag from the base plate and pulled out a head harness and boom throat microphone. A palm sized display monitor came next and she attached her half of the bracelet to the curved receptacle on top, and then pressed a tiny button.

Markoff watched the screen shimmer into life.

Vasily had his binoculars levelled on the Library, elbows resting on the balcony's balustrade. 'There is movement, I see a man standing by the window.'

'Pouring drinks?' Helena asked.

Markoff squinted at the distant lights, but the range was too great for the naked eye.

Vasily spoke, an edge to his voice. 'I think he makes drinks, yes.'

'And are the others there yet?' she demanded.

Markoff waited for him to answer and glanced at the time, seventeen minutes to nine; they were slipping behind schedule.

'I see more hands. No . . . wait, they gather now.'

Helena adjusted the throat mike and lifted the Electronic Controller. She reached forward, hand hovering above the base plate's launch control.

Markoff gritted his teeth, willing her to fire.

Her finger twitched, followed by a muffled blast. The weapon catapulted into the night sky and was gone.

His eyes reverted to Helena's face, a grey-green phosphorescent glow lighting her pupils. The voice commands came rapidly.

'Up . . . level . . . go right . . . centre . . . glide . . , steady.' She paused, peering closely at the screen.

'Target acquisition . . . left . . . steady . . , paint target.' A hesitation. 'Target acquired.'

Vasily uttered a warning. 'They're moving away!'

Markoff saw her blink, squinting intently at the screen. He held his breath, anticipating the moment.

'Execute.' A single word command.

The Unmanned Module simultaneously switched from a stabilised auto-robotic glider and transferred maximum energy to the Graphene Accelerator. The brushless impeller sucked greedily at an unrestricted flow of electromagnetic current. It rapidly rotated to a spin greater than any conventional rotor. Instantly converting internal suction into a whirlwind of external thrust, Lightning powered itself across the intervening space.

The pressure activated primer slammed into the window and a kilogram of high explosive erupted. An instantaneous fireball swept through the Library. Outside, an armed officer somersaulted across the lawn. A glass shard severed his right leg. Lethal fragments impacted his face, sliced a neck artery. Blood pumped and he died before coming to rest.

Inside the Library, chairs turned to matchwood, the conference table obliterated. Heavy curtains burst into flame, thick smoke choked the air. The lights shattered, only the flames to see by.

Brian Gilmore misjudged his escape and took the full force of the explosion. He was hurled bodily across the room and flung against the far wall. His lifeless remains crumpled to the floor, battered beyond recognition.

In the gatehouse, Jim recovered from his initial shock and activated an emergency call that automatically linked to the SAS, fire service, ambulance and police. A secondary call went out to the Army Bomb Squad.

Mike Bowman lay face down near the main doors, right arm shielding Sarah's head. He struggled with his breathing, lungs crushed by the power of the blast. She moved beneath his outstretched arm and he raised his head to look around. Emergency lighting kicked in, a pale blue glimmer. Smoke curled slowly, coiling uneasily along the devastated bookshelves. Sarah groaned and he came to his knees.

'Angel?'

She groaned again, followed it with his name. 'Mike?'

'It's alright,' he said. 'Let me see you.' He helped her turn over. The beautiful smoke blackened face gazed at him, bewildered, and he smiled gently. 'You hurt?'

'Don't think so,' she said, and pushed herself into a sitting position.

Bowman squinted through thick smoke. The idea to pretend 'happy hour' was proceeding as normal had not quite gone according to plan. They'd left it too long before seeking shelter. But who knew it would be a bomb? Where was the Old Man? Were they alive? He needed to get them out, might be another attack. Struggling to his feet, he reached for her hand and pulled her upright. They coughed in unison, acrid smoke biting their lungs. Flames crackled as the curtains suddenly flared, books catching fire. The stench of smouldering wood caught him, stinging his eyes, watering with tears.

A pair of legs stuck out from underneath the partially collapsed conference table and Bowman stepped over a mass of debris and bent to peer beneath. It was Winslow Palmer, and his left arm was strangely bent at the elbow, his jacket charred and smouldering. A residue of pale white dust smothered the black skin of his face. But he was alive, eyes open and screwed up in pain. There didn't appear to be any blood.

'Hold on,' Bowman said, 'we'll get you out.' The main door crashed open and he reached for his gun, crouching in readiness. Two of the armed patrol burst in, weapons up, moving sideways at speed.

Bowman called out. 'We've got injuries in here, need help.' He turned, wanting to find the Old Man. Aided by the draught from the shattered windows, the bank of smoke rolled towards the open door, and two inert forms appeared, huddled together at the base of the bookshelves. He lunged over and recognised Fraser's charcoal grey suit under a layer of fine dust, his face turned to the wall.

Kneeling to the side Bowman touched the Old Man's shoulder. When there was no response he shook him and raised his voice.

'Commander Fraser, sir?'

The Old Man coughed and Bowman felt the spasm under his hand. 'Sir?' he queried again, louder. The iron-grey head of wiry hair lifted and slumped, lifted once more and turned, dropped to the floor.

Bowman bent lower meeting his eyes. 'Where are you hurt?'

Fraser managed a feeble grunt. 'In the guts,' he whispered faintly.

Bowman glanced down and could see blood oozing out onto the floorboards. He looked round found Sarah swaying on her feet. 'Help me, Angel.'

He pointed at the blood and gestured to turn Fraser on his back. She knelt with him and they gingerly rolled the Old Man over. He gasped in agony, clenching his teeth, and Bowman cradled his head to the floor. Not a pretty sight and Sarah turned her head away.

A ragged splinter of wood had embedded itself into Fraser's left abdomen and his shirt was a bloodied mess. Bowman teased away some of the material, peeled back his jacket and allowed himself a small smile. The splinter had sliced in at shallow angle and broken out of the side wall. No deep penetration. A lot of blood, but no serious damage.

He told Fraser who blinked and attempted a grin. 'I'll live then?'

'Yes, sir. Stretcher case, and nil by mouth for a week.' He softened the statement with a terse grin.

The Old Man forced his head up. 'What about Montague?' he asked, eyes straying to the other man next to him.

Sarah leaned across and shook him roughly. A quiet moan escaped his lips and his eyes flickered open. He squirmed up onto one elbow and shook his head, staring at the carnage. 'My God,' he said slowly. 'Where did that come from?'

Bowman got to his feet. Two missing, Monroe and Gilmore. He picked his way toward the blazing curtains, searching the room, and spotted the mangled body of Brian Gilmore. He knew instantly that he'd perished, no one survived that much damage.

He crunched across broken glass, pistol raised. A molten mess of burnt curtains slithered to the floor and he felt the heat. Peering out into the darkness his gaze landed on a shapeless figure sprawled on the grass, and Bowman caught the vague outline of body armour. The heat from the flames proved too much and he backed off.

A scratching sound made him glance left. Below the shelves, books and chairs lay piled haphazardly in a smouldering heap. An inverted chair-back moved, slid sideways, and a charred hand pushed at the pile of books. Bowman edged forward, cautious, pistol outstretched. He kicked the chair, sent it skidding. Gun aimed, he scraped books with his foot. A filthy white shirt and blue tie appeared with part of a jacket and he remembered   Jock Monroe had been dressed in something similar. Bowman tucked away the gun and stooped to clear more rubbish.

A head of hair and eyes surfaced, and Bowman paused. Even he was unprepared for what met his eyes. Monroe's face had been lacerated to a bloody pulp, eyebrows singed, teeth red, gaps. A garbled nonsense came from his mouth as he tried to speak.

Bowman hid his revulsion. 'Easy,' he said, 'don't try to talk.' He brushed ash from Monroe's hair, picked out pieces of glass, and then removed some heavier books from on top of his thighs. 'Lie still,' he said, and looked for someone to take over. An armed officer walked up and Bowman gestured to Monroe.

The officer took one look and nodded. 'I've got him,' he said, and knelt to help.

Free of responsibility, Bowman made for the double doors. A fire extinguisher foamed as someone dealt with the flames and he caught sight of Sarah coughing.

He grabbed her by the arm. 'Come on, fresh air.'

Striding through the Library doors he forced her through the foyer and out beyond the entrance porch. Night had become day under a phalanx of security lights, bathing their immediate surroundings in dazzling brightness. Cool night air filled their lungs and they both took a breather. Sarah stopped coughing.

A Land Rover came careering towards them from the gatehouse, headlights swaying over the gravel drive. It skidded to a halt and Jim jumped out from the driver's seat. Four heavily armed officers joined him.

'Mike,' Jim called, 'there was nothing on the acoustic sensors. Must have been a mortar, or a missile fired from outside the fence.'

Bowman nodded searching the brightly lit grounds. Accurate, he thought, almost like a guided missile. But if so, from where? And under these arc lamps he felt highly vulnerable. 'Can we kill the lights?'

Jim spoke into his radio and a moment later the lights fizzled out.

It took longer for night vision to reassert itself and Bowman walked away onto the grass and round to the west side of the Hall. He drew level with the dead officer in body armour and swept his gaze out to the perimeter fence. Lights were on in the few upmarket houses beyond. He aligned himself with the Library window and looked again at the houses. There was something odd, and he squinted in concentration, fighting to understand what his eyes told him.

And then it came. The Atkinson's house lay in total darkness. Not a light anywhere. The sound of the explosion would surely have carried that distance, natural curiosity should come to the fore, kids waking up. Miranda would certainly have gone to her balcony for a look. He stared for a good thirty seconds; was there some sort of shadowy movement on that balcony? Come to that, where was Hugh, still in his office or caught in the blast?

Sarah came over, avoiding the dead officer. 'What gives?'

'Wondering why the Atkinson house is in pitch darkness. Have you seen Hugh?'

'No, he went upstairs.'

Bowman rubbed his eyes. There'd been no follow up to the explosion, no squad of gunmen closing in for the kill. Jim could be right; maybe from outside the boundary, and the Atkinson house might be just the place. He reminded himself that the balcony had a direct line of sight.

'The Land Rover, come on!' They sprinted for the vehicle.

Bowman slammed the door of the Defender, hit the starter and put peddle to the metal. Slewing round in a flurry of spinning wheels he flicked on main beam and powered across the manicured lawns. The Land Rover bounced wildly over a concrete kerb and he yanked the wheel to accelerate up the gravel drive. In minutes they made the iron gates and Jim's colleague activated the electrics.

He tore out onto the road, wrenched the wheel to the right, and almost lost control tilted on two wheels. He glanced at Sarah; grim faced and silent. He rammed the stick into top gear and swept headlong into the night. A mile on and he took a right hand curve, fighting the wheel to retain traction. It left him with a straight run for Atkinson's lane and he gripped the steering, willing them on.

He braked at the last possible moment, tyres squealing, and swung violently down the lane. He switched off the lights. It had been three years since he'd visited the family and in the darkness he slowed to get his bearings. A white van had parked on the right and instinctively he knew it was involved. Beyond the van a solitary street light helped illuminate the scene. Braking to a halt, he reached for his Sig and checked the magazine. Beside him Sarah did the same, made sure of the silencer then looked over in the semi-darkness, and he gave her a confident nod.

'I'll go for the door, you cover me. Stay sharp, I don't know what we'll find but that van doesn't fit. You okay?'

'I'm good,' she said, and he detected an edge to her reply.

He reached out and touched her cheek. 'Stay loose, Angel,' he said, and opened the door. They slipped out and moved forward, ghostlike in the gloom.

Helena Goreya found herself trembling with adrenaline. Her mission had been achieved, the technology proved in action, and the explosion had come as a relief. Even Markoff, the great doubter, reluctantly nodded his approval and congratulated her on the outcome.

She asked Vasily for the binoculars, to see for herself the end result of the explosion. It was almost an anticlimax. The window no longer existed and from what she could see of the interior, the blast had wreaked havoc on the occupants. Thick smoke curled from the flickering flames, orange-red in the darkness. Arc lights cast a brilliant beam of incandescent light around the immediate vicinity of the walls, and were then suddenly extinguished. She panned down the length of the building, broken windows and the vague shadows of movement inside. Three or four armed men hovered near the entrance, and what appeared to be a man and woman wandered about outside the target window.

Lowering the binoculars she offered them to Markoff who shook his head.

'I've seen enough, time to get out.'

She saw Pushkin standing the other side of Vasily, a broad smile etched on his face. He had earned his laurels. 'Thank you, Anatoly. It was a good job.'

He bobbed his head, basking in the accolade, then turned to Markoff, head tilted in query.

Markoff nodded. 'As soon as we can,' he said, and Helena recognised their impatience to move on.

'We must clear away the rest of this equipment,' she said, and bent to pick up the launcher and base plate. Vasily and Pushkin joined her, but Markoff went inside to the landing and she frowned. He seemed to be distracted. At the same time, it was not her place to interfere.

She shook her head and returned to gathering the evidence. They must leave no trace of the technology.

Markoff stood by the door to the young girl's bedroom. A faint glow from a child's night-light reflected off the walls, outlining the mother's shape on the bed. The thought crossed his mind she might be useful as a hostage. He entered the room and moved to the bedside. Above the gag her wide eyes stared, fear and loathing in equal measure. His main problem would be the woman's ability to identify her intruders. It might be better to kill them all, no witnesses. Glancing at the kids he toyed with the idea of using his gun, make it quick. As for the mother, and he narrowed his eyes with a malicious grin, the knife would be more fun.

Bowman heard a man speaking, and he knew enough to recognise a Russian dialect. A woman's voice answered, full of authority. It certainly wasn't Miranda. He remembered the promise he'd made after losing Jessica, and swore blind he wouldn't allow it to happen to Sarah, not if he had anything to do with it. No more collateral damage on his watch. He turned to her and whispered: 'I'll give 'em one chance. If they don't play the game, shoot to kill. Don't do nice, Angel, they won't.'

Sarah commented. 'There's a woman.'

He grimaced. 'So are you, but they won't hesitate.'

Pistol raised he stepped closer to Atkinson's driveway. The voices came nearer and he flicked the safety to off. With a silencer attached the gun's balance tended to be nose heavy and he made an adjustment to his grip.

Footsteps, louder.

They appeared from behind the hedge, two shadows in the ambient light, hands full of equipment.

'Hey!' he called softly.

For an instant they froze, and then reacted. The man dropped everything, dived for the ground and rolled; the woman throwing what she carried at Bowman and running for the house. He fired twice, reflex action, and heard her cry out. She staggered and went down, crawling. He changed position, dropping into a crouch.

By his left shoulder Sarah's gun thumped, spitting bullets at the man. He grunted but then returned fire. Bowman felt the draught of a bullet. He took a calculated risk. The woman had gone down and Sarah might be vulnerable. At that moment

228

Sarah jinked to her left away from Bowman, and he fired two shots as a distraction.

Sarah bent at the knees, gun arm stretched forward as she took deliberate aim, and the pistol belched. Her hand jumped with recoil, recovered, and she fired again. The target lurched backwards and then slumped forwards onto his knees, chin on chest, and collapsed.

'Nice shot,' Bowman said, and switched his attention back to the woman, crawling desperately for the door. Her right leg trailed uselessly, unable to assist with her forward momentum. He ran to catch her, caught a glimpse of a gun and kicked it clear. She looked up into the muzzle of his Sig, eyes glinting; whether with pain or anger he had no way of knowing. He stooped and hauled her off the ground, and she stood wincing, hopping on one leg. She spat in his face. He wiped it with his forearm and grinned. He patted her down and found a lethal looking knife. Wary now, pistol held with intent, he bent and scooped up her gun, tucked it inside his belt.

'Sarah,' he called quietly. 'What gives?'

'Two hits, kneecap and chest. Might not survive the chest wound.'

Bowman dragged the woman bodily across to the van. 'Search her,' he said. 'We need the keys.'

Sarah went through the woman's clothing, without success. She bent to the man and after a moment came up smiling, dangling the keys in front of her face.

Bowman nodded in relief. 'Good, let's get 'em inside, tie 'em up.'

Sarah unlocked the back doors and Bowman forced the woman inside. He bound her with the reams of electric cable and lashed her to the ribs of the van walls. He and Sarah then lifted the groaning man into the back, propped him seated against the side, and repeated the tying operation. Lastly they gagged the pair of them, even though the man needed every lungful of air he could get.

Bowman leaned out from the back of the van and peered at the house. Still no lights, maybe more Russians inside. And then there were Miranda and the kids, with luck, unharmed. He jumped down with Sarah, locked the van, and together they made a cautious approach to the front door.

22
Duty Calls

Inside the house, Markoff sat on the foot of the bed, still pondering the future of the Atkinson family, enjoying his thoughts on how to inflict the most pain on the woman. In Russia, the Spetsnaz were trained in many things, the sophisticated art of torture being high on the list. He liked to think of himself as a leading advocate of the practice. The blade of his knife gleamed as he rubbed it gently on the bare skin of her ankle.

The small girl again began to cry, and he hissed threateningly for her to stay silent.

'Alex!' It was Pushkin, in hushed alarm.

'What?' he answered, angered by the disturbance, but reluctantly moving to the landing.

Pushkin crouched at the top of the stairs, his assault rifle aimed at the door below. 'I thought I heard something,' he explained.

Markoff frowned. Pushkin had enough experience not to be spooked easily. He would take into account Vasily and Helena outside and yet still sounded a warning.

'Where are the other two?'

His voice carried in the silence of the house. 'Kitchen,' came an answer from one of them.

'Lounge,' said the other.

Markoff bent over the landing railings and called down in hushed tones. 'Use the kitchen door and circle round the front, see what you can find.'

He heard their affirmatives and sank down on one knee. 'We wait,' he said to Pushkin, and wiped the sweat from the palm of his hand. The pistol grip seemed more secure.

Bowman held up a hand in warning and touched the door. Unlatched, it moved a fraction under his fingers. He felt perspiration standing out on his forehead and glanced at Sarah.

'Ready?' he mouthed.

Before she acknowledged her hand touched his shoulder, forewarning of danger, her head turning to look the other way,

Then Bowman heard a faint rustling from the far corner of the house. He backed off from the door, leaving space between them, and aimed head-high at the brickwork. He felt the rise and fall of his lungs and fought to control his breathing, hands steady.

The movement came, a fleeting impression of head and shoulders, and the gun bucked in his fist. A plume of brick dust flew from the bullet's strike and he cursed as the target ducked back. Hot fumes wafted across his face. He dodged left, widening the angle of attack, changing position from where he'd fired. Sarah advanced along the wall, staying tight to the brickwork, crouching past a window ledge. She stopped a few paces from the corner, gun at shoulder height.

Bowman refocused, waist high down the brickwork, the tension tightening his neck muscles. When it happened he was caught out by the speed. The target darted clear of the corner, bounding across the low bushes and fired on the run, a short burst from an assault rifle.

Bowman snapped off a couple of shots in reply and dived for the ground, hit and rolled. The target made it to the van and hid out of sight.

Sarah fired, a double tap, and a second man squealed in agony as he crashed headlong into the bushes. His sub-machinegun sprayed bullets haphazardly, then buried its muzzle in the soil, stopped. Sarah moved up and put a round in the man's temple, and he nodded. Better safe than sorry.

And taking his eyes off his own target almost cost him his life. A bullet fanned past his ear, too close, and he dived forward into the prone position. But now the man had left himself silhouetted against the glow of the street lamp and Bowman wasn't about to let that sort of opportunity slip.

Finger caressing the trigger he raised the Sig in line with the dark outline, aligned the foresight, and squeezed. At the front of the van the target jerked. He slipped from view and Bowman heard a weapon clatter onto the road. Rising to his feet he ran for the back of the van, stopped short and walked slowly round the front. The man lay on his back, and where once there'd been a nose and mouth, now only an open gash, sightless eyes staring up at the street light.

Bowman took a breath and picked up the gun. He frowned in surprise. It was a British variant of the Heckler & Koch MP5, chambered for a 9mm round. He looked down at the dead man.

He heard the muffled blast of a silenced gun and Sarah cried out with pain. He glanced up and spotted the open front door, the shape of a man withdrawing inside. Sarah made it round the end of the house clutching her arm to her side, head bent in pain.

Bowman shook his head in anguish. He'd sworn to keep her safe, and failed. Unclipping the MP5's magazine he searched the dead man for a spare, found two, and slapped on a fresh one. The same for the Sig.

Sarah looked to be suffering with the wound, but still on her feet, leaning back against the end wall. Her predicament worried him, how bad was the wound? Did she need a tourniquet? A forbidding stillness settled over house and garden, eerily quiet after the shootings.

Mike Bowman didn't do 'brave', it never entered his consciousness. Courage belonged to an exceptional few, a nebulous thing awarded to others. The heat of the moment demanded a prescribed course of action; either face up to the challenge or succumb to the paralysis of fear.

He steeled himself for the next move.

The front door to the house lay open, not fully, but far enough that a person inside might well be able to see out. A prickling sensation ran up his spine. Edging cautiously alongside the van, he brought the butt of the rifle into his shoulder and prepared to launch himself across the void. Sarah, hugged her pain, in need of his help. To hell with duty, he decided, this time he would lend a hand. Braced against the side of the van, he coiled himself for the effort, and lunged into danger. A bullet hissed past his eyes, and he flinched, feet pounding over the ground. He heard shells slash through the leaves to his left and he twisted to fire a burst at the doorway. The bullets cracked bricks into fragments and smashed at the door.

Leaping over the bushes, he lost his footing and landed hard on his left shoulder. He swore as the old wound stabbed pain through his neck, a few well chosen words to accompany the hurt.

Despite her own pain, Sarah giggled. 'Language!' she said.

Bowman staggered to his feet. 'Let me see that arm,' he insisted, and propped the rifle against the wall. She gingerly removed her supporting hand and pointed to her left forearm. Blood dripped from her fingers and Bowman pushed the sleeve of her jacket up the arm. She winced. He found the wound, a nasty laceration above her wrist, but it appeared not to have hit tendons or broken a bone.

'Can you move your fingers?'

She wiggled them, screwing up her face at the pain.

'Good,' he said with an enormous sense of relief. 'Just a scratch,' and grinned sideways at her indignant moan of disbelief.

Grabbing the rifle, he straightened, face close to hers. 'Can you defend this corner from the front?'

She looked at him in defiance. 'If I have to. Where are you going?'

'Round the back. I'm sure those two came out of the kitchen. Might give me the element of surprise.'

'Might get you very dead too,' she said, frowning.

'Nah,' he said, 'not me. Too old and too ugly, they wouldn't waste bullets.' He leaned a fraction closer, drinking in the liquid eyes, and quickly kissed her lips. Grinning at her surprise, he winked, and turned for the rear of the house. It was time to turn the tables.

Markoff called softly down the stairs. 'What's happening?'

'Not sure,' Pushkin said. 'At least two armed Britishers. I wounded one, a woman I think.'

'And Helena? What about the others?'

Pushkin answered with his head turned over his shoulder. 'No sign of Helena. The other two are down, one dead for sure. I can't see Vasily.'

'Where are the British now?' Markoff demanded, short tempered with uncertainty.

'The woman made it to the end of the house and a man joined her. I don't see them.'

Markoff thought rapidly. 'You go watch the back door, I'll cover the front. Go!' He waited at the top of the stairs and Pushkin walked under the landing and into the kitchen. He and Pushkin had the advantage of darkness and staring down at the front door, Markoff knew he had a perfect firing solution. Any one attempting an entry would be outlined against the light.

He heard a whimper from the girl's bedroom, reminding him of the hostages. The mother might yet prove to be useful. What did they call it in Syria? He struggled to bring it to the forefront of his mind, then remembered with a grim smile. Hostage fodder, because any hostages tended to be fodder for the guns, or send them down the road if it was mined. When the time came they could be very useful indeed.

Mike Bowman skirted round a rose bush and walked through a trellised pergola. The sweet scent of the roses followed as he knelt to study the French doors at the rear of the kitchen. One half had been left open, pitch black inside, and now, knowing what armament they carried, what waited for him? He could do with some kind of diversion. It gave him a moment of indecision, his choice of weapon. The Sig 9mm or an assault rifle? Close quarters combat . . . , he settled for the pistol, not so bulky.

For all his experience, he knew the odds were against him. His personal exposure to 'house clearance' as the lads used to call it, was negligible, just the once in live combat, and not at all since he'd joined the NDSO.

Heart in his mouth he took a step forward and stubbed his toe on something solid. A small clay flower pot wobbled precariously, giving him pause for thought. With a small glimmer of hope, he frowned and glanced at the open door. Grabbing the pot, Bowman eased to his right until he touched the wall and then crept towards the open door. For a moment he paused to listen, and then moved.

He took a quick pace to his left and lobbed the pot through the door. It crashed onto a worktop. Bowman dived into the kitchen, hit the floor and rolled right. The muffled thump of an automatic stammered, bullets ricocheting off the wall, a suppressed flash of gunfire. It was enough to locate the target and Bowman triggered the gun. The Sig jumped in his hand, a jolt through his wrist. He squeezed off three more rounds for good measure. In an acrid smell of lingering gunsmoke he rose to one knee, and held his breath in the silence.

'Pushkin?' A subdued call from elsewhere. 'Pushkin?' Impatient.

Bowman came to his feet, bent double, and took a step forward. As his eyes grew accustomed to the darkness he found the quiet glow of the cooker's green display helping to illuminate the room. By the inner door a dark lump lay on the floor, no movement. He moved left, to the work surface, slid along the front until the hall and the front door came into view. The door hung open, light from the distant street lamp penetrating the gloom. No sign of any targets, and the voice had sounded as if it were upstairs. And the stairs had danger written all over them. He remembered a landing surrounded by bedroom doors, all potential hiding places.

Listening carefully, he wondered about Miranda and the kids. Where were they?

Standing alone at the corner of the house, Sarah weighed the gun in her hand and glanced along the front wall. From where she stood the front door was obscured from view. She wondered what Mike was up to, and although she understood his determination to go solo, felt somewhat disconcerted by being abandoned to hold the fort. He faced danger while leaving her to feel isolated and useless.

The pain in her forearm had eased off to a burning ache, an odd sensation of weakness. She flexed the hand, opening and closing her fingers. The initial blood flow had diminished, congealing into a sticky mess, and she decided it had become a case of mind over matter, ignore the pain. She again looked along the front wall, there must be a way to help. The least she could do was to see if that door was open. And the safest way to do that would be from a distance, use the Ford Focus as cover. If nothing else, she could surely force the gunmen to split their firepower.

Mind made up, Sarah moved into the open, crouching forward in a diagonal run for the car. She made it across and went to ground. Bending low, she bent to peer under the right rear wheel arch. The splintered door stood ajar, darkly hostile. That's where she'd been shot from, so whoever hid inside knew their business, no amateur. Pondering her options, she cursed under her breath. Whatever she chose, she would be down the route of maximum risk for little reward.

Sarah levered herself to squat on her heels and raised the pistol. She aimed inside the door and into the darkness, to where a target ought to be, where she *hoped* a target would be. With measured control she pulled the trigger, and a bullet tore through the opening. She heard the impact, and it wasn't the sound of flesh. Another minute and again the gun jumped in her hand; same result, and no one made any effort to return fire. She checked her ammunition, two full magazines equalling thirty rounds, and whatever remained in the pistol. To attempt an indefinite period of sustained fire was out of the question.

If only Mike would make a move, something tangible she could react to.

She loosed off another round, this time deliberately aiming at the door, and heard a satisfying crack of breaking plastic. Loud enough to attract attention, friend or foe.

A stab of intense pain shot up her arm and she winced, compressing her lips in agony. Screwing up her eyes, she waited, and the moment passed, leaving her hot and light headed. A body didn't need too much of that.

Refocusing on the front door, Sarah steadied the Glock and let go another shell. At least it served to distract, effective or not.

She might still be isolated, but she no longer felt quite so useless.

Alexander Markoff sat on the carpeted landing at the top of the stairs and prepared to fight it out. There'd been no reply from Pushkin, only a sudden noise followed by suppressed gunfire, and then that silence. He guessed a Britisher now controlled the rooms downstairs.

A fifth bullet shattered the front door and Markoff nodded; Pushkin had been correct. One enemy outside, and one enemy inside, he had faced many odds worse than two Britishers. He tapped the side of his British 7.62mm Self Loading Rifle, a relic of the Cold War, a powerful weapon and easy to acquire in England

He eased the fighting knife in his boot and then loosened his pistol ready for use. If these Britishers wanted him, let them come and get him. Let's see what they're made of when faced with a veteran.

Bowman heard bullets striking the front door and made the assumption Sarah had changed location. Not that it would influence the outcome, but it signalled her intent. So how could he turn those random shots to his advantage? But first things first; he crept across to check on the body by the door. No sound, no breathing, and with his pistol extended he found a limp wrist. No pulse, no threat.

Another bullet smacked the door and he took the chance on a quick look into the hall, and glanced up at the landing. No sign of life and he withdrew.

It was then that he remembered the balcony overlooking the rear garden. If he could get up there . . . ? Only one way to find out. Moving swiftly, Bowman stepped out through the French doors, took a few paces across the lawn and turned to look overhead. Squinting into the gloom, he could see the balcony to his left and a bathroom window above the French doors. In between, a heavy duty, vertical waste pipe ran from ground level to up and beyond the guttering, securely fixed to the wall. He estimated the gap from pipe to balcony and thought he might manage it.

He tucked away the Sig and strode over to the pipe, and with both hands took a firm grasp above his head. He tugged, hard. Everything seemed solid so he jumped for a higher hand hold and hauled himself upwards. Finding purchase with his feet, he reached again, straightened his legs and pushed himself up level with the base platform. The balustrade and handrail were still out of reach above him and he stretched once more over his head until he was head and shoulders above the handrail. He scrabbled with his feet, feeling for grip, and found a pipe bracket for support. He leaned to his left, reaching for the rails, and cursed. Too far away. It would have to be an awkward lunge from pipe to balcony, no guarantee of success. He didn't have time to mess about, so gritting his teeth, he let go the pipe with his left hand, braced for the jump and launched himself at the ironwork.

Bowman's right hand missed and knuckles banged painfully into steel, but he managed to grab on with the fingers of his left. His body dangled in mid-air, the weight pulling on his left shoulder, and he felt the healing wound give way. Desperately, he fought for a second hold, swung his right arm for the balustrade. His fingers found metal, clamped round the bar and he hoisted his right foot onto the platform. For a second he hung, then heaved upwards and bellied onto the handrail. With an agile flip he landed on his feet and crouched.

Reaching for his gun, he brushed his knuckles against the jacket and flinched at the pain. A layer of skin had been torn off by his clumsiness. But gun in hand he stepped over to the open glass door and quietly let himself in. As far as he could tell the room was empty. Without a sound he edged cautiously round the double bed. An almost imperceptible lifting of the darkness came through the bedroom door from the landing. The door had been left open just a crack and he put en eye to the gap. There on the landing, at the top of the stairs, sat a man with his back to Bowman. All his attention appeared to centre on the front door below.

And Bowman smiled as Sarah sent another bullet into the door. But even though the man concentrated on the stairway, Bowman reminded himself he hadn't yet established how many Russians were in the house, or for that matter, where Miranda and the kids were. Even so he couldn't let this situation linger on indefinitely. He pulled the door open and stepped onto the landing.

Beneath the carpet a floorboard squeaked, and the man reacted with lightning reflexes. He dropped straight onto his back, aimed a rifle upside down and fired. Bowman threw himself left and the bullet creased his right hip. He automatically aimed the Sig and fired, pumping shells at the target. The man grunted as a bullet hit, and rolled onto his belly. He slithered down a few steps, a controlled slide, feet first, and the rifle thumped off another round. Bowman involuntarily ducked, but the bullet went high, hit the ceiling.

Mike Bowman got angry. He wasn't supposed to lose control, but now he got angry. The old wound in his shoulder hurt, his knuckles hurt, and he felt a pain in his side. He'd had enough. Dropping to one knee he pursed his lips and aimed at the man's forehead.

'Die you bastard,' he shouted and squeezed the trigger.

The bullet caught the man's right eye and buried itself deep inside his skull. He lurched to the side, feet slipping from beneath and tumbled down the stairs.

Sarah came running, saw the man rolling towards the door and hit him with two rounds. Alexander Nickolai Markoff died at her feet, an impotent bloody mess.

Bowman sagged against the wall, then spun around to a noise from behind a closed bedroom door. It was a child's whimper, a muffled sobbing. He beckoned for Sarah to join him. A moment later she stood at his side.

He whispered. 'I think the kids are in there. Might be guarded, I don't know. I'll go in fast, to the left. You take the right.' He met her eyes in the gloom. 'Three . . . two . . . one . . . Go!'

He slammed open the door, powered into the room, and pulled up short. Sarah stormed in behind him going to the right, and stopped, lowering her weapon. By the warm glow of a child's nightlight they grinned at one another. The danger had passed, non-existent. The family were safe, all tied up, but safe. Bowman collapsed with his back to the wall.

Sarah came round to the little girl, spotted the cable ties and paused. She undid the gag and asked her for scissors. The girl nodded to a chest of drawers.

'Mummy keeps them in the top drawer,' she sniffled. A moment later Sarah began to cut the family free. Bowman straightened up and left her to it, walked onto the landing and switched on the lights. Mechanically, without thinking, he moved from one room to the next until he'd turned on every light in the house. Finally, he strode into the kitchen, found a bottle of vodka and unscrewed the top. He put the neck to his lips and swallowed, three times. With deliberate precision he screwed the top back on and returned the bottle to where he'd found it. The fiery liquid hit him and he coughed, reached for his cigarettes and moved out into the night air. Slowly, after what seemed an eternity, the adrenaline dispersed from his system and he found himself able to stand quietly, at peace.

23
Reckoning

Commander Robert Fraser sat in the Medical Centre of Salerton Hall's east wing and demanded a situation report. Naked from the waist up, and with a makeshift bandage dressing his wound, his patience had run out. The medic and his assistant were coping as best they could and as far as Fraser could see, making a damn good fist of it. The emergency services had been notified and a unit of the SAS at Hereford had been despatched by helicopter.

'Has anyone seen Bowman?' he snapped at the nearest unfortunate to get too close.

It was an armed officer helping bring in Jock Monroe.

'Last I saw he and the girl went off in the Land Rover, bit of a hurry.'

'Where, which way?'

'Main gate. I think they turned right.' The officer waited for the medic to indicate where to place Monroe, and then slipped out before any more questions.

Fraser scowled at his own misfortune, he did not make for a good patient. He slid forward in the seat and tested his weight on his left leg. His abdomen let him know he was injured, but it didn't seem so bad. Snatching up his jacket, he picked his way through the casualties and limped out into the corridor. Threading his arms into the jacket, he hugged it round his bare torso and made for the Library.

Arriving at the entrance, he could see a sense of order had been established from the shambles of the explosion. A fire engine and its dismounted crew had already dealt with the flames and were now damping down and checking for hot spots.

Jim stepped out from the doorway and Fraser called. 'Everybody accounted for?'

'No, sir. Can't find Carol or   Hugh Atkinson.'

'Bloody hell' Fraser muttered, and then said, 'Bowman and Sarah on some wild goose chase, and now these two missing.'

Jim answered. 'I'm pretty sure Bowman went round to Atkinson's house. I overheard them talking about it.'

Fraser frowned in an effort to understand. 'Why . . . ? Oh, never mind, leave that with me. See what you can do to find Carol and Hugh.'

Jim nodded. 'Will do, sir,' and he turned to re-enter the library.

Fraser hobbled round outside the library to where the fire engine had parked and studied the scene of devastation. At that moment the sound of beating rotor blades made him look up and a Eurocopter Dauphine hovered into view from over the Hall. A powerful beam of light erupted from the nose and the chopper circled wide before coming in to land. It had barely touched down when an eight man SAS team swarmed out from beneath the blades. They wore full kit, helmets, night vision, the lot, and Fraser detected they were armed to the teeth. A tall, rangy soldier loped over to the fire engine and Fraser attracted his attention.

The man looked him over, saw the bandage and hastily thrown on jacket, and raised an eyebrow. 'Who're you,' he asked abruptly.

'Commander Robert Fraser, this is my headquarters. And you are?'

'Cunningham,' he said. 'SAS, D Squadron, 22 Regiment. Heard you were in a spot of bother.'

Fraser grinned at the informality and quickly ran him through the relevant details. He finished by pointing to the Atkinson house. 'I believe our man Bowman went to investigate.'

The enigmatic 'Cunningham' looked across and squinted through the darkness. 'Is that beyond the perimeter fence?'

'It is' Fraser agreed.

'Okay, we'll try roping in. I'll take three with me, the others are at your disposal.' He turned away and began calling. 'Jack, I want you Chris and Tom on the chopper. Bill, you hang in here with the rest, try and make yourselves useful.'

With that, he loped back to the waiting helicopter and boarded with his men.

Fraser watched as the rotors picked up speed, the tail lifted and the machine rose into the air, nose down and climbing rapidly. It banked left and headed away.

An ambulance careered up the long drive and Fraser turned to oversee the loading of casualties. He put Bowman and Sarah to the back of his mind, more concerned with Carol and Hugh's whereabouts, than whether his two 'deniables' could cope. He hobbled off to find Jim, see if he could get any answers.

Colonel-General Viktor Leonid Zherlenko sat in his customary seat in the Tactical Operations Centre and watched a live feed coming in from a geo-stationary satellite. At the allotted hour, he and his senior compatriots had seen the explosion at Salerton Hall and followed the subsequent happenings in real time. And Colonel-General Zherlenko now extracted a fresh Cuban cigar from his case and allowed himself the pleasure of a well earned celebration. Operation Lightning had passed off without a hitch, not quite in accordance with the expected sequence of events, but nevertheless successful.

A ripple of applause rang out round the table, his subordinates quick to congratulate the man who had the ear of the Kremlin, the General who held their future careers in the palm of his hand.

Zherlenko held up a hand in modest appreciation. 'Thank you, thank you. I am sure when my report reaches the President, all your names will be included for his consideration. I can guarantee decorations and promotions.' He looked sideways at Major Oleg Stapanovich. 'Is that not so, Major?'

Stapanovich half stood to acknowledge his role in the proceedings. 'I am assured by the Kremlin that in the event of a successful mission, many of those present in this room may rely on the Motherland to show her gratitude.' He sat down.

More clapping followed this announcement and Zherlenko puffed on his cigar and beamed.

A momentary bright light on the satellite image caught his attention and he leaned forward, agitated. 'What's that?' he inquired, waving the cigar at the screen.

'Helicopter,' someone replied.

Zherlenko stared hard, unable to relax. Helicopters often meant elite formations in England, the SAS or armed police reinforcements. The Operations Centre fell silent as they watched the figures dismount, and then half their number climb back in. The helicopter took off and swung towards a house on the perimeter, and General Viktor Zherlenko anxiously bit his bottom lip. The helicopter slowed and hovered directly over the rear garden of the Atkinson house, and everyone in the room realised the white van remained parked in the lane. Markoff's team had not yet made their escape.

He chewed on the cigar until the end turned soggy.

Bowman heard the distinctive beat of a helicopter's blades, instinctively recognised the probability of assistance, albeit a little late, and walked out into the back garden. The brilliant beam of a spotlight lanced into his eyes and he raised his arms away from his body. No need for anyone aboard to get excited. Through the glare he made out the dropped coils of rope, and four men hit the ground in rapid succession. A tall, loose limbed man in combats emerged from the brightness, an assault weapon aimed at Bowman's stomach.

He kept his arms in full view. 'The name's Mike Bowman, NDSO.'

'Uh huh,' the man said, 'I'll take your word for it. Commander Fraser reckoned I might be useful.'

Bowman grinned. 'That sounds like the Old Man. Mind if I put my arms down.' He didn't wait for an answer and let them drop.

The man jerked a hand and waved it sideways. 'Leave it, Jack! He's a friend.'

As the helicopter swung away and the bright light diminished, Bowman saw the other three men poised with weapons aimed at his head. They relaxed and walked in smiling.

Bowman beckoned them forward and turned to the kitchen. They filed in behind him and he pointed to the body by the front door. 'Russian,' he said, 'part of a hit squad, you'll find more out front, and there's two live ones in the back of a white van. Well, they were alive.'

The tall man gave him a strange look, peering at him with renewed interest. 'How many are we talking about?'

Bowman wrinkled his nose, thinking, trying to remember the sequence of events, adding them all up. 'Six all told, four dead; five if the other one didn't make it.'

The man called Jack whistled softly. 'Regular one man army.'

'Not just me,' Bowman said, 'her too.'

They turned to look at the stairs. Sarah sat halfway down, concentrating on the pistol in her hands, twisting it over and over, lost in thought.

They looked from Sarah to Bowman, plainly uncomfortable with her behaviour.

He dismissed their concerns with a brief, 'She'll be okay,' and led them out towards the van. 'We caught two and tied 'em up. There's a woman, could be important. Our Sigs Intel suggested she's the one who gave the orders.'

'Got the keys?'

Bowman patted his pockets and handed them over. 'Here you go'

'Alright, we'll take it from here.'

Bowman nodded and tagged along in the rear.

The tall one unlocked and stepped to the side as he opened the van door. Three assault weapons covered the inside and Bowman waited.

The soldier called Jack climbed in and gave the captives a perfunctory once over. 'Tom,' he called, peering closely at the man in the back. 'See what you can do, he might not make it.' He turned to the woman.

'Careful,' Bowman warned, and Jack gave him a wry smile.

'A bad 'un?'

'Could be,' he said. 'She didn't take kindly to be being shot.'

246

Jack obviously wasn't in the mood to be messed with and produced a vicious looking knife. He handed his gun to the tall soldier outside and leaned in close to the woman. He grabbed a handful of her short hair, forced her head down and hacked through the electric wiring tying her to the side of the van. Ignoring her wounded leg, he dragged her roughly out to the ground and then propped her against the van door.

She spat at him, and Jack slapped her face, with venom. His knife came up under her throat and he applied just enough pressure to puncture the skin. A trickle of blood ran down her neck.

Bowman smiled grimly as the woman stopped struggling, wide eyed with fear. Jack definitely had no qualms about using a bit of force.

Tom called, shaking his head. 'Nothing I can do, Boss. He's bled out.'

The 'Boss' handed Jack his gun and turned to Bowman. 'That it?' he asked.

'Yep,' he said, 'but we'll need her for interrogation.'

'No problem,' said the man and held out a hand. 'I'm Cunningham, supposedly in charge of these reprobates.' He chuckled easily, a broad smile lighting his face. 'Good to know you.'

Bowman accepted the handshake, remembering the feeling of kinship he had with these tough professionals. 'Glad you could come.'

Cunningham let out a sharp laugh and glanced around him. 'Didn't really need us though, did you?' He dropped the smile and a serious frown took its place. 'If you ever need a job, look me up.'

It was Bowman's turn to laugh. 'Tried your lot for a while, proper soldiering isn't my style.'

Cunningham's sombre face nodded. 'Each to his own, I guess,' he said, and patted Bowman's shoulder. 'We're done here. Want me to drop the woman off with your boss?'

'That'd be useful,' Bowman said. 'And if you'd let the Old Man know all's well. Atkinson's family are okay too. He's our GCHQ boffin. Wife and kids are all good.'

'Will do,' Cunningham said, and pressed a button on his belt pack. 'Hello Skyranger, this is Delta-Foxtrot. Ready for extraction.'

Bowman heard a faint reply and the tall soldier raised a hand in farewell, gathered his men, and with the woman in their midst, made for the back garden. And this time the helicopter came in slowly, cleared the fence, and landed in the centre of the lawn. Four men and a Russian woman bent their heads under the rotating blades and climbed aboard. The noise of the engine increased in volume, lifted into a hover and peeled away for Salerton Hall.

Bowman glance at his watch, astonished to find it was only twenty past ten. He sighed and reached for another cigarette. Once news got to the Old Man, it wouldn't be long before the place was swarming with people from 'logistics'. He walked back round the end of the house, stepped over one of Sarah's victims, and ambled over to the Ford Focus.

The sound of an engine made him turn, and Hugh Atkinson's Audi swept into the drive and skidded to a halt. He flung open the car door.

'Where are they?' he shouted running for the house.

'In the living room,' Bowman called after him, and made a move for the Land Rover. Halfway there he almost tripped over a large holdall of equipment. It was what the woman had thrown at him. Bending to retrieve it, he saw what appeared to be a glorified games controller lying nearby. Gathering as much as he could carry he took it all to the back of the Land Rover and piled it on the floor. It took a second trip to recover the last bits, including an odd looking square tube.

He flopped into the driving seat and drummed his fingers on the steering wheel. With Hugh now home to see to his family, Sarah wouldn't be long. Bowman leaned back to wait and closed his eyes.

At Salerton Hall, somebody somewhere again switched on the floodlights and turned black of night into glaring day.

Robert Fraser heard the distinctive throb of the returning helicopter and walked away from the ambulance to stare up into the night sky. The brilliance of the lights lit up his craggy features, his iron-grey head of hair glinting in the beam. For half a minute he stood gazing upwards before spotting the incoming chopper. He watched it down and limped over to meet the dismounting SAS.

His eyes were drawn to a fifth person, a woman, supported by two of the men.

Cunningham came forward. 'Found your man, Commander. All's good. Said for me to tell you the Atkinson family are unharmed.' He half turned and indicated the woman. 'And he said you'll want to ask her a few questions, something about her being the leader of the pack.'

Fraser thanked him and called to Jim. 'Lock this woman in the gatehouse, and be sure you keep her away from Webster.'

Cunningham touched the rim of his helmet with one finger. 'We'll stick around for a while. Never know what might turn up.'

'Of course,' Fraser said, grateful for their timely response. 'I appreciate your help.'

Cunningham grinned. 'All part of the service,' he said, and turned to his men, stopped, and looked back. 'By the way, that man of yours, Bowman.' He paused for a second, searching for the right phrase. 'One of the best.' And with that, he marched off to join his men.

Fraser watched him go, a warm feeling of pride in Mike Bowman's continued allegiance to not only NDSO, but also a curmudgeonly old boss like himself. He shook his head, disconcerted by his affection for a man of Bowman's calling, then grinned and limped away. Still, he thought, it was good to know that another man who also knew how to handle himself would pay Bowman such a compliment.

He hugged his jacket tighter ignoring the blood trickling down his thigh, and went off in search of Carol. It was the pain in his side that slowed him down.

Colonel-Viktor Zherlenko threw away the damp cigar and thumped the table with his fist. On the wall the main screen displayed a freeze-frame image of a man staring up at the sky, his face lit by the full glare of floodlights, and Zherlenko cursed in helpless disappointment. He knew that face better than that of his own dead mother. Commander Robert Fraser had survived the assassination and all the General's hopes for the future glories of Presidential favour had, in that moment, ended in abject failure. A year of planning, four months of surveillance, his promise to annihilate Bullseye, all for nothing. He hung his head in defeat.

'General!'

He raised his eyes to the screen. It had reverted to real time and he swallowed in anguish.

The helicopter had returned to land and in the centre of a small squad of soldiers, Helena Goreya was being escorted forward. Zherlenko gritted his teeth, incensed. Her capture in such circumstances was the final straw, the ramifications too bitter to contemplate. He buried his head in his hands. Early retirement into mind numbing obscurity had just been confirmed.

Sarah Campbell stood quietly at the door to Hugh and Miranda's living room. No words of hers could describe the heart warming reunion of these two lovely people. They sat on the sofa holding hands and staring into each others eyes. Tina and Christopher, initially subdued by the trauma of violence, had quickly come through the worst and now vied with one another for control of the remote, the first happy giggles coming from Tina.

Sarah was loathe to interrupt but felt she ought to warn them.

'There will be people coming soon. They'll have to lock down this area while they carry out their work. I don't know if you'll be able to stay.'

Miranda looked up and smiled gently. 'That's alright, Sarah. After this, I'm not sure I want to stay. It might be better to find somewhere new.'

Hugh turned and nodded. 'For the sake of the kids, it might be the right thing.'

Sarah inclined her head in agreement, not willing to argue otherwise. It all seemed very sensible. 'Well, if you're alright, I'm going now. I'll wait outside until the police get here, explain things.'

Hugh stood up and came to stand in front of her. 'Thank you, Sarah. Thanks for saving Miranda and the kids.'

Before she could reply, he leaned forward and kissed her cheek. 'Without you and Mike . . . ,' he shook his head. 'I wouldn't like to think what might have happened.'

She placed a hand on his chest and eased him away. 'Get on with you, we were only doing our job.' She smiled and turned to go. 'Bye kids,' she called, and two smiling faces waved from the floor.

'Bye-bye, Sarah,' they called in unison, instantly forgot she existed, and glued themselves to the TV screen.

Miranda raised a hand, and Sarah walked out. She hadn't got past the Ford Focus before the first of the investigating teams began to arrive.

Between them, she and Mike gave them all the answers they needed, made their excuses, and fired up the Land Rover. She sat with her wounded arm across her lap and grimaced. It had been quite a day. She glanced at Bowman from the corner of her eye and marvelled at his disciplined self control. Twice now, they'd been caught up in dangerous situations, life threatening conflict, and not once had he questioned her competence. For that alone Sarah's admiration for this man knew no bounds. She leaned over and lolled her head against his arm and smiled contentedly.

24
Backwash

Jim called to Bowman from the window of the gatehouse. 'Take it easy up at the Hall, there's a lot of guns over there.'

'Right. How's the Old Man?'

'Like a bear with a sore head,' he said, grinning. 'Issuing orders like they were confetti.' The big gates swung inwards and Jim waved them through.

Bowman drove slowly towards the brightly lit building. The helicopter sat quietly, rotors stopped, but everywhere he looked men carrying guns patrolled the grounds. Even a Royal Engineer Bomb Disposal lorry had parked up near the entrance porch.

As the Land Rover drew closer an ambulance drove out from the Hall under flashing blues, and Bowman squeezed over to allow it free passage. Then he drove on and parked up on the grass, staying clear of the emergency services.

John Cunningham saw them arrive and strode across.

Bowman stuck his head out of the window. 'Seen the Old Man?'

'Yep, on his way to hospital, and not happy about it. You just passed him.'

'Who's in charge?'

Cunningham shook his head. 'Not sure, but I think somebody called Montague is filling in.'

Bowman glanced meaning fully at Sarah, knowing Sir Hillary didn't think much of his two 'deniables'.

'Problem?' Cunningham asked.

Bowman grinned. 'No, not really. Internal politics, but I better report in.' He gestured at the back of the Defender. 'Can you see this stuff gets to the investigation teams. The woman had hold of it, taking it back to the van.'

'I can do that.'

'Cheers. We'll go and face the music.' He and Sarah got out and made their way over to the Hall. They found Sir Montague monitoring the situation in the Old Man's office, issuing a string of instructions via the phone.

Bowman waited patiently until Montague looked up to acknowledge their presence. 'You're back then?'

'Yeah, five dead and a woman for interrogation.' Bowman deliberately dropped any pretence of respecting the man's authority.

'So I've heard.' He stared at them for a long moment. 'You'd better report to the Medical Centre, looks like you both need patching up. After that, it's up to you. The investigating teams are taking responsibility now, so as far as I'm concerned you can go home. There'll be a Board of Inquiry, and there'll be questions. Make sure you're available.' The phone rang and he picked it up. 'Montague?'

They were dismissed. Bowman nudged Sarah and gestured with his chin. With his hand in the small of her back, he guided her out into Carol's empty office and then led off in the direction of the Medical Centre.

An hour later, having both refused the offer of being taken to Gloucestershire's Royal Infirmary, they walked out to the Land Rover.

Bowman stopped her from getting in. 'Angel,' he began, hesitant. 'You coming with me, or would you prefer going home? You might be more comfortable at your own place, my cottage is a bit lacking.'

She raised her bandaged arm to rest her hand on his chest, peering closely into his eyes. 'Are you trying to get rid of me?'

Bowman swallowed; why did women always put their own spin on things, all he wanted was for her to choose, for her own good. He held both her arms and fixed her with an imploring look. 'No that's not what I meant. I just want what's best, I'm not asking you to leave.'

She laughed quietly and touched the side of his face. 'I'd prefer to be with you, let's go home.'

He breathed a sigh of relief and then gallantly opened the passenger door. 'Your carriage awaits,' he smiled, closed it behind her and walked round to the driver's door. He started the engine and they sat for a moment staring at the brightly lit Hall.

Bowman looked at all the activity, the bright lights and the chopper, the emergency services all flashing blue lights.

'Won't ever be the same again you know,' he said, bemused by the thought. 'The NDSO were the only service not in the public eye, but not any more. We might have survived this particular operation, but if you stop to think about it, the Russians have exposed us to the world. Not very 'deniable' now.'

Major John Cunningham of 22 Regiment, Special Air Service, watched the Land Rover drive away and nodded with respect. Those two had earned their laurels this night. Between them they'd doled out the kind of body count his own unit would have been proud of. And it had been managed in the dark with pistols. He smiled grimly and shook his head in disbelief. Astonishing, he thought, they deserved a medal.

In Gloucester Royal Infirmary, a senior consultant of the medical team, personally saw to it that Commander Robert Fraser received the best treatment available. Not that the irascible Old Man thought any more favourably about those tending his wounds. The nursing staff smiled politely and got on with their ministrations, immune to his string of obscenities.

Angus Jock Monroe spent two hours in the operating theatre having a multitude of glass shards removed from his face. Expected to make a full recovery, he was nonetheless kept in for observation.

Winslow Palmer would not prove to be so fortunate. His leg had to be amputated above the knee.

It was late the following morning when Mike Bowman stood at the back door of the kitchen and gazed at the familiar sight of the distant flock of sheep. The warm aroma of Brazilian coffee drifted on the air. He heard a floorboard creak upstairs as Sarah made a move and he turned to the cafetiere. Depressing the plunger, he poured two mugs, found a fresh pack of cigarettes, and took his mug out to the garden, basking in the heat of the sun.

His mind took him back to a mountain in southern Russia, and the moment he'd been unable to save Jessica Stewart from an assassin's bullet. Had he made up for that mistake? That was for others to judge. But right now, in the peaceful surrounds of the English countryside, it felt like he'd gone some way to restoring the balance.

A minute later and Sarah joined him, coffee in hand.

'Morning, Mike,' she said, and reached up a hand to hang on his shoulder.

He glanced sideways enjoying the intimacy of the moment. She stood with her face raised to the sun, eyes closed to the warmth, her tousled hair framing the beautiful, elfin features.

'Morning, Angel. Sleep well?'

'Like a log. You?' She sipped the hot coffee.

'Yeah, pretty good.' He allowed his gaze to linger, as if seeing her for the first time. There was an indefinable something about this woman that continually crept under his skin, and he struggled with conflicting emotions. It wasn't as if they had a lot in common. She had a strong will, fiercely independent, quick to temper, and yet somehow beneath that confident exterior, there existed a vulnerability that made him want to protect her, to ward off the harshness of the world. The thought crossed his mind that this was more than just a casual relationship, that he felt something for this alluring woman.

She seemed to sense his thoughts and turned to look at him. 'What?'

He smiled sheepishly, momentarily caught off guard. 'You and me . . . , we make a good partnership.'

Sarah gave him a long probing look, her liquid dark eyes searching his. 'Is that all we are, Mike? I thought we were maybe more than a just a partnership, more like . . .?' She left it hanging in the air, tilting her head for an answer.

Michael Richard Bowman, a tough maverick who put his life on the line for others, a spy in all but name, succumbed to a sensual pair of waiting lips.

-- ---- --

255

More by this Author

WW2 Naval fiction; **THE WAVES OF WAR**

and companion piece, **WHEN D-DAY DAWNS**

Made in the USA
Las Vegas, NV
12 December 2021

36990970R00144